Robert W. Chambers

The Haunts of Men

Robert W. Chambers

The Haunts of Men

ISBN/EAN: 9783743348745

Manufactured in Europe, USA, Canada, Australia, Japa

Cover: Foto ©Andreas Hilbeck / pixelio.de

Manufactured and distributed by brebook publishing software (www.brebook.com)

Robert W. Chambers

The Haunts of Men

THE HAUNTS OF MEN.

" How shall we seem, each to the other, when,
On that glad day, immortal, we shall meet—
Thou who, long since, didst pass with hastening feet—
I, who still wait here, in the haunts of men ? "

THE HAUNTS OF MEN

BY
ROBERT W. CHAMBERS

Author of "The King in Yellow," "The Red Republic," "A King and a Few Dukes," "Lorraine," etc., etc.

NEW YORK
FREDERICK A. STOKES COMPANY
PUBLISHERS

To Elsa.

As a Black Veil of Lace,
Parted in sombre grace,
Shadows a pallid face,
So shall the Veil of Night,
    Dimly withdrawn,
Shadow the coming Dawn.

Changed are the ashen skies,—
    The clearer blue
Deep mirrored in thine eyes
    Is changing too.

If the dim Dawn be fair,
Can its pale flames compare
In glory to thy hair?
    What, in the jewelled skies,
    Matches the dyes
In thine uplifted eyes!

Out from the splendid night
Bright as a spirit's flight
Thou com'st with the Light.
And in the East the World spins, grey and old,
And in the West wait Life and Death; behold!

Bend down with me; behold!
    This is the World,—
This tattered scroll unrolled,—
    This chart unfurled.
    Here at thy feet,
The Seven Oceans part and meet.

Trace with thy finger tips
    The round World round,
Free as a shadow slips
    Over the ground.
    The World sleeps there
Steeped in the shadow of thy hair.

CONTENTS.

THE GOD OF BATTLES

Ah, who could couple thoughts of war and crime
 With such a blessed time ?
Who in the West wind's aromatic breath,
 Could hear the call of Death ?
TIMROD.

THE HAUNTS OF MEN.

THE GOD OF BATTLES.

Sovereign of the world. . . . these sabres hold another language to-day from that they held yesterday. —VATHEK.

IT happened so unexpectedly, so abruptly, that
she forgot to scream. A moment before, she had
glanced out of the pantry windows, dusting the
flour from her faded pink apron, and she saw the
tall oats motionless in the field and the sunlight
sifting through the corn. In the heated stillness a
wasp, creeping up and down the window pane, filled
the dim house with its buzzing. She remembered
that,—then she remembered hearing the clock ticking in the darkened dining-room. It was scarcely a
moment; she bent again over her flour pan, wistful,
saddened by the summer silence, thinking of her
brother; then again she raised her eyes to the window.

It was too sudden; she did not scream. Had
they dropped from the sky, these men in blue,—
these toiling, tramping, crowding creatures? The
corn was full of them, the pasture, the road; they
were in the garden, they crushed the cucumbers and

3

the sweet-peas, their muddy trousers tore tender tendrils from the melon vines, their great shoes, plodding across the potato hills, harrowed the bronzed earth and levelled it to a waste of beaten mould and green-stuff. They passed, hundreds, thousands,—she could not tell,—and at first they neither spoke nor turned aside, but she heard a harmony, subtile, vast as winds at sea,—a nameless murmur that sweeps through brains of marching men,—the voiceless prophecy of battle.

Breathless, spellbound, she moved on tiptoe to the porch, one hand pressed trembling across her lips. The field of oats shimmered a moment before her eyes, then a blue mass swung into it and it melted away, sheered to the earth in glimmering swathes as gilded grain falls at the sickle's sparkle. And the men in blue covered the earth, the world, her world, which stretched from the orchard to Benson's Hill.

There was something on Benson's Hill that she had never before seen. It looked like a brook in the sunshine; it was a column of infantry, rifles slanting in the sun.

Somebody had been speaking to her for a minute or two, somebody below her on the porch steps, and now she looked down and saw a boy, slim, sunburnt, wearing gauntlets and spurs. His dusty uniform glittered with gilt and yellow braid; he touched the vizor of his cap and fingered his sword hilt. She looked at him listlessly, her hand still pressed to her lips.

"Is there a well near the house?" he asked. After a moment he repeated the question.

Men with red crosses on their sleeves came across the grass, trailing poles and rolls of dirty canvas. She saw horses too, dusty and patient, tied to the front gate. A soldier, with a yellow ornament on his sleeve, stood at their heads, holding a red flag in one hand.

Something tugged gently at her apron, and, "show me the well, please," repeated the boy beside her.

She turned mechanically into the house; he followed, caking the rag-carpet with his boots' dry mud. In the woodshed she started and turned trembling to him but he gravely motioned her on, and she went, passing more swiftly under the trees of the orchard to the vine-covered well-curb.

He thanked her; she pointed at the dipper and rope; but already blue-clad, red-faced soldiers were lowering the bucket and the orchard hummed with the buzz of the wheel.

She went back to the porch, not through the house but around it. Across the little lawn lay crushed stalks and dying flowers; the potato patch was a slough of muddy green.

Soldiers passed in the sunshine. She began to remember that her brother, too, was a soldier, somewhere out in the world; he had been a soldier for nearly a week, ever since Jim Bemis had taken him to Willow Corners to enlist. She remembered she had cried and gone into the pantry to make bread and cry again. She remembered that first night, how she had been afraid to sleep in the house, how at dusk she had gone into the parlour to be near her mother. Her mother was dead, but her picture hung in the parlour.

Soldiers were passing, clutching their rifle butts with dirty hands, turning toward her countless sun-dazzled eyes. The shimmer of gun-barrels, the dancing light on turning bayonets, the flicker and sparkle on belt and button dazed and wearied her.

Somebody said, " We're the boys for the purty girls! Have ye no eyes for us, lass ? "

Another said, " Shut up, Mike, she's not from the Bowery ; " and, " G'wan ye dead rabbit ! " retorted the first.

A flag passed, and on it she read " New York," and another flag passed, dipped to her in grim salute, while the folds shook out a faded " Maine."

She began to watch the flags ; she saw a regiment plunge into the trampled corn, but she knew it was not her brother's because the trousers of the men were scarlet and the caps hung to the shoulders, tasselled and crimson.

" Maryland, Maryland, Maryland, 60th Maryland," she repeated, but she did not know she spoke aloud until somebody said: " It's yonder," and a blue sleeve swept towards the west.

" Yonder," she repeated, looking at the ridge, cool in the beechwoods' shadow.

" Is it the 60th Maryland you want, Miss? " asked another.

"Silence," said an officer, wheeling a sweating horse past the porch.

She shrank back, but turned her head toward the beechwoods. As she looked a belt of flame encircled the forest, once, twice, again and yet again, and through the outrushing smoke, the crash! crash! crash! of rifles echoed and re-echoed across the valley.

All around her thousands of men burst into cheers; a deeper harmony grew on the idle breeze—the solemn tolling of cannon. The flags, the bright flags spread rainbow wings to the rising breeze; they were breasting the hills everywhere. The din of the rifles, the shouting, the sudden swift human wave, sweeping by on every side, thrilled her little heart until it beat out the long roll with the rolling drums.

In the orchard the rattle of the bucket, the creak and whirr of the well-wheel, never ceased. A very young officer sat on his horse, eating an unripe apple and watching the men around the well. The horse stretched a glossy neck toward the currant bushes, mumbling twigs and sun-curled leaves. A hen wandered near, peering fearlessly at the soldiers.

The girl went into the kitchen, reached up for her sun-bonnet, dangling on a peg, tied it under her chin, and walked gravely into the orchard. The men about the well looked up as she passed. They admired respectfully. So did the very young officer, pausing, apple half-eaten; so perhaps did the horse, turning his large, gentle eyes as she came up.

The officer wheeled in his saddle and leaned toward

her deferentially, anticipating perhaps complaint or insult.

In Maryland "Dixie" was sung as often as "The Red, White, and Blue."

Before she spoke she saw that it was the same officer who had asked her about the well; she had not noticed he was so young.

"I am sorry," he said,—and, as he spoke, he removed his cap—"I am very sorry that we have trampled your garden. If you are loyal, the Government will indemnify you—"

The sudden crash of a cannon somewhere among the trees drowned his voice. Stunned, she saw him, undisturbed, gather his bridle with a deprecatory gesture. His voice came back to her through the ringing in her ears: "We do not mean to be careless, but we could not turn aside, and your farm is in the line of advance."

Her ears still rang, and she spoke, scarcely hearing her own voice: "It is not that—I am loyal—it is only I wish to ask you where my brother's regiment—where the 60th Maryland is."

"The 60th Maryland—oh—why it's in King's Brigade, Wolcott's Division; I think it's yonder." He pointed toward the beechwoods.

"Yonder? Where they are firing?"

Again the cannon thundered and the ground shook under her. She saw him nod, smiling faintly. Other mounted officers rode up; some looked at her curiously, others glanced carelessly; the attitudes of all were respectful. She heard them arguing about the water in the well and the length of the road to Willow Corners. They spoke of a turning movement, of driving somebody to Whitehall Station. The musketry on the hill had ceased; the cannon, too, were silent. Across the trampled corn a regiment moved listlessly to the tap, tap of a drum. On the road that circled Benson's Hill, mounted soldiers were riding fast in the dust; several little flags bobbed among them; metal on shoulder and stirrup flashed through the dust, burnished by the mid-day sun.

She heard an officer say that there would be no fighting, and she wondered, because the musketry began again, little spattering shots among the beeches on the ridge, and behind the house drums rolled and a sudden flurry of bugle music filled the air. Other officers rode up, some escorted by troopers who bounced in their saddles and grasped long-staffed flags, the butts resting in their stirrups.

She reached up and bent down an apple bough, studded with clustered green fruit. Through the leaves she looked at the officers.

The sunshine fell in brilliant spots, dappling flag and cap and the broad backs of horses; there was a jingle of spurs everywhere. The hum of voices and the movement were grateful to her, for her loneliness was not of her own seeking. In the pleasant summer air the distant gunshots grew softer and softer; the twitter of a robin came from the ash-tree by the gate.

Out on the road by Benson's Hill, the cavalry were still passing, the little flags sped along, rising and falling with the column, and the short clear note of a trumpet echoed the robin's call.

But around the house the last of the troops had passed ; she could see them, not yet far away, moving up among the fields toward the ridges where the sun burned on the bronzing scrub-oak thickets. The officers, too, were leaving the orchard, spurring on, singly or in groups, after the disappearing columns. From the main road came a loud thudding and pounding and clanking ; a battery of artillery, the long guns slanted, the drivers swinging their thongs—passed at a trot. After it rode soldiers in blue and yellow, then waggons passed, ponderous grey wains covered with canvas, and on either side clattered more mounted troopers, their drawn sabres glittering through the heated haze.

She stood a moment, holding the apple bough, watching the yellow dust hanging motionless in the rear of the disappearing column. When the last wain had creaked out of sight and the last trooper had loped after it, she turned and looked at the silent garden, trodden, withered, desolate. She drew a long breath, the apple bough flew back, the little green apples dancing. A bee buzzed over a trampled geranium, a robin ran through the longer grass and stopped short, head raised. Beyond Benson's Hill a bugle blew faintly ; distant rifle shots sounded along the ridge ; then silence crept through the sunlit meadows, across the levelled corn, across dead stalks and stems, a silence that spread like a shadow, nearer, nearer, over the lawn, through the orchard to the house, and then from corner to corner, dulling the ticking of the clock, stifling the wasp on the window, driving her before it from room to room.

On the musty hair-cloth sofa in the parlour she lay, flung face down, hands pressed to her ears. But silence entered with her, stifling the sob in her throat.

When she raised her head it was dusk. She heard the murmur of wind in the trees and the chirr of crickets from the fields. She sat up, peering fearfully into the darkness, and she heard the clock ticking in the kitchen and rustle of vines on the porch. After a moment she rose, treading softly, and felt along the wall until her hands rested on her mother's picture. Then, no longer afraid, she slipped silently across the room, and through the hallway to the pantry.

It was nearly moonrise before she had cooked supper ; when she sat down alone at the long table, the moon, yellow, enormous, stared at her through the window.

She sipped her tea, turned the lamp-wick a trifle lower, and ate slowly. The little grey dusk moths came humming in the open window and circled around her. The porch dripped with dew; there was a scent of night in the air.

When she had sat silent a little while dreaming over the sins of a blameless life, there came to her, peace, so sudden so perfect, that she could not understand. How should she know peace? What thought of the past might bring comfort? She could just remember her mother,—that was all. She loved her picture in the parlour. As for her father, he had died as he had lived, a snarling drunkard. And her brother? A lank, blue-eyed boy, dissipated, unwholesome, already cursed with his father's sin—what comfort could he be to her? He had gone away to enlist; he was drunk when he did it.

She thought of all these things, her finger tips resting on the edge of the table. She thought too —of the soldiers passing, of the rippling crash of rifles, the drums, the cheering, the sunlight flecking the backs of the horses in the orchard.

There was a creak at the gate, a click of a latch, and the fall of a foot on the moonlit porch. She half rose; she was not frightened. How she knew who it was, God alone knows, but she looked up, timidly, understanding who was coming, knowing who would knock, who would enter, who would speak. And yet she had never seen him but once in her life.

All this she knew,—this child made wise in the space of time marked by the tick of the kitchen clock; but she did not know that the memory of his smile had given her the peace she could not understand, she did not know this until he entered, dusty, slim, sunburnt, his yellow gauntlets folded in his belt, his cap and sabre in his hand. Then she knew it. When she understood this she stood up, pale, uncertain. He bowed silently and stepped

forward, fumbling with his sabre hilt.   She motioned
toward a chair.

He said he had a message for the master of the
house, and glanced about vaguely, noting the single
place at table and the single plate.   She said he
might give the message to her.

"It is only that—if I do not inconvenience you
too much—" he smiled faintly,—"if you would
allow me,—well, the truth is I am billeted here for
the night."

She did not know what that meant and he explained.

"The master of the house is absent," she said,
thinking of her brother.

"Will he return to-night?" he asked.

She shook her head ; she was thinking that she
did not want him to go away.   Suddenly the thought
of being alone laid hold of her with fresh horror.

"You may stay," she said faintly.   He bowed
again.   She asked him if he cared for supper, with
a gesture toward the table, and when he thanked
her she took courage and told him where to hang
his cap and sabre.

There was a small room between the parlour and
the dining-room.   She offered it to him, and he accepted gratefully.   While she was in the kitchen,
toasting more bread, she heard him go to the front
door and call.   There came a clatter of hoofs, a
quick word or two, and, as she re-entered the dining-room, he met her.   "My orderly," he explained,
—"he may sleep in the stable, may he not?"

"My own bed-room is all I have here," she said.

"Not—not the one you gave me!" he asked.

She nodded. "You may have it,—I often sleep in the parlour,—I did when my brother was home."

"If I had had any idea—" he burst out. She stopped him with a gesture; but he insisted and at last he had his own way. "If I may sleep in the parlour, I will stay," he said, and she nodded and seated herself at the table.

He ate a great deal; she wondered a little, but nodded again at his excuses, and insisted that he must have more tea. She watched him; the lamp-light fell softly on his boyish head, on his faint moustache, and bronzed hands. He ate much bread and butter and many eggs; he spoke about his orderly and the horses, and presently asked for a lantern. She brought him one; he lighted it.

When he had gone away with his lantern, she rested her white face in her hands and looked at his empty chair. She thought of her brother, she thought of the village people who leered askance when she was obliged to go to the store at Willow Corners. The mention of her father's name, of her brother's name in the village aroused sneers or laughter. As long as she could remember the one great longing of her life had been to be respected. She had seen her father fall at night in the village street, drunk as a hog; she had seen her brother reel across the fields at noonday. She knew that all the world knew—her world—that she was merely one of a drunkard's family. She never spoke to a

neighbour, nor did she answer when spoken to. She
carried her curse,—and her longing,—supposing
that she was a thing apart.   In the orchard at mid-
day a man, a young boy, a soldier, had spoken to
her and looked at her in a way she had never known.
All at once she realised, dreaming there in the lamp-
light, that she was a woman to him, like other
women ; a woman to be spoken to with deference,
a woman to be approached with courtesy.   She had
read it in his eyes, she had heard it in his voice.   It
was this that brought to her a peace as gracious,
as sweet, as the eyes that had met her own in the
orchard.

He was coming back from the stable now,—she
heard his spurs click across the grass by the orchard.
And now he had entered, now he was there, sitting
opposite, smiling vaguely across the table.   A rush
of tears blinded her and she looked out into the
night where the yellow moon stared and stared.

She found herself in the parlour after a while,
silent, listening to his voice ; and all about her was
peace, born of the peace within her breast.

He told her of the war.   She had never before
cared, but now she cared.   He spoke of long marches,
of hunger and of thirst, with a boyish laugh, and
she laughed too, not knowing how else to show her
pity.   He spoke of the Land, and now, for the first
time, she loved it ; she knew it was also her Land.
He spoke of the flag and what it meant.   In her
home she had no symbol of her country, and she
told him so.   He drew a penknife from his pocket,

cut a button from his collar, and handed it to her. On the button was an eagle and stars, and she pinned it over her heart, looking at him with innocent eyes.

She told him of her mother,—she could not tell much but she told him all she remembered.   Then, involuntarily, she told him more,—about her life, her hopes long dead, her brother bearing his father's name and curse.   She had not meant to do this at first; but as she spoke she had a dim idea that he ought to know who it was that he treated with gentleness and deference.   She knew it would not change anything in him, that he would be the same. Perhaps it was a vague hope that he might advise her,—perhaps be sorry, she could not analyse it, but she felt the necessity of speaking.

There is a time for all things except confession. But, to the lonely soul, long stifled, time is chosen for confession when God sends the opportunity.

She spoke of honour as she understood it; she spoke of dishonour as she had known it.

When she was silent, he began to speak, and she listened breathlessly.   Ah, but she was right! The God of Battles had sent to her a messenger of peace.   Out of the smoke and flame he had come to find her and pity her.   Through him she knew she was worthy of respect, through him she learned her womanhood, from his lips she heard the truths of youth, which are truer than the truths of age.

He sat there in the lamplight, his gilt straps gleaming, his glittering spurs ringing true with every movement, his bronzed young face bent to hers. She knew he knew everything that man could know; she drank in what he said, humbly. When he ceased speaking, she still looked into his eyes. Their brilliancy dazzled her; the lamp spun a halo behind his head. Wondering at his knowledge, she wondered what those things might be that he knew and had not told. He was smiling now. *She felt the power and mystery of his eyes.

It is true that he had not told her all he knew,— although what a boy of eighteen knows is soon told. He had not told her that her brother lay buried in a trench in the beech-grove on the ridge, shot by court-martial for desertion in the face of the enemy. Yet that was the very thing he had come to tell her.

About midnight, when they had been whispering long together, he told her that her brother was dead. He told her that death with honour wiped out every stain, and she cried a little and blessed God,—the God of Battles, who had purified her brother in the flames of war.

And that night, when he lay asleep on the musty hair-cloth sofa, she crept in, white, silent, and kissed his hair.

He never knew it. In the morning he rode away.

2

PICKETS.

" Hi, Yank ! "

" Shut up ! " replied Alden, wriggling to the edge of the rifle-pit. Connor also crawled a little higher and squinted through the chinks of the pine logs.

" Hey, Johnny ! " he called across the river, "are you that clay-eatin' Cracker with green lamps on your pilot ? "

" Oh, Yank ! Are yew the U. S. mewl with a C. S. A. brand on yewr head-stall? "

" Go to hell ! " replied Connor sullenly.

A jeering laugh answered him from across the river.

" He had you there, Connor," observed Alden with faint interest.

Connor took off his blue cap and examined the bullet hole in the crown.

" C. S. A. brand on my head-stall, eh ! " he repeated savagely, twirling the cap between his dirty fingers.

" You called him a clay-eating Cracker," observed Alden ; " and you referred to his spectacles as green lanterns on his pilot."

" I 'll show him whose head-stall is branded," muttered Connor, shoving his smoky rifle through the log crack.

Alden slid down to the bottom of the shallow pit and watched him apathetically.

The silence was intense; the muddy river, smooth as oil, swirled noiselessly between its fringe of sycamores; not a breath of air stirred the leaves around them. From the sun-baked bottom of the rifle-pit came the stale smell of charred logs and smoke-soaked clothing. There was a stench of sweat in the air and the heavy odour of balsam and pine seemed to intensify it. Alden gasped once or twice, threw open his jacket at the throat, and stuffed a filthy handkerchief into the crown of his cap, arranging the ends as a shelter for his neck.

Connor lay silent, his right eye fastened upon the rifle-sight, his dusty army shoes crossed behind him. One yellow sock had slipped down over the worn shoe heel and laid bare a dust-begrimed ankle.

In the heated stillness Alden heard the boring of weevils in the logs overhead. A tiny twig snapped somewhere in the .forest; a fly buzzed about his knees. Suddenly Connor's rifle cracked; the echoes rattled and clattered away through the woods; a thin cloud of pungent vapour slowly drifted straight upward, shredding into filmy streamers among the tangled branches overhead.

" Get him ? " asked Alden, after a silence.

" Nope," replied Connor. Then he addressed himself to his late target across the river:

" Hello, Johnny ! "

" Hi, Yank ! "

" How close ? "

" Hey ? "

" How close ? "

" What, sonny ? "

" My shot, you fool ! "

" Why, sonny !" called back the Confederate in affected surprise, " was yew a shootin' at me ? "

Bang ! went Connor's rifle again. A derisive cat-call answered him, and he turned furiously to Alden.

" Oh, let up," said the young fellow ; " it 's too hot for that."

Connor was speechless with rage, and he hastily jammed another cartridge into his long, hot rifle, while Alden roused himself, brushed away a per-sistent fly, and crept up to the edge of the pit again.

" Hello, Johnny ! " he shouted.

" That you, sonny ? " replied the Confederate.

" Yes. Say, Johnny, shall we call it square until four o'clock ? "

" What time is it ? " replied the cautious Con-federate ; " all our expensive gold watches is bein' repaired at Chickamauga."

At this taunt, Connor showed his teeth, but Alden laid one hand on his arm and sang out : " It 's two o'clock, Richmond time ; Sherman has just telegraphed us from your State-house."

" Wa-al, in that case this crool war is over," re-plied the Confederate sharpshooter ; " we 'll be easy on old Sherman."

" See here!" cried Alden; "is it a truce until four o'clock?"

" All right!   Your word, Yank!"

" You have it!"

" Done!" said the Confederate, coolly rising to his feet and strolling down to the river bank, both hands in his pockets.

Alden and Connor crawled out of their ill-smelling dust wallow, leaving their rifles behind them.

" Whew! It's hot, Johnny," said Alden pleasantly.   He pulled out a stained pipe, blew into the stem, polished the bowl with his sleeve, and sucked wistfully at the end.   Then he went and sat down beside Connor who had improvised a fishing pole from his ramrod, a bit of string, and a rusty hook.

The Confederate rifleman also sat down on his side of the stream, puffing luxuriously on a fragrant corn-cob pipe.

Presently the Confederate soldier raised his head and looked across at Alden.

" What's yewr name, sonny?" he asked.

" Alden," replied the young fellow briefly.

" Mine's Craig," observed the Confederate; " what's yewr regiment?"

" Two hundred sixtieth New York; what's yours, Mr. Craig?"

" Ninety-third Maryland, *Mister* Alden."

" Quit that throwin' sticks in the water!" growled Connor; "how do you s'pose I'm goin' to catch anythin'?"

Alden tossed his stick back into the brush-heap and laughed.

"How's your tobacco, Craig?" he called out.

"Bully! How's yewr coffee 'n 'tack, Alden?"

"First-rate!" replied the youth.

After a silence he said: "Is it a go?"

"You bet," said Craig, fumbling in his pockets. He produced a heavy twist of Virginia tobacco, laid it on a log, hacked off about three inches with his sheath knife, and folded it up in a big green syca-more leaf. This again he rolled into a corn-husk, weighted with a pebble, then stepping back, he hurled it into the air, saying: "Deal squar, Yank!"

The tobacco fell at Alden's feet. He picked it up, measured it carefully with his clasp-knife, and called out: "Three and three-quarters, Craig. What do you want, hard-tack or coffee?"

"'Tack," replied Craig: "don't stint!"

Alden laid out two biscuits. As he was about to hack a quarter from the third he happened to glance over the creek at his enemy. There was no mis-taking the expression in his face. Starvation was stamped on every feature.

When Craig caught Alden's eye, he spat with elaborate care, whistled a bar of the "Bonny Blue Flag," and pretended to yawn.

Alden hesitated, glanced at Connor, then placed three whole biscuits in the corn husk, added a pinch of coffee, and tossed the parcel over to Craig.

That Craig longed to fling himself upon the food and devour it was plain to Alden, who was watch-

ing his face. But he didn't; he strolled leisurely
down the bank, picked up the parcel, weighed it
critically before opening it, and finally sat down to
examine the contents. When he saw that the third
cracker was whole, and that a pinch of coffee had
been added, he paused in his examination and remained motionless on the bank, head bent. Presently he looked up and asked Alden if he had made
a mistake. The young fellow shook his head and
drew a long puff of smoke from his pipe, watching
it curl out of his nose with interest.

"Then I'm obliged to yew, Alden," said Craig;
"'low, I'll eat a snack to see it ain't pizened."

He filled his lean jaws with the dry biscuit, then
scooped up a tin-cup full of water from the muddy
river and set the rest of the cracker to soak.

"Good?" queried Alden.

"Fair," drawled Craig, bolting an unchewed seg-
ment and choking a little. "How's the twist?"

"Fine," said Alden; "tastes like stable-sweep-
ings."

They smiled at each other across the stream.

"Sa-a-y," drawled Craig with his mouth full,
"when yew're out of twist, jest yew sing out,
sonny."

"All right," replied Alden. He stretched back
in the shadow of a sycamore and watched Craig with
pleasant eyes.

Presently Connor had a bite and jerked his line
into the air.

"Look yere," said Craig, 'that ain't no way foh

to ketch ' red-horse.' Yew want a ca'tridge on foh
a sinker, sonny."

"What's that?" inquired Connor suspiciously.

" Put on a sinker."

"Go on, Connor," said Alden.

Connor saw him smoking and sniffed anxiously.
Alden tossed him the twist, telling him to fill his pipe.

Presently Connor found a small pebble and improvised a sinker.   He swung his line again into the
muddy current with a mechanical sidelong glance
to see what Craig was doing, and settled down again
on his haunches, smoking and grunting.

" Enny news, Alden?" queried Craig after a
silence.

" Nothing much—except that Richmond has
fallen," grinned Alden.

"Quit foolin'," urged the Southerner ; " ain't thar
no news?"

" No.   Some of our men down at Long Pond got
sick eating catfish.   They caught them in the pond.
It appears you Johnnys used the pond as a cem-
etery, and our men got sick eating the fish."

" That so?" grinned Craig ; "too bad.   Lots of
yewr men was in Long Pond, too, I reckon."

In the silence that followed, two rifle-shots sounded
faint and dull from the distant forest.

" 'Nother great Union victory," drawled Craig.
" Extry! extry! Richmond is took!"

Alden laughed and puffed at his pipe.

" We licked the boots off of the 30th Texas last
Monday," he said.

"Sho!" exclaimed Craig. "What did you go a lickin' their boots for?—blackin'?"

"Oh, shut up!" said Connor from the bank, "I can't ketch no fish if you two fools don't quit jawin'."

The sun was dipping below the pine-clad ridge, flooding river and wood with a fierce radiance. The spruce needles glittered, edged with gold; every broad green leaf wore a heart of gilded splendour, and the muddy waters of the river rolled onward like a flood of precious metal, heavy, burnished, noiseless.

From a balsam bough a thrush uttered three timid notes; a great gauzy-winged grasshopper drifted blindly into a clump of sun-scorched weeds, click! click! cr-r-r-r!

"Purty, ain't it," said Craig, looking at the thrush. Then he swallowed the last morsel of muddy hard-tack, wiped his beard on his cuff, hitched up his trousers, took off his green glasses, and rubbed his eyes.

"A he-cat-bird sings purtier though," he said with a yawn.

Alden drew out his watch, puffed once or twice, and stood up, stretching his arms in the air.

"It's four o'clock," he began, but was cut short by a shout from Connor.

"Gee-whiz!" he yelled, "what have I got on this here pole!"

The ramrod was bending, the line swaying heavily in the current.

"It's four o'clock, Connor," said Alden, keeping a wary eye on Craig.

"That's all right!" called Craig; "the time's extended till yewr friend lands that there fish!"

"Pulls like a porpoise," grunted Connor, "damn it! I bet it busts my ramrod!"

"Does it pull?" grinned Craig.

"Yes,—a dead weight!"

"Don't it jerk kinder this way an' that," asked Craig, much interested.

"Naw," said Connor, "the bloody thing jest pulls steady."

"Then it ain't no 'red-horse,' it's a catfish!"

"Huh!" sneered Connor,—"don't I know a cat-fish? This ain't no catfish, lemme tell yer!"

"Then it's a log," laughed Alden.

"By gum! here it comes," panted Connor; "here, Alden, jest you ketch it with my knife,—hook the blade, blame ye!"

Alden cautiously descended the red bank of mud, holding on to roots and branches, and bent over the water. He hooked the big-bladed clasp knife like a scythe, set the spring, and leaned out over the water.

"Now!" muttered Connor.

An oily circle appeared upon the surface of the turbid water,—another and another. A few bubbles rose and floated upon the tide.

Then something black appeared just beneath the bubbles and Alden hooked it with his knife and dragged it shoreward.

It was the sleeve of a man's coat.

Connor dropped his ramrod and gaped at the thing: Alden would have loosed it, but the knife-blade was tangled in the sleeve.

He turned a sick face up to Connor.

"Pull it in," said the older man,—"here, give it to me, lad—"

When at last the silent visitor lay upon the bank, they saw it was the body of a Union cavalryman. Alden stared at the dead face, fascinated; Connor mechanically counted the yellow chevrons upon the blue sleeve, now soaked black. The muddy water ran over the baked soil, spreading out in dust-covered pools; the spurred boots trickled slime. After a while both men turned their heads and looked at Craig. The Southerner stood silent and grave, his battered cap in his hand. They eyed each other quietly for a moment, then, with a vague gesture, the Southerner walked back into his pit and presently reappeared, trailing his rifle.

Connor had already begun to dig with his bayonet, but he glanced up at the rifle in Craig's hands. Then he looked suspiciously into the eyes of the Southerner. Presently he bent his head again and continued digging.

It was sunset before he and Alden finished the shallow grave, Craig watching them in silence, his rifle between his knees. When they were ready they rolled the body into the hole and stood up.

Craig also rose, raising his rifle to a "present." He held it there while the two Union soldiers

shovelled the earth into the grave. Alden went
back and lifted the two rifles from the pit, handed
Connor his, and waited.

"Ready!" growled Connor, "aim!"

Alden's rifle came to his shoulder. Craig also
raised his rifle.

"Fire!"

Three times the three shots rang out in the wilder-
ness, over the unknown grave. After a moment or
two Alden nodded good night to Craig across the
river and walked slowly toward his rifle-pit. Connor shambled after him. As he turned to lower
himself into the pit he called across the river;
"Good night, Craig!"

"Good night, Connor," said Craig.

AN INTERNATIONAL AFFAIR

AN INTERNATIONAL AFFAIR.

"...Brown-bear clam' de ole fence rail,
Rabbit holler; " Whar yoh tail?..."
Banjo Song.

I.

WHEN the gunboats entered Sandy River, Cleland's regiment was ordered to garrison and recon-
struct the forts at the Landing, evacuated by the
Confederate troops as soon as the gunboats crossed
the bar.

The gunboats tossed a few shells after the leisurely retreating Confederates, then dropped anchor
below the Landing, and waited for something to
turn up. A week later they steamed out of the
river, promptly stuck on the bar, churned and
thrashed and whistled and signalled, and finally slid
out into blue water where a blockade runner tempted
them into a chase that contributed to the amusement of the Southern Confederacy.

By Thanksgiving time, Cleland's regiment had
finished the forts at Sandy Landing. Cleland did
it because he was told to, not because either forts
or town were of the slightest military value to anybody. The Landing itself was a skunk-haunted
village, utterly unimportant as supply depot, strat-
egical pivot, or a menace to navigation. It was a

35

key to nothing; its single railway led nowhere, its whisky was illegal, illimitable, and atrocious.

Cleland's report embodied all of this. He was ordered to hold his ground, establish semaphores, and plant torpedoes. So he built his semaphores as directed, planted torpedoes, and reported. Twenty-four hours later orders came to go into winter-quarters. Then he was notified that he was to be reinforced, so he built barracks for two more regiments, as directed, and wondered what on earth was coming. Nothing came except the two regiments; one arrived on the first of December, by rail,—an Irish regiment;—the other turned up a week later in two cattle trains, band playing madly from the caboose. It was a German regiment full of strange oaths—and aromas.

Now Cleland was enlightened; he understood that the Landing was to be used as a species of cage for these two foreign regiments, raised, Heaven knows where, and destined to prove a nuisance to any army that harboured them. The Irish possessed an appalling record of pillage, bravery, and insubordination. The German regiment, raised " to march mit Siegel," had an unbroken record of flight to its discredit. It had run at Grey's Ford, at Crystal Hill, at Yellow Bank, and at Cypress-Court-House. It fled cheerfully, morning, noon and night; its band stampeded naively and naturally; it always followed its band, adored by all; and the regiment bore no rancour when scourged in general orders. Fallbach was its colonel,—known to the sarcastic and unin-

structed as Fallback,—a rosy, short-winded, peaceful
Teuton, who ran with his regiment every time, and
always accepted censure with jocular resignation.

" Poys will pe poys, ain't it ?" he would say with
a shrug ; " Der band iss a fine band alretty. Dot
trombone iss timid, und der poys dey follow der
trombone."

When Cleland understood that the authorities had
rid themselves of the two regiments by interring
them at Sandy Landing, he wrote a respectful protest, was snubbed and ordered to begin housekeep-
ing for the winter, which meant that his regiment
was now on police duty, stationed at the Landing
to keep the peace between the Germans and their
Irish neighbours.

Trouble began promptly ; Bannon, colonel of the
1st Irish, met Fallbach of the 1st Jägers, and mispro-
nounced his name with an emphasis unmistakable.
An hour later the two regiments knew the war was
on and made preparations accordingly. Hogan of
the 10th company, crossing the street, hustled Franz
Bummel of the Jägers and called him a " dootch
puddy-fud ! "

Quinn, listening to the Jägers' band concert that
afternoon, whistled " Doolan's Wake," and imitated
Fritz Klein's piccolo, aided and abetted by Phelan
and McCue. That night there were three scuffles
and a fight, and the provost-marshal had his work
cut out for him.

Little by little the two regiments were installed
in distant sections of the town. Cleland dealt jus-

tice untempered with mercy, and the rival regiments understood that their warfare would have to be carried on by stealth.

When Phelan, Quinn, Hogan, and McCue were released from the guard-house, they rejoiced with their comrades of the 10th company, and prepared future calamity for the Jägers. But Fate was against them. Their regimental fetish, a strong young goat, disappeared, and that night the Jägers were reported to have revelled in a strangely suggestive stew.

A day or two later, Quinn, fishing for suckers in the Sandy River, was assaulted by three Jägers, his fishpole and three fish confiscated, and he himself ducked amid grunts of universal satisfaction.

The fury of the 10th company passed all bounds when Quinn was relegated to the guard-house for conduct unbecoming a soldier; but the Teutons never strayed from their barracks except in force, and, as night leave was forbidden both regiments, the 10th company hesitated to inaugurate riot by daylight.

Quinn, squatting in the guard-house found plenty of leisure to hatch revenge. He did not waste thought on mere individual schemes for assault and battery; he meditated a master stroke, a blow at the entire regiment calculated to tear every Teuton bosom. The two objects most cherished by the Jägers were their cat and a disreputable negro who cooked for the colonel. How to combine damage to these centres of Teutonic affection occupied

Quinn's waking hours. To kidnap the cat; that was not enough,—the Teutons must be beguiled into eating their cat—and liking it too. How? Quinn sucked at an empty pipe and brooded. Bribe the negro Cassius, first to kidnap the cat, then to cook it? Quinn writhed maliciously at the prospect; he hated Tom, the black and white cat who sang every night on the Jägers' barrack roof— sang to each individual star in the firmament to the indignation of every Irishman in Sandy Landing.

When Quinn emerged from the guard-house he took council with Phelan and McCue; and that evening Hogan was despatched to tempt Cassius with promises and a little cash.

The affair was easier than Hogan had dared hope; Cassius took the cash and promised to betray, and Hogan, lips compressed, to stifle all outward mirthful symptoms, went back to the barracks where Quinn, Phelan, and McCue sat waiting in pessimistic silence.

" He'll not kill the cat," said Hogan, " he'll fetch ut in a bag to the shanty foreninst the hill,—d'ye mind the hut, McCue? "

" I do," said McCue impressively.

" Thin be aisy," continued Hogan; " we'll skin ut an' co-ook ut an' the naygur can take the stew to thot Dootch runaway sodger, Fallback, bad cess to him an' his! Pass th' potheen, McCue."

" Sure there's not stew in wan cat for all! " objected Phelan.

" There is! There is," said Quinn: " there's cats

in town to be had for the askin', an' nary a Dootch-
man will starve! Usha! but they'll be crazy, th'
omadhouns!"

"'Twill choke them," said Phelan.

"Did they choke wid the goat they shtole?"
demanded McCue angrily.

"I met Bummel an' Klein," continued Quinn:
"Sure, 'I sez, "'tis dhirty thricks ye play on the
Irish.' 'Phwat's that?' sez Klein. 'Ye ate our
goat,' sez I. Wid that they grinned an' me phist
hurrt wid the timptayshun of Bummel's nose."

"'Sure,' sez I, "'tis frinds we should be!' 'Sorra
th' day!' sez Klein. 'Phwy not?' sez I. 'Ye hate
us an' bate us,' sez Klein; 'I'll not thrust ye, Mike
Quinn.' 'Take me hand,' sez I, extindin' me fingers;
wan touch of nature, me lad! 'Tis a crool war
entirely, an' it's frinds we'll be, an' no favor!' 'Prove
ut,' sez he. 'I wull,' sez I, 'an' be th' same token
'tis huntin' we go this day week, so look fur a
Christmas dinner to shame the Pope's cook.' 'A
dinner,' sez he, 'wid th' town betchune us!' 'Ye'll
dine wid us, yet,' sez I. 'An' how,' sez he, a lickin'
the chops av him. 'Whin ye dine wid the Irish ye
should have a long spoon,' sez I, laughin' friendly
like. 'We'll sind ye a shtew, me b'y, if God sinds
us the rabbits.' Thin,' continued Quinn, "we
parrted genteel; an' they'll hear we have lave to
hunt on Christmas day—musha, bad luck to th'
Dootch scuts!—'tis cats they'll be eatin' this blessed
hour come Christmas, an' may the howly saints sind
them the black cramp of Drumgoole!"

II.

Christmas eve, while Hogan and Phelan lay slumbering, and Quinn and McCue walked their rounds, gloating over revenge, Cassius the disreputable sat in the kitchen of the Jäger barracks counting the advanced payment of cash received from Hogan, and leering at the black and white tom-cat who dozed peacefully by the dying fire.

" Pore ole Tom," muttered Cassius guiltily, " hit's gwinter 'sprise dishyere kitty. 'Spec ole Tom gwinter git riled."

The cat opened its yellow eyes.

" Gwinter 'sprise ole Tom," repeated Cassius, compassionately pursing up his lips.

The cat began to purr.

" Pore ole Tom," sighed the darkey, tremulous with remorse.

The cat rose and began to march around, purring and hoisting an interrogative tail.

Cassius continued to bemoan Tom's fate and recount the money until he had hardened his heart sufficiently. Finally he pocketed the coins, wiped his eyes, and approached the cat with seductive caution. Tom permitted caresses, courted further endearments, and suffered himself to be seized and dropped into a potato sack. But, once imprisoned, he scrambled and squalled and clawed until Cassius, unable to bear the sight and sound of Thomas's distress, deposited the sack in the pantry and fled from the barracks to the street.

Guilt weighed heavily on the darkey's soul; he shuffled ᵣalong, battling with conscience, trying to think of some compromise to save the cat and his money at the same time. Moonlight flooded hill and valley; he heard the sentries calling from post to post, the stir of the horses in the artillery stables across the square, the creaking of leafless branches overhead. He went around to the chicken coop; he often went there to enjoy the thrill of a temptation that he dared not succumb to, also to keep stray cats from doing murder on their own account. For, though he dared not steal a single chicken, he could at least have the bitter pleasure of foiling the feline marauders of Sandy Landing. This he was accustomed to do with a tin box, placed on its side, a trip-stick, a string, and a bit of bone for bait. Cat after cat he had trapped and committed to the depths of Sandy River, highly commended by his colonel and the rank and file of the Jägers. Now, as he stepped softly around the corner, his eyes fell on a black and white object, stealing toward the window where the long tin box stood temptingly baited. The next instant the trip-stick clicked, the weighted box-lid fell and snapped, and Cassius seized the box with a chuckle of triumph.

"Cat! Cat!" he repeated, addressing the frantic

inmate of the box, "doan' yoh count yoh chickens fore dey's hatched !—"

Cassius stopped short, pulsating with a new idea. Why sacrifice Tom when here was a victim ready at hand, doubtless provided by Providence in the nick of time to save a poor darkey from treachery? And it was a kind of treachery that even Cassius found uncongenial.

"Pit-a-pat ! Pit-a-pat !" mocked Cassius derisively listening to the manœuvres of the imprisoned victim; "Stop dat scratchin' on de box! He! He! He! I'se gwineter let ole Tom outen de bag,—pore ole Tom! Dishyere nigger ain't no Judas! Lan's sakes !—dat ole cat smell kinder funny ! "

He wrinkled his nose, sniffed, turned a pair of startled eyes on the big box under his arm, then a sickly smile of intelligence spread over his face and he placed the box gently on the ground.

"Had mah s'picions 'bout dat black an' white kitty-cat," he muttered.

The animal inside scratched and writhed and scrambled.

" Lan's sake !" chuckled Cassius, grinning from ear to ear, " 'spec dat ole pole-cat gwine twiss he tail off'n 'bout two-free minutes ! Yah ! yah !—he ! he ! yiah—ho ! "

And, as he entered the servant's quarters he smote his knees and shook his head, and laughed and laughed and laughed.

About midnight he took his banjo from the nail, thumbed it, and began to croon to himself :

Bob-cat he caynt wag he tail—
Ain got no tail foh to wag !
Brown-bear clam' de ole fence rail,
Rabbit holler ; " Whar yoh tail ? "
Bob-cat larf like he gwinter bus' ;
Pole-cat stop for to see de fuss,
De bob-cat scoot, de bear turn pale,
ᴄAn' de rabbit he skip froo de ole fence rail.

" Ef yoh wanter see a tail, " sez de pole-cat ; " see !
" Mah tail's long 'nuff foh mah folks an' me ! "

III.

About three o'clock on Christmas afternoon,
Hogan's rifle exploded prematurely and killed a rabbit.   The intense astonishment of McCue, Quinn
and Phelan nerved Hogan for more glory, and he
fired at every tuft of hill-weed until his cartridges
were gone, and his temper too.

" Bad cess to me goon ! " he shouted, " 'tis twisted
it do be, an' I'll thank ye for th' loan av yere piece,
McCue."

"G'wan," said McCue, " 'till I show ye a thrick ! "
—and he blazed away at a rapidly vanishing cotton-
tail and missed.   Occasionally, firing by volleys, they
scored a rabbit to four rifles, and, at sunset, McCue
spread out a dozen or so cotton-tails on the newly
fallen snow before the door of the hill shanty.
Phelan wiped his brow with the back of his
fist.

" Phwere's th' naygur ? " he demanded.

Hogan looked at his watch and began to swear, just as Cassius appeared over the hilltop, a tin box under his arm, and on his face a smile of confidence.

" Have ye th' ould Tom ! " demanded Quinn, as Cassius shuffled up and, depositing the tin box on the doorstep, looked cheerfully around.

" Evenin', gemmen, evenin'," said Cassius, licking his lips and leaning down to pinch the fat rabbits lying in a row; " Kinder cold dishyere Chris'mus, gemmen. 'Spec we gwinter 'sperience moh snow——"

" Have ye the cat ? " repeated Quinn sternly.

" 'Cose I has " said Cassius indignantly, " an' I'se come foh de cash——"

" Phwat's that ! " snarled Hogan.

" Hould a bit ! " interposed Quinn ; " is the tom in the box now ? "

" 'Cose he is," repeated Cassius ; " yaas, sah, dasser mighty fine kitty, dat is ! Hit ain't no or'nary cat, hit ain't,—no sah. Dasser pole-cat, sah, dat is ! "

" 'Tis a Dootch cat ! " said Phelan.

" Sure Poles is Dootch, too," observed McCue ; " Phwat are ye waitin' for I dunno ? " he added, scowling at the darkey.

" I'se lingerin' foh mah cash," said Cassius.

" G'wan ! " said Phelan briefly.

Cassius turned an injured face from one to the other. There was a hostile silence. Phelan produced a flour sack and threw the rabbits into it, one by one.

"'Scuse me, gemmen," began Cassius,—when an exclamation from Quinn silenced him and drew the attention of all to a black-and-white object advancing across the snow toward the shanty.

"Lan's sake!" muttered Cassius, "pole-cat in de box gwineter draw all de pole-cats in dishyere county !"

"'Tis a rabbit!" said McCue, seizing his gun.

"It's a cat!" said Hogan, "d'yez mind th' tail of ut !"

"Dat ain't no cat," said Cassius contemptuously, "dasser skunk."

"Skoonk is it? An phwat's a skoonk, ye black mutt?" demanded McCue. At the same instant Phelan fired and missed; Quinn, paralysed with buck-fever, clutched his rifle, mouth agape, while Hogan, in an access of excitement, began shouting and kicking the darkey from snowdrift to snow-drift.

"Now will ye grin!" he yelled; "G'wan home ye omadhoun !—"

"Leggo mah wool!" retorted the darkey, and rose from the snow with sullen alacrity: "Wha' foh yoh yank mah kinks?"

"Faith then, fur luck an' bad-luck," said Hogan and followed McCue into the deserted shanty.

A moment later, Quinn and Phelan came back after an eager but fortunately fruitless quest for the game, and McCue and Hogan issued from the shanty, bearing the tin box, ready to return to the barracks.

" Me heavy hand on th' naygur ! " growled Mc-
Cue : " he's gone, where ?—I dunno, but he'll carry
the bag o' rabbits or me name's not McCue ! Call
him, Hogan."

" Come out, ye bat-o'-th'-bog, ye ! Where are
ye now !—the Red Witch o' Drumgoole follow ye !"
shouted Hogan, tramping around the shanty and
poking under the steps.

" Lave th' black scut," said McCue with dignity,
" I'll carry the sack. Have ye th' sack ? " he added,
turning to Phelan.

" I have not," said Phelan, " 'twas there foreninst
the shanty."

" Now the red itch o' Drumgoole on him !"
shouted McCue. " Usha, musha, he's gone wid the
sack, an' divil a bit or a sup av a shtew ye'll eat
the night ! Sorra the rabbit he's left !—me heavy
hand on him an' his !—may the saints sind him sorrow this blessed night ! "

" We have th' ould tom in th' box," said Quinn,
with a significant flourish of his rifle.

" There's no luck in it—Care killed a cat, an'
worrit the kittens. Begorra !—I'll kill no cat at all,
at all !" replied McCue superstitiously.

" May the Dootch robbers choke whin they sup
this night !" shouted Phelan ; " Wirra the day I set
eye on the naygur an' his Dootch whippets ! "

" They'll have no luck, mark that !—McCue !"
said Hogan : " We've their Tom in a box an' they'll
have no luck ! "

They gathered up their rifles in silence ; McCue

carried the box; one by one they filed down the darkening hillside toward the village where already a lantern or two glimmered along the stockade and the bugles were sounding the evening call.

When the sportsmen reached the barracks, and it became known that the Jägers' tom-cat had been captured, the regiment went wild with enthusiasm. It was decided not to open the box at once, because the cat might hastily migrate toward the familiar barracks of the Jägers; but Quinn, the prime mover in the capture of Thomas, was selected a delegate of one to present the box to Colonel Bannon as a surprise and a Christmas gift from the whole regiment.

So, that night, the regiment ate their Christmas dinner in eager anticipation, and their hilarity was scarcely marred by Hogan's report that the Jägers' barracks resounded with a joyous din of feasting and song.

" May th' banshee worrit thim! Let them be wid their futther—an'—mutther! May the red banshee sup with them in hell ! " said Quinn as he rose in obedience to the orderly who said the Colonel would receive him.

He took the tin box gingerly, for the animal inside was very lively, and he followed the orderly to the door of the messroom in the officer's quarters.

Here the orderly left him a moment but returned directly and whispered :

" The colonel knows it's the Dootch cat ye have, —but ye'll say ye bought it. Sure he's a dacent man, is Colonel Bannon, an' no love lost betwixt him an' Fallback. Are ye ready now?"

"Yis," said Quinn firmly, forage cap in one hand, box in the other : "is the rigiment outside on the parade?"

"It is, an' ready to cheer."

"Then in I go," said Quinn.

The colonel sat at the head of the table, flanked by his staff and line officers. His face, a little red with Christmas cheer, was gravely composed for the occasion. His officers, to a man, beamed with anticipation.

"Quinn," said the Colonel.

"Sorr," said Quinn, standing at attention.

"This is a very pleasant occasion," said the Colonel, "and I am gratified that my men have remembered their colonel upon this blessed day. I am told you have a surprise for me, Quinn."

"Yis sorr,—a cat, sorr."

"A cat!" said the Colonel in affected surprise.

"We've lost our goat, sorr, but we'll conshole our sorrow wid a cat, sorr—Colonel Bannon's cat if you plaze, sorr."

The Colonel's eyes twinkled.

"'Tis a dacent kitty, sorr," said Quinn, undoing the rope that held the lid ; "a Dootch Kitty they do say from Poland, sorr, where we sint for a dozen an' this is the pick o' them."

The Colonel suppressed a smile ; the officers gurgled.

"I have the spachless honor, sorr," said Quinn,

4

placing the box on the table before the Colonel,—
" I have the unmintionable deloight in presinting to
our beloved Colonel in the name av his beloved
rigiment, this illegant kitty ! "

And he took off the lid.

There was a silence. Suddenly a long slender
black and white creature sprang from the box to
the table, flourishing a beautiful bushy tail; there
came a yell, a frightful stampede, a crash of glass,
a piteous shriek from the Colonel under the sofa:
"Quinn! Quinn! Ye murtherin' scut! 'Tis a
skoonk! Usha, but I'll have yer life fur this night's
work ! "

And Quinn, taking his nose firmly in both hands,
pranced away like one demented—fled for his life
through the falling snow of that blessed Christmas
night.

*   *   *   *   *

In the barracks of the Jägers was song and jest
and Christmas cheer:—shouting and feasting and
heart-friendships, and the intermittent din of trombones.

Cassius, feeding to repletion in the kitchen with a
bowl of rabbit stew between his knees, paused to
hold his aching sides because it hurt him to laugh
when he ate. Beside him on the floor, Thomas
licked his whiskers, and yawned and stared into the
dying fire.

SMITH'S BATTERY

A new warre e're while arose —

LOVELACE.

SMITH'S BATTERY. •

Impotent Pieces of the Game He plays
Upon this Checker-board of Nights and Days ;
Hither and thither moves, and checks, and slays,
And one by one back in the Closet lays.
FITZGERALD.

ON the evening of the 15th the cavalry left by moonlight, riding along the railroad toward Slow-River-Junction. The bulk of the infantry followed two days later, leaving behind them "The Dead Rabbits,"—a New York regiment,—a squad of cavalry, and Smith's four-gun battery, to garrison a hamlet inhabited principally by mosquitoes.

The hamlet of Slow-River contained a red brick church, some houses, a water-tank, and a race-track. The " Dead Rabbits " established their warren in the race-track sheds, the cavalry guarded the railway and water-tank, and Smith's battery decorated the graveyard around the red brick church.

The inhabitants of Slow-River, barring the mosquitoes, had mostly disappeared toward Dixie before the arrival of Wilson's division. When Wilson moved on toward the Junction, leaving behind him the " Dead Rabbits,"—and Smith's Battery to take

53

care of them—the non-combatant population of
Slow-River numbered two,—not including an
Ethiopian of no account.

Smith, of Smith's Battery, had constituted himself an inquisition of one. The Reverend Laomi
Smull, pastor of the brick church took the oath of
allegiance and smacked the Book with moist thick
lips. Mrs. Ashley, the remaining inhabitant of
Slow-River, widow of a Union officer killed in the
early days of the war, took the oath earnestly, then
told Smith who she was and received his apologies
with sensitive reserve.

"I wished to take the oath," she said: "I have
not had my country brought so near for many
months."

The Reverend Laomi Smull, clasped his soft
fingers together and surveyed the firmament while
Mrs. Ashley brushed the tears from her blue eyes.
When she thanked Smith for the privilege of pub-
licly acknowledging her country, the Reverend
Laomi nodded and closed his small eyes as though
in ecstatic contemplation of a soul regenerated.

"Where's the nigger?" inquired Smith when Mrs.
Ashley had gone back to her cottage below the
church.

"Do you refer to our unfortunate coloured
brother?" suggested the reverend gentleman.

"Oh yes—of course," said Smith, fidgeting with
his sabre.

"Abiatha is angling from the bridge," said Smull
wagging his double chin till his collar creaked.

"What is he fishing for," inquired Smith, who was an angler.

"Fish," said the Reverend Laomi, and entered his church with more agility than his fat bulk appeared to warrant.

At the door he turned to cast one last sly glance at the firmament.

Smith, distrustful, and of the earth earthy, walked back to the graveyard, lifting his sabre to prevent the clanking of the scabbard on fallen grave-stones.

"Look out for that pastor," he said to Steele: "if I know a copperhead from a copper kettle he's one with double fangs."

"You think he may play tricks?" asked Steele, toasting a rasher of bacon on the coals before his feet.

"Yes, I do. He'll get no passes from me, I can tell you. I'm going up into the church tower. Is there a bell there?"

"A cracked one," said Steele.

"I'll take the clapper out," observed Smith. He accepted a bit of bacon from Steele, laid it on a morsel of hardtack, munched silently for a few minutes, then washed his breakfast down with a tin of coffee, returned Steele's salute, and entered the church through the vestry. Climbing the belfry ladder on tiptoe, cap in hand, he could not prevent the ladder from creaking. So, when he stepped out on the loosely laid planks beside the bell, he found the Reverend Laomi Smull leaning on the belfry-ledge, preoccupied with the sky.

"Oh," said the reverend gentleman with a start, "is it my young friend, Captain Smythe?"

"Smith," said the officer dryly, and felt in the bell for the iron clapper.

"Where is the clapper?" he added turning on Smull.

The Reverend Laomi regarded him calmly.

"I do not know," he said.

To search the person of the minister was Smith's first impulse; Smull divined it and smiled sadly.

"He's thrown it from the tower where he can find it," thought Smith. Then he drew a jackknife from his blouse, cut the two bell-ropes and let them drop to the tiled floor far below. The thwack of the ropes echoed through the silent church; Smith apologised for the military precaution and stepped to the tower parapet. There he could look out over the ravaged country toward the Junction where rumour reported an ominous concentration of Union troops. He could see the water-tower and the railroad and cavalry patroling the embankment in the morning sunshine. He could see the weather-stained sheds of the race-track where the "Dead Rabbits" prowled, a nuisance and sometimes a terror to everybody except the enemy. Behind him he heard the Reverend Laomi pattering about over the loose planks that formed the belfry flooring.

"I shall station a signal officer here," he said without turning.

"Sir," stammered the minister.

" I am sorry," said Smith impatiently : " we need the church more than you do."

" I agree with you," said Smull in a peculiarly soft voice.

" I am sorry to exclude you—" began Smith turning,—and those words had wellnigh been his last, for one leg slipped through an unexpected fissure between the planks, and he clutched a beam beside him and drew himself up, deadly pale.

He looked at Smull ; the clergyman overwhelmed him with congratulations on his escape from pitching headlong to the tiled floor below. He spoke of the mercy of Providence, of the miracles of the Most High ; he deplored the condition of the belfry floor ; he reproached himself for not noticing the fissure.

" I did not notice it either—when I came up," said Smith.

He followed Smull down the ladder and out of the church, returning the reverend gentleman's salute gravely. Then he ordered Steele to use the church for barracks and march his men in without delay.

" Into the church ? " repeated Steele.

" I guess Union soldiers won't desecrate this church or any other church," said Smith savagely, and turned on his heel.

On his way to the river he passed Mrs. Ashley's cottage ; she was hanging a home-made flag over the porch ; the stars and stripes were not symmetrical, but they were stars and stripes.

She stood on the top of a ladder, hammering tacks and holding the red, white, and blue folds in her pretty mouth. Occasionally she hammered one pink-tipped finger instead of a tack; at such moments she repeated, "Oh dear!"

Smith, cap in hand, offered to hold the ladder; Mrs. Ashley thanked him and continued to hammer serenely, until she remembered her ankles and descended precipitately. Then Smith climbed the ladder, drew out all the tacks Mrs. Ashley had hammered in, rehung the "symbol of light and law," draped and nailed it with military rigidity, and descended, covered with perspiration and mosquito bites.

Mrs. Ashley, cool and sweet in a white gown and black sash, thanked him and offered him a cup of tea under the magnolias. He accepted and sat down, sabre between his knees, to mop his face and evade mosquitoes until she returned with two cups of cold tea, creamless and sugarless.

"I have some limes—if you wish,—Captain Smith," she ventured, holding out the golden-green fruit in her smooth palm.

He thanked her and squeezed a lime into his tea.

Overhead, among the magnolia blossoms, the summer harmony had already begun with the deep symphony of bees; butterflies hovered under the perfumed branches; a grasshopper clicked incessantly among the myrtle vines.

Mrs. Ashley rested her chin on her wrist and looked at nothing. A breeze began to stir the folds

of the draped flag over the porch ; the crimson
stripes undulated, the stars rose and fell.

"We hear nothing in Slow River," said Mrs.
Ashley : " has anything important happened, Captain
Smith?" Her voice was almost inaudible.

"Nothing important. The last battle went
against us."

"Will there be a battle here?"

"No—I don't know—I have no reason to suppose
so," he said with conscientious precision. "If by
any possible chance the rebel cavalry should ride
around our army we might be visited here, but,"
he added, "the contingency is too remote for speculation."

"Too remote for speculation?" repeated Mrs.
Ashley under her breath.

Smith looked up at her—he had been watching a
file of ants bearing off minute crumbs from the biscuit he was nibbling. Smith's shoulder-straps were
too recent to admit of trifling, and he had an instinct
that Mrs. Ashley considered him young.

"Too remote for speculation," he repeated, and
touched the down on his upper lip with decision.
The faintest flicker of amusement stirred Mrs.
Ashley's blue eyes.

They spoke of the war, of battles on land and sea,
of sieges and blockades, of prisons and of death.
Listening to her passionless voice he forgot his
shoulder-straps for a while. She noticed it. She
spoke now as a very young hostess to a distinguished
guest, and he appreciated it. Little by little they

dropped into the half frank, half guarded repertoire peculiar to conventional civilisation ; he recognised her beauty; she conceded his gallantry ; the bees buzzed among the magnolias ; the warm breeze stirred the flag.

Sitting there with white fingers interlaced, and blue eyes demurely fixed on his, she wondered at the pains she took to wind him around the least of those white fingers of hers. Yet there was reason enough for her; her reason, in concrete form, skulked up-stairs under a mound of bedclothes,— a sallow faced, furtive young man, reported killed at Bull Run,—a deserter from the Union army, a Rebel at heart, too cowardly to back his convictions, —the blight and sorrow and curse of her young life —her husband.

From the day of their marriage, she had found him out and loathed him, yet, when he marched with a loyal regiment, she had bade him God-speed.

When the news came from Bull Run she had wept and forgiven him the past, because he had been good to her in death,—he had left her the widow of a Union soldier. His apparition in Slow River almost killed her. The Reverend Laomi Smull sarcastically bade her rejoice and put off her widow's weeds. She did neither.

Suddenly Wilson's advance was signalled from the hills beyond the river ; the population of Slow River fled Dixie-ward,—all except young Ashley, who lay sleeping off a debauch in his own gutter. The Reverend Laomi preferred to remain for several reasons. Hours after the Union cavalry dashed into the village, Ashley awoke to consciousness. When he comprehended what had happened he crawled into bed and cursed his wife and his luck and the Union Army impartially.

With what loathing did she aid in concealing him! With what desperation did she evade questions and intrusive patrols and the quiet questions of officers, courteous young fellows in blue, who accepted her word of honour with a bow and went away, deceived by a loyal woman—the wife of a coward and traitor—for that traitor's sake.

But she must play the frightful comedy to the end; she was doing it now, smiling back at Smith with eyes that caressed; with death in her heart.

When he rose to go she dropped him the quaintest and stateliest courtesy that can be dropped by a girl of twenty. His cap swept the tall grass-blades; Southern chivalry is infectious. So he passed on his way to the river.

Five minutes later the Reverend Laomi Smull appeared at the gate, smirked at the young wife, entered the cottage, and ascended the stairs with a parodoxical nimbleness that displayed two white cotton socks and inadequate attention to personal ensemble.

Smith pursued his way to the river through a weed-tangled path choked with rank marshy stalks, mint, elder, and wild lady-slipper. The little brown honey-bees hummed from bud to bud; dragon-flies, balanced in mid-air on quivering wings, selected plump mosquitoes from the cloud that wavered above Smith's head, and darted so close to his ears that he dodged like a new recruit at a bullet. When he came to the narrow sluggish river, where a foot-bridge swayed in the amber eddies, he took his cigar from his mouth and his Bible from his pocket.

A dilapidated individual of African descent, legs dangling over the water, fishpole clasped in both black fists, glanced up at the young officer and said : " Mohnin' suh !" Smith nodded, looked hard at the darkey, shrugged his shoulders, and restored the cigar to his lips and the Bible to his pocket.

" What are you fishing for, Uncle ? " he asked.

" Fishin' foh bass, suh," replied the dilapidated one.

" Catch any ? "

" I done cotch free bass an' a tarrypin turkle, suh."

" Want to sell them ? "

" No, suh,"

" Going to eat them all yourself, Uncle ? "

" I's gotter right ter," said the angler combatively.

Smith glanced down on the river sand where, anchored to a string, three plump bass floated out in the current.

" Are you going to eat the terrapin, too, Uncle ? "

" Co's I is," sniffed the darkey ; " I's gotter right ter."

" Let's see it," said Smith.

The angler climbed down to the strip of sand, picked up the terrapin, and held it out to Smith.

"How much?" asked Smith.

"Two dollahs, suh."

Smith paid the money grimly, picked up the terrapin, and stood a moment watching the darkey climb back to his perch on the footbridge.

"You'll leave your footprints on the sand of time," said Smith; "you'll be in Wall Street in a month—or in Sing-Sing."

"Wha's dat yoh's a-sayin' 'bout leabin' shoeprints on de san's ob time, suh?" asked the sable one, much interested.

"Nothing. If you get any more terrapin, bring them to the artillery camp. What's your name, Uncle?"

"Nuffin', suh?"

"No name?"

"No suh, jess 'Biah, suh."

"Oh—Alcibiades? No? Then Abiatha?"

"Yaas, suh."

"Whose darkey are you?"

"Mis' Ashley's niggah, suh."

"Oh! And the fish are for Mrs. Ashley?"

"Yaas, suh. Gwineter tote 'em back foh dinner, suh."

"Then," said Smith, "take back your terrapin too, you rascal! How dare you sell your mistress's property!"

'Biah watched the terrapin fall on the sands again, then he ruefully fished out the two dollars from some rent in his ragged coat. For a moment he struggled to tell the truth,—that Mrs. Ashley, in the present state of her finances, would rather have twenty-five cents than a dozen terrapins. Perhaps he feared Mrs. Ashley's wrath, perhaps a spark of Mrs. Ashley's pride had lodged beneath his own shirtless bosom. He said nothing, but rose, holding his fishpole in one hand, and sidled along the footbridge toward Smith, money clutched in one outstretched fist.

Smith glanced at the four silver half-dollars.

" Keep them and buy a coat, 'Biah," he said, relighting his cigar. At the same instant a big bass seized 'Biah's hook and made off with it, and 'Biah, losing his balance, dropped the silver coins into the river. Then the tattered African lost his head, too ; for a minute, bass, darkey, pole, and line became a blurr on the bridge, on the sands below, and finally in the water.

When 'Biah emerged, he had the bass by the gills ; later he fished out pole and line, while Smith, wading through the shallows in his cavalry-boots, poked about for the lost coins with the butt of his sabre-scabbard.

Ten minutes later 'Biah had recovered three of the half dollars. Smith had found something else, —a bundle of soaked clothes bearing United States army buttons and a second lieutenant's shoulder straps.

Instinctively he tossed the soaked packet into the alders and walked carelessly back to the footbridge where 'Biah, absorbed in disentangling his tackle, breathed hard and deep and muttered maledictions on "dat ole bull-bass what fink he know a heap moh'n ole 'Biah."

"Done drap mah hook in de hole," he puffed; "gwine ter gitter hook an' tote mah fish, suh. Mohnin', suh, mohnin'," ; and 'Biah scrambled to his feet and shuffled back along the weed-grown footpath that led to Mrs. Ashley's cottage.

When the negro had disappeared, Smith leaped lightly to the sand below, parted the alders, found the bundle of clothes, and cut the cord with his sabre.

"New clothes," he muttered: "not a patch, not a rag—hello—what's this?"

He drew a soaked bit of paper from the breast-pocket of the jacket, and, standing in the alders, read the pencilled memorandum.

It was a receipt signed by the Reverend Laomi Smull for pew-rent received from Anderson Ashley. But what troubled Smith was the date, for, if Mrs. Ashley's husband had been killed at Bull Run, how could he be renting pews from the Reverend Laomi in Slow-River? Smith examined the paper closely ; it read:

"Received from Anderson Ashley, Esquire, $3.75, pew-rent for Mr. and Mrs. Anderson Ashley."

The date, two months back, startled him. As he stood, holding the paper, staring vacantly at the motionless leaves on the alders, far away he heard the noon call from the artillery bugles, taken up by the cavalry trumpets at the water-tank, and passed on to the infantry around the race-track. He shoved

5

the wet clothes under a fallen log, opened the Bible in his pocket, placed the folded receipt between the leaves, and, carrying the Bible in one hand, sword in the other, went back along the tangled footpath toward Mrs. Ashley's cottage.

III.

When the Reverend Laomi Smull displayed un-expected agility on Mrs. Ashley's staircase, Ashley himself, hearing the ascending footsteps, cowered under the bed quilts and turned cold to the marrow of every bone.

"It's me," said the reverend gentleman, enter-ing the bed-room and waving his fat hands at the pile of quilts under which Ashley squirmed in fear: "it's me, Ashley," he repeated, disregarding the finer points of grammatical construction: "Moseby's men is in the hills and I don't know what to do."

Ashley's dissipated face emerged from the bed-covers. Fear stamped every feature with a grimace that amused Smull.

"What did you say about Moseby's men?" stammered Ashley.

"They're in the hills across the river," repeated Smull: "I seen smoke on Painted Rock."

"It's a blockade still," suggested Ashley.

"No it ain't," retorted Smull; "it's green wood burnin'—don't I know a still, hey? It's Confede-rate cavalry, an' they've ridden around the Yankee army, that's what they've done."

Ashley protruded his long pallid neck, looked around like an alarmed turkey, in a weed patch, and finally stared at Smull.

"What are you going to do?" he asked.

The fat cunning on Smull's face was indescribable.

"Do?" repeated Smull.

"Yes, do! Didn't Moseby tell you to ring the church bell on Sunday as many times as there was Yankee companies in Slow-River? Didn't he tell you to hang out your washing according to code,—a shirt, 'come,' two shirts 'run,' a red undershirt, 'run like the devil'—say, didn't he and you fix up the code?"

Smull's small eyes rested on the door, then on Ashley.

"The Yankee Battery Captain came to look at the bell. I threw the clapper out into the bushes," he said.

After a moment he added: "He came near falling through the plank floor. Frightened me to death—most."

Ashley's eyes met his; Smull raised a fat white hand to conceal the expression of his mouth.

"That's all very well," said Ashley petulantly, "but I reckon you'd better go. If I'm caught I'm toted out to a shootin' match—and I'll be the target too."

This observation appeared to start a new train of thought in Smull's mind. And, as he cogitated, his expression changed from sly malice to complacence, and then to that sanctimonious smirk with which, in the garden below, he had greeted Mrs. Ashley.

"Ashley," he said gravely, "I can't give no signals to Moseby, nohow. I regret," he continued piously, "I regret and see the error that the South has made in this here unchristian war."

Ashley started and fixed his bloodshot eyes on Smull, who immediately raised his own to the ceiling and addressed it unctuously: "This here unchristian war to disrupt the sacred union of the States is a offence against God and man, my young friend, and I now am brought to see, by God's grace, the sin of secession an' slavery, an' Jefferson Davis an' his wicked ways. Surely the wicked shall perish and be cut down like the grass; in the morning it flourisheth and groweth up, in the evenin' it is cut down an' withereth, my young fren'."

Ashley had grown paler and paler; his fingers clutched at the bedclothes, and he watched Smull's increasing exaltation with a horror that pinched every feature in his face.

"No!" bawled Smull: "no! no! I have took the oath of allegiance to these here United States! Blessed is the merciful, for they shall obtain mercy!"

"Shut up!" gasped Ashley, "do you want to have the Yankee provost here?"

Smull raised his hands and wept on; "Behold I am utterly enlightened! Blessed are the meek for they"—

"Stop!" shrieked Ashley, starting up in bed.

Smull glanced sharply at him, then sat down with
a sigh.

"Are you going to give me up to the provost-
marshal because you took the oath?" quavered
Ashley, beside himself with fright and fury.

"No," said Smull wagging his double chin and
meeting Ashley's glance squarely; "no, I will not
bring the centurions for fear they utterly destroy
thee with the sword."

Ashley, sweating with terror, looked at the reverend gentleman and wondered whether he could
kill him without undue disturbance. That fat neck
could not be strangled with Ashley's slender fingers;
the revolver under the pillow was surer—and surer
still to bring the Yankee soldiers pell-mell into the
house. He had been jealous of Smull when that
gentleman made his weekly call on Mrs. Ashley.
He, besotted as he was, noticed the expression of
Smull's small eyes when Mrs. Ashley entered the
room, her innocent heart filled with plans for char-
ities suggested by the minister. Would the Reverend Laomi like to see Mrs. Ashley a real widow?
Would he even aid fate toward the accomplishment
of her widowhood?

"What the hell made you holler like that!" stammered Ashley fiercely. "Damn you," he added,
"if the Yankees had come into this room, you
would have left it feet first an' fit for a hole in the
ground?"

The Reverend Laomi Smull looked sadly at the
young man. There were tears on his fat cheeks.

"Yes, I tote a gun," sneered Ashley, tapping the pillow under his head. "Don't be a fool. Hang out your shirt and let Moseby come and clean out these Yankees, for God's sake, before they shoot me and hang you on my evidence."

"Moseby's men can't face cannon," observed Smull with sudden alacrity.

"Then lock the cannoniers in the church when Moseby signals. You can do it ; you've got the keys, haven't you?"

Smull nodded.

"They'll come at night, of course ; you can go and whine hymns in the church by special permit, and lock the door when the first carbine goes off."

"And the bell on Sunday?" inquired Smull : "the clapper's gone, the ropes are cut, and the Yankee Battery Captain wouldn't let me ring it no-how."

"Never mind the bell. If Moseby sees the shirt he'll attack by night, unless he's in force. If the whole Confederate cavalry has ridden around Wilson, then he'll come by day and send the Yankees packing, battery or no battery. All you've got to do is to hang out that shirt. Now go away, d'you hear?"

Smull rose and walked softly to the door.

"And," added Ashley, "if you play tricks on me you'll hang on my evidence."

Smull opened the door.

"And you'll not get my wife anyway, damn you!" finished Ashley triumphantly from the bed.

Smull turned and looked at him, then went out, quietly closing the door behind him.

At the foot of the stairs he met Mrs. Ashley, and he smirked and opened his thick moist lips to speak, but the young wife's face startled him and he closed his mouth with a snap of surprise.

"You intend to betray my husband," she said breathlessly.

"You have been listening at your husband's door," he retorted savagely.

She clenched her small hands: "What of it! With cowards and traitors and hypocrites as guests, honest people need be forewarned! Shame on you! Shame on your cloth! Shame on your oath of allegiance! You'll sell my husband to steal his wife! You'll break your oath to bring the rebel cavalry down on us!"

She brushed the tears from her eyes with both trembling hands.

"God knows," she said, "I thought I was right to hide my husband, and I think so now. Yet, if he or you betray these soldiers I shall denounce you both to the first picket!"

"Madame," began Smull in thick persuasive tones, "you wrong me——"

"Leave this house!" she said, trembling.

The Reverend Laomi bowed low, raised his eyes to the sky, sighed, and stepped out into the garden. There, before he could rearrange his expressive features, Smith met him face to face and returned the clergyman's disconcerted salute gravely.

"One moment, my dear young friend," stammered Smull.

Smith wheeled squarely in his tracks and stood rigid. Smull hesitated, passed a fat tongue over his lips, and weighed the chances. The next moment he made up his mind, glanced at the door, saw Mrs. Ashley entering the house, then leaned swiftly toward Smith and whispered.

Smith drew himself up sharply; the Reverend Laomi Smull turned and left the garden, head bowed on his breast as though in anguish of spirit. A few minutes later he brought a wash basket out of his house and pinned a single shirt to the line with a wooden clothespin. Then he ran to the woods, as fast as he could, and squatted under a rock where a tangle of brambles fell like a curtain to screen him from the eyes of the impious, indiscreet, and importunate.

IV.

Smith, holding his sabre very stiffly, raised the bronze knocker on Mrs. Ashley's door and rapped three times. Then he loosened the chin-strap of his forage-cap; drew off both gauntlets, folded them, and placed them in his belt.

As he waited for admittance he saw the flag over the porch, motionless in the still air; he heard the wild bees' harmony overhead, he heard the rustle of a summer gown behind the door. But the door did not open. He waited. A burr stuck to the crimson stripe on his riding breeches; he flicked it off with his middle finger. Presently he knocked again, once; the door opened, and Mrs. Ashley came out, smiling faintly.

"I hope you want another cup of tea," she said with the slightest gesture toward the table under the magnolias where the two chairs still stood as they had left them in the morning.

He attended her, cap in hand, to the table; when she was seated, he stood beside her.

"Is it tea, Captain Smith?" she asked, looking up at him.

He grew suddenly red, but did not reply.

"What is it then?" she repeated, smiling: "not the mere honour of my poor presence I am sure. But, as a gallant officer, you must contradict me, Captain Smith."

Fear whitened her lips that the smile had not left; she faced him with the coquetry of desperation; and the pathos of it turned him sick at heart.

"I brought the Bible to you," he said; "it is the one you swore on—the oath of allegiance. You kissed it."

She inclined her throbbing head and took it.

"Open it," he said.

She obeyed. The wet bit of folded paper caught her eyes and she held it out to Smith, saying: "This is yours."

"No!" he said, "it is yours."

She glanced swiftly up at him, caught her breath;

and sat motionless, the paper clutched nervously in her fingers.

"Read it," he said in a scarcely audible voice.

She opened it; one glance was enough. Then she dropped it on the grass at her feet. Presently he stooped and recovered it.

"Yes," she said, obeying his eyes' command, "my husband is not dead. What of it?"

"Where is he?"

She was silent.

"A deserter."

"Yes."

"A traitor."

"Yes."

Smith walked to the gate, looked down the road toward the church where the artillery pickets paraded, naked sabres drawn. Then he came back.

"You are under arrest," he said, looking at the ground.

She turned a bloodless face to his, and raised one slender hand to her forehead.

"Do you doubt my loyalty?" she stammered.

He turned his back sharply.

"My loyalty?" she repeated as though dazed.

He was silent.

"But—but you administered the oath—you saw me kiss the Book," she persisted with childlike insistence.

"And your husband?" he asked, turning abruptly.

"What of him!" she cried, revolted; "I am myself!—I have a brain and a body and a soul of my

own! Do you think I would damn my soul with a
kiss on that Book! Do you think if I were a Rebel
I would deny it to save my body?"

"You have denied it," he said. He took the
Bible from her hand and opened it at a marked
page:

"By their acts ye shall know them," he read
steadily, then closed the Book and laid it on the
table. Their eyes met; the anguish in his bore a
message to her that pleaded for forgiveness for what
he was about to do.

"Not *that!*—" she stammered, half rising from
the chair.

He turned, drew out a handkerchief, and signalled
the artillery picket, flag-fashion. Then, before he
could prevent it, she was on her knees to him, there
on the grass, her white face lifted, speechless with
horror.

"For God's sake don't do that," he said, trying to
raise her, but she clung to him and pushed him toward the gate murmuring, "Go! Go!"

Furious at the agony he was causing her, tortured
by the agony it cost him, he held her firmly and
told her to be silent.

"Your husband is hidden in that house," he said:
"he is attempting to add to his treason by com-
municating with the Rebel cavalry. He tried to
force your own pastor, at the point of a pistol, to
hang a red shirt on his clothesline, which means
'attack!' The pastor is a good man; he had
taken the oath; such villainy horrified him. To

save his life in the room above he consented to hang
out a signal, but the signal he hung out is a white
shirt which means 'retreat.' There it is! '

He pointed angrily at the white shirt hanging on
the minister's clothes-line down the road.

" Now," he said, " let me do my duty."

He took her by the wrists, and looked straight into
her eyes, adding:

" I'd rather be lying dead at your feet than doing
what I've got to do."

" But," she cried, struggling to free herself, " but
the signal! Can't you understand? The man
lied! He lied! He lied! The white rag means
'attack!'"

Stupefied, he dropped her wrists and stepped
back.

" Run to your battery!" she wailed, " run! run!
Can't you understand! They're coming! They'll
kill you!"

Scarcely had she spoken when a rifle-shot rang
out from the race-track, another, another, then a
scattered volley.

An artillery guard approached the garden, halted,
turned, then scattered pell mell toward the church.
The next moment Smith was running for his battery
and shouting to Steele, who, mounted, cantered
among the grave-stones, and hurried the panic-
stricken cannoniers to their stations.

A frightful tumult arose from the race-track, where
the " Dead Rabbits," taken utterly unprepared by
a cloud of Confederate cavalry, ran like rabbits very

much alive. Through them galloped the Confederate riders, heavy sabres dripping to the hilt. The
Union cavalry at the water-tank was overwhelmed ;
the gray-jacketed troopers, shouting their " Hi! yi!
yi ! yi !" wheeled into the village, shaking a thousand glittering sabres ; but here they met a blast of
cannister from the churchyard that sent them reel-
ing and tumbling back to the race-track, now swarming with the entire Confederate division.

Smith's battery, limbered up, filed out of the
churchyard, while Smith, looking annihilation in
the face, saw the last of the " Dead-Rabbits " leg-
ging it for the woods. He turned with a groan
to Steele, and Steele said, " Ride for it, if we're
to save the guns ! The whole rebel cavalry is
here ! "

Bullets begin to sing into the bewildered column ;
the cannoniers struggled with the horses and swore.
Suddenly a shell fell squarely on the church tower
and burst.

" They've got artillery ; we're goners ! " shouted
a teamster.

Smith drew his sabre and raised it high above his
head : " Battery forward ! " he cried : " by the left
flank ! Gallop ! "

" God help us," gasped Steele.

Team after team dashed into position, dropped
their guns, and wheeled into station behind. Smith
dismounted and, standing by gun No. 1, began to
make calculations, pad and pencil in hand. Presently he gave his orders; a shrapnel shell was

rammed home, the screw twisted to the elevation, then :

" Fire ! "

A lance of flame pierced the white cloud, the shell soared away toward the race-track and burst beyond it.

Before gun No. 2 could be fired, a roar broke from the wooded heights close to the left, and a flight of shells struck Smith's battery amidships. For a moment it was horrible; teams were butchered, guns dismounted, cannoniers torn to shreds.

" Steele, bring that limber up ! " shouted Smith; " they shan't have every gun ! "

Steele seized the bridle; the terrified animals lashed out right and left, threatening to kick the traces to bits. A cannonier tried to hook up the gun but fell dead under the limber. A caisson blew up, hurling a dozen men into the air and stunning as many more. With blackened face and jacket, Steele reeled toward the gun again but fell on his face in the long grass.

" Bring off that gun ! " shouted Smith, standing straight up in his stirrups. Crack ! went the wheel, and the gun sank to its axle. Then Smith sprang from his horse and helped the gunners take the spare wheel from the caisson, roll it up over the grass, and mount it on the broken pieces. Smith hammered it on the axle, then drove home the linchpin, brushed the sweat from his half-blinded eyes, and looked around.

What he saw was the wreck of three guns and
caissons, the blackened fragments of gunners and
horses, and a mess of trampled grass; and beyond,
between his single gun and the race-track, a long
gray line, glittering with naked steel, sweeping
straight upon him.   ⸲

Of his battery there remained three men with
him; the others were lying dead around Steele or
stunned and mangled somewhere in the rank grass.

Scarcely conscious of what he did, he helped his
three gunners hook the gun to the limber, then
mounted and followed the gun back into the village
through a constantly increasing rain of bullets. One
of his men fell to the earth.

"I guess the whole Rebel army's here," he said,
as though speaking to himself : "I guess I'd better
get this gun to the Junction damn quick."

In front of Mrs. Ashley's cottage, as the cannon
passed, Ashley, in his shirt-sleeves, fired from the
window point-blank at a cannonier and shot him
out of his saddle. The dead man's clutch on the
team's bridle brought the gun to a halt, and the remaining gunner sprang from his saddle with an oath
and dashed into the house, sabre unsheathed.

"Come back!" shouted Smith, reining in ; "man!
man! we've got to save the gun! Come back!"
He climbed from his own saddle into the saddle of
the nigh battery horse and seized the heavy rawhide. A bullet broke his wrist as he lifted it.

There was a struggle going on in the room from
which Ashley had fired, but Smith did not see it;

his head swam and he looked at his gun with sick eyes. For a second all round grew black, then he found himself rising from his horse's neck, and, in the road beside him, he saw Mrs. Ashley and 'Biah, holding the bridles he had dropped.

" Tho/'ve hit me, I can't guide the team," he said vacantly. " I've got to save the gun, you know."

His eyes fell on the dead body of her husband, lying where it had been flung from the window among the flowers below.

" He's dead," said Mrs. Ashley; " I can't stay. Don't leave me! I can sit a horse if you will let me. I'll go with you. Don't refuse me!"

She sprang into the limber seat and clutched the railing with both hands; 'Biah followed with a howl of terror. There was a whip there; she swung the heavy rawhide and, seizing a horse by the mane, drew herself forward to the saddle, calling; "here they come! Gallop! gallop!"

With a plunge the six horses leaped forward, and tore down the road, Smith swaying in his saddle with a broken arm, the young girl, enveloped in a torrent of dust, riding the nigh horse of the wheel-team, limber and gun swaying and crashing on behind, 'Biah bouncing, jouncing, and howling intermittently.

" Guide!" called Smith faintly: " I can't."

She seized the bridles and lashed the horses. 'Biah shrieked.

" There are soldiers ahead!" she cried to him,— " Rebel infantry! They're going to fire!"

" Drive over them!" he gasped.

With a rumble, a roar, and a tearing crash, the train broke into the shouting mass of men, the scurrying wheels crunched on something, there came a flash of rifles, and Smith staggered. Before his eyes all was a blurr; he still heard the hoofs clink, the chains clash, the wheels thump and pound. Gun and limber struck an opposing body and leaped into the air; Smith's glazing eyes opened; he clung to his mount and attempted to turn.

He tried to say: " Is the wheel broken ? "

She could not reply, nor did she dare turn her head to that heap in the road already far behind. Terror sealed her lips—had sealed her lips when, through the dust ahead, she saw Smull, almost under the head team's hoofs, start to run, then go down to death beneath her very eyes.

     *   *   *   *   *   *

Six wild horses, a runaway limber and gun, two half-dead creatures hanging to the saddles, and a frantic darkey on the limber,—that was all of Smith's battery that tore into the Junction to the horror of Wilson and the scandal of the rank and file.

It all happened years ago; too long ago to fix the year or the date. Perhaps the incident is recorded in the archives of the Nation. Perhaps not. At all events when they had picked some stray bullets out of Smith and set his wrist in splints, he went North on furlough.

I think Mrs. Ashley went with him; and 'Biah being of no account, toted their luggage and breathed hard.

6

AMBASSADOR EXTRAORDINARY.

Alas! he's gone before,
Gone to return no more,

Whose well-spent life did last
Full ninety year and past,

Crowned with Eternal bliss
We wish our souls with his.

Ancient Epitaph

AMBASSADOR EXTRAORDINARY.

Sing again the song you sung
When we were together young—
When there were but you and I
Underneath the summer sky.

GEORGE WILLIAM CURTIS.

I.

IT was the season when our beloved motherland undergoes a quadrennial Cæsarian operation and presents a new president to a pardonably hysterical people.

Installed in the several departments of the national incubator, newly hatched cabinet officers, destitute of the Roman Augur's sense of humour, met around the "Oracle," and parted, without the shadow of a smile; brand-new heads of departments gazed solemnly at each other, government clerks cast owlish eyes on brand-new chiefs, gloomily alert for new cues.

The Ambassador to England was named, and sent forth; at parting the President intimated to him that he was a statesman; they shook hands and looked into each other's eyes; neither relaxed a muscle. The Ambassador to Germany departed; the Ambassador to Russia followed. Other statesmen-patriots expatriated themselves with serious

85

alacrity; a Minister descended on Brazil, another on Spain, another on Belgium; no guilty land escaped.

When His Excellency the United States Ambassador to France presented his credentials to the President of the French Republic, the guard at the Elysée presented arms, a nurse-maid wheeling a baby-carriage stopped to look, and there was a paragraph in the Figaro several days later.

In the Latin Quarter the American students discussed the new Ambassador.

Selby said to Severn: "There's a new Ambassador, you know; I hear he's red-headed."

Severn said to Rowden: "There's a new Ambassador, you know. I understand his family have red hair."

Rowden observed to Lambert: "I am told that the new Ambassador's daughter has red hair."

That morning the pale April sunshine, slanting through the glass-roofed studio in the rue Notre Dame, awoke Richard Osborne Elliott from refreshing slumbers. That young man, in turn, aroused Foxhall Clifford from a lethargy incident on a nuit blanche and a green table.

" Black can't turn up every time; red is bound to assist the lowly," muttered Clifford on his pillow.

At that moment Elliott, reading the Figaro, encountered the paragraph concerning the new Ambassador.

" Red is going to assist us," he remarked; " they say he has red hair."

" Who? " yawned Clifford.

An hour later Elliott, swathed in a blue crash bath-robe, sat in the studio sipping his morning coffee and perusing the feuilleton in the Figaro.

His comrade entered a moment later carrying a pair of shoes, and sat down on the floor.

"New Ambassador," repeated Clifford, lacing his patent leathers; "what do I care for Ambassadors!"

"They're good to know," observed Elliott, "they give receptions."

"Yes," sneered Clifford, "fourth of July receptions, where everybody waves little flags at every body else. I've seen trained birds do that."

"Ambassadors," insisted Elliott, "can get you out of scrapes. If you're broke they can send you home. You're not much of a patriot anyway."

"Yes, I am," snapped Clifford, "I'm loyal to the spinal marrow, but I draw the line at our diplomats."

He laced the other shoe, tied it, straightened up and rose, kicking out gently first with one leg then with the other until his trousers fell over each instep with satisfying symmetry.

"Patriot?" he went on, "I am too patriotic to countenance the status quo at our consulate, where the United States Consul sits in his shirt-sleeves and practises at a cuspidor, and where you can't get a consular certificate without being bullied by an insolent roustabout! So your new Ambassador," he continued reflectively, "can go to the devil!"

"Now you're too hasty," said Elliott; "Ambassadors are not consuls." He added dreamily, "His Excellency has a daughter—I understand."

Clifford, loitering before the mirror, unconsciously gave a smarter twist to his tie, and buttoned the snowy waistcoat in silence. When he was ready, gloved, hatted, and faultlessly groomed, he selected a blossom from a pot of fragrant pinks on the window and drew it through the lapel of his morning coat.

"Going to see Jacquette?" asked Elliott, pouring out more coffee.

"No," replied Clifford. He hummed a bar of a wedding march, strolled to the great glass window, mused a moment, sighed, whistled softly, and sighed again. There was a cock-sparrow out in the garden, hopping around, chirping and trailing his dusty wings through the gravel. A lady sparrow pecked him at intervals. The innocent courtship of the little things stirred Clifford with amorous wistfulness. He flattened his nose against the window glass and watched them, gently humming:

> " The fox and the bear,
>   The squirrel and the hare,
>   The dickey-bird up in the tree,
>   The roly-poly rabbits,
>   So amazing in their habits,
>   They all have a mate but me,
>   But me !
>   They all—
>   They a—a—a—ll—
>   Oh, they all have a mate but me ! "

Elliott listened scornfully.

"Why," said Clifford, twisting suddenly around,

" should I go to school and paint Italian models—
on a day like this?"

"You haven't been to the atelier in a week," said
Elliott morosely.   "Oh, I know what you're going
to say!   "

" No, I'm not," retorted Clifford.

" You are!   You're going to tell me that you've
seen the most wonderful girl in the Luxembourg,
who must be some foreign countess!   Don't I
know!   Haven't I heard it a thousand times?
And hasn't the countess always turned up with you
at some cheap restaurant?"

Clifford sat down on a camp-stool and pointed his
cane toward the floor.   Squinting along it at a spot
of sunlight on the velvety Eastern rug, he listened
in silence to Elliott's reproaches.

" Have you finished?" he asked.

Elliott girded up his bath-robe and moved off.

" Because," continued Clifford, " I have a proposition to make."

" Make it then," said Elliott, scowling.

" Well, sit down."

Elliott squatted Turk fashion on a divan, saying
bitterly, "Last week you moaned and protested
that you had been wasting your time.   Now go on
with your proposition,—but I'll not be a party to
any new infatuation, let me tell you—"

Clifford began to walk up and down the studio,
gloved hands clasped behind his back, head thoughtfully bent as far as his collar permitted.   As he
walked he twiddled his cane.

" Well?" inquired Elliott sarcastically.

Clifford came up to him and stood a moment in silence. Then he said: " Elliott, suppose we get married to twins?"

"Married!" bawled Elliott in angry astonishment. •

" Irretrievably," continued Clifford gently, " suppose we go into the thing thoroughly. Suppose we become respectable!"

" I am," broke out Elliott, but the other held up five expostulating gloved fingers.

" In a way—yes, in a way. But do you know what I think? I think no man is absolutely and hopelessly respectable unless he has a wife!— Elliott, a wife—a little wifey—"

" Rubbish!" replied Elliott, rising from the divan. "And let me inform you I don't want a wife. I'm well enough as I am—if anybody should ask you. Let go of my bath-robe; I'm going to paint."

" Think," urged Clifford,—" think of being really and legally married—think of the joyful anguish— no more suppers, no more Bullier, no more tzing! la! la!—"

He removed his silk hat, skipped playfully, and pretended to kick it.

" But," he continued, with sudden soberness, "a wife—a little wifey--is recompense for all pleasure—"

" Antidote, you mean—"

" No, I don't! Joy is born from the nuptial blessing. I desire to wed—"

" Who?   What?"

" A lovely, spirituelle, delicate vision—unworldly and—er—passably provided for—"

" By you?"

" Partly by me—partly by an adoring father,—a fine silvery-haired old patrician, borne down by the weighty cares of his millions—do you know any of that kind, Elliott?"

" I know some silvery-haired patricians."

" Tottering under the weight of millions?"

" Yes."

" With daughters?"

" Never asked 'em."

" What about the new Ambassador? You said his daughter—"

Elliott laughed :

" Oh, he's tottering under millions, but his hair is red and I think that hers—"

" You annoy me," said Clifford, and left the studio. He paused in the garden, sniffed at the lilacs, eyes raised in contemplation of the firmament.

" Nevertheless," he said to himself, " red hair or silver hair—I'm not bigoted on the silver question. And," he added with sprightly humour, " it's 16 to 1 I call on his Excellency before the week is out."

II.

His Excellency the United States Ambassador was a sheep-faced old gentleman who became hope-lessly mixed up in some railroads and escaped with

impaired health and most of the stock. Wheat hit
him hard a year later, and oil nearly ended him, but
he became entangled in trolley wires and put them
underground to save future annoyance to his legs.
This naturally set him on his feet again; and he
went to Washington where there is honour among—
financiers, and where they practise statesmanship as
she is taught. When his wife died and his daughter
Amyce began to go to school, his future Excellency
bobbed up and down in Congress with the caprice
and abruptness of a bottled imp. The see-saw continued year after year; sometimes he had a bill
passed, sometimes he blocked a bill; now and then
he got other people's money, now and then other
people got his money; but it evened up in the end
like dominoes—if you play long enough.

Then came the new administration, the stampede
for office. Before his future Excellency made up his
own mind, fate shoved him into the front rank, and
he asked for the French mission and the odds were
against him. The President weighed him—the
scales of the mint are exquisitely adjusted—and,
separating the dross from the pure metal, the mind
from the material, the President found him avail-
able for the diplomatic mission and told him he
might have it. So he took it and went.

His Excellency's income permitted him to keep
up his establishment in the rue de Sfax. Two neat
attachés, military and naval, played croquet with
him; his first secretary read Ollendorf to him, his
daughter played hostess on national holidays, and

Massenet every morning from ten to twelve. From three to four she swung in a hammock in the garden, and read Henry James.

It was at that hour and under those circumstances that Clifford first met Amyce. He was permitting his Excellency to beat him at croquet on the lawn; he loathed the game with a loathing untranslatable. He sat on the butt-end of his mallet, watching his Excellency pattering about from stake to stake, adjusting the balls with a chuckle, stooping to peer through wickets, calculating angles and split-shots.

His Excellency's heavy, sheep-like face with its silvery tuft of side-whiskers was ruddy and minutely shaved. Always scrupulously dressed, he had the air of having been neatly attired by a doll's costumer, then varnished. There was something about the old gentleman that recalled the irresponsible inertia of a manikin,—something, when he moved that resembled the automatic trot of a marionnette. He left an impression of not being responsible for either his clothes or his movements, but mutely referred you to his maker for guarantees that both were O. K. His hair was the glossy white that red hair frequently changes to; his eyes were pale hazel, lambent and vitreous as the eyes of a middle-aged sheep. His upper lip, also, seemed as though it were intended for cropping short grass.

He had taken to Clifford at once; he introduced him to the naval attaché and to the military attaché, to the first, second, and third secretaries of the Embassy. He did this partly because Clifford came armed with three good letters of introduction, partly because the United Service began to fight shy of the croquet-ground, and a substitute was necessary.

He did not, however, present him to his daughter; in fact Clifford had never even caught a glimpse of her, although on two occasions he had been bidden to dine at the Embassy. Stanley of the cavalry, the military attaché, had been pumped by Clifford without result. All he learned was that the young lady sometimes dined by herself.

However, that afternoon in early May, as Clifford sat glum and impatient on his mallet, and the Ambassador trotted about mauling the lawn, a young lady suddenly appeared under the trees by the hammock, glanced nonchalantly at his Excellency, languidly surveyed Clifford, and then, placing a hammock-pillow where it would do the most good, sat down in the hammock. It was gracefully done; she appeared to dissolve among a cloud of delicate draperies; her head indented the feather cushion; one small patent-leather toe glistened in the sunlight.

"She *is* red-haired," was Clifford's first thought; the next was: "She is a beauty,—oh, my conscience!"

She was. Her eyes were those great tender grey eyes that must have been forgotten when Saint Anthony was tortured; her skin was snow and roses. But her hair, her splendid, glistening hair, heavy and red gold!—dazzling as sunlight on floss-silk!

"It's your shot," said his Excellency for the third time.

The Ambassador won the game; he proposed another and Clifford assented with a sickly smile. Inwardly he swore that he would be presented, willy-nilly, even though he had to drag h͟i͟s Excellency to the hammock.

"Confound him," he thought; "have rumours of my reputation in the Quarter penetrated my country's Embassy?"

They had not; yet, it was exactly because Clifford was an artist and inhabited the Latin Quarter that the Ambassador avoided taking him to the bosom of his family. Vague and dreadful stories had been afloat in the Embassy concerning the Quarter. His Excellency had read Trilby too. This may have weighed with him; he had that distrust of art and artists prevalent among Anglo-Saxons. He also had the Anglo-Saxon desire to explore the Quarter for himself, one day,—if all was true as rumour had it. Therefore Clifford was doubly welcome, for his croquet, and for what the future promised when his Excellency needed a companion to the veiled mysteries of the Rive Gauche. So, on the whole, Clifford was a good man to amuse him, but not at all the kind of man to amuse Amyce.

But Fate, busy, as usual, with other people's business, began to meddle with the hammock cords where Amyce swung serenely reading Henry James.

Amyce rose just in time; there came a rapid unravelling of cords, and the collapsed hammock fell with a flop.

Flushed at the nearness of undignified disaster, Amyce shook out her fluffy skirts, Henry James tightly clasped in one hand, and looked appealingly at his Excellency.

The Ambassador started to rehang the hammock; Clifford said : " Permit me—"

" Not at all," returned the Ambassador,—but that was where he collided with Fate.

Amyce smiled and looked relieved; Clifford re-hung the hammock; Amyce thanked him. Then there was a pause during which both looked expectantly at his Excellency.

The Ambassador sullenly did his duty and took Clifford back to the lawn and beat him five games of croquet. But even this triumph was wet-blank-eted, for Amyce, holding Henry James to her chin, came out to the lawn to " watch papa " and encourage " papa," and condole with Clifford for his bad fortune. Only he knew how good that fortune had been—and, perhaps, she suspected it.

Amyce suggested tea on the lawn ; his Excellency began to object, but Fate was there and took another fall out of his Excellency, for Amyce had already ordered it, and a servant appeared with tables and trays on the porch.

The Ambassador cropped thin slices of bread-and-butter; Amyce poured tea; Clifford, in a daze of love, saw everything through pink haze. From this dream he was abruptly roused by the advent of

Captain Stanley of the cavalry.   He saw Amyce feed the brute with tea ; he heard her laugh softly when the Captain told some imbecile story or imitated Count Fantozzi.   He measured the Captain, he accorded him six feet two, a pair of superb legs, and a cavalry moustache.

"Granted him cards and spades," thought Clifford, "I'll beat him yet.   I know I can."

He was an honest youth with no more vanity than you or I.

III.

In the Quarter, Clifford's attitude became unbearable.   Rumours were afloat that he had outgrown the Quarter and its simple lurid pleasures ; that he had put away childish things ; that he consorted exclusively with the ostentatious great.   When garden parties were given at the English Embassy, Clifford's name figured among the guests,—and the Quarter read it in the Figaro and chafed.

Elliott, incredulous at first, observed the absence of Clifford from all Quarter rites with astonishment and grief.   The studio grew lonelier and lonelier. Elliott drank cocktails and brooded.

"See here," he blurted out, one day, "how long are you going to keep this up?"

"What?" replied Clifford, placing violets in his buttonhole.

"This confounded pose of yours—this tolerating the Quarter—this Embassy nonsense!"

"I prefer it to Bullier," said Clifford—"or," he added maliciously, "to the ' Bal à l'Hôtel-de-Ville.' "
Then he put on his gloves, humming:

> "Des chapeaux melon et des chapeaux rond!"
> Dame! c'est pas d'la petite bière!—eu!
> Tous ces gueux là
> Ils ont pigé ça
> 'A la Belle Jardinière!—eu!"

Elliott arose in fury.

"Very well," he said, "go and eat thin bread-and-butter and talk to fat princesses!—go and learn baccarat from that yellow mummy Fantozzi!—go and play imbecile croquet games with his Excellency and marry his daughter and live in the Parc Monçeaux. But you'll regret it! oh yes, you'll be sorry. And you'll think of the Luxembourg and of Jacquette and the old studio, and you'll hear a nursery full of babies squawling and you'll see Fantozzi leering at your wife and—"

Clifford looked around with gently raised eyebrows.

"I won't be back to dinner," he said amiably.

"Where are you going—dressed like that!" burst out Elliott with new violence.

"Going to shoot pigeons in the Bois."

They stood for a while in silence. Presently Elliott arose, went over to his manikin, and began to dress it; the manikin at present was doing duty as a French fireman for Elliott's great picture, "Saved!"

He mechanically placed the brass pot-helmet on

the manikin's papier-maché head, twisted the neck viciously, straightened out a sawdust stuffed arm, placed a rope in the hand, and closed the jointed fingers. Then he hauled out his easel, opened his colour box, and clattered the brushes.

Clifford watched him.

Elliott set his palette rainbow fashion, touched the canvas with the tip of his third finger, rolled a badger brush in rose-dorée, and began to glaze.

" Don't glaze yet," said Clifford.

" Why ? " snapped Elliott without turning.

" Because you make the flames too pink."

" What do you know about flames or pictures or glazing?" said Elliott bitterly. " Go and shoot pigeons and get married."

Clifford went out haughtily ; yet there was an un-accustomed pang in his breast. He suddenly realised how utterly out of it he was ; he began to com-prehend that he was afloat on the Rubicon in a very leaky boat. There was nothing to warrant his hopes of Amyce except a superb self-confidence. He saw he was alienating the Quarter ;—he noticed it now, as he walked, when Selby passed with a constrained smile, when Lambert bowed to him with unaccus-tomed rigidity, when, as he crossed the Luxembourg, Jacquette, passing with Marianne Dupoix, averted her pretty eyes.

He knew that an announcement of his engage-ment would be followed by excommunication from the Quarter. He had intended, in the event of be-trothal, to confine his Quarter visits to Elliott and

Selby and Rowden, but the prospect of involuntary exclusion had small attraction for him. He thought of Jacquette; the odour of violets from a street flower-stand recalled her.

He was in a bad humour when he reached the Tir aux Pigeons. Before he entered he saw Captain Stanley laughing on the lawn with Amyce. That, and the apparition of Fantozzi, completed his irritation and his score at the traps was ridiculous.

"You play croquet better," observed his Excellency, at his elbow.

That was the last straw, and Clifford forced a smile and went across the lawn.

"What was your score?" asked Amyce, looking up at him from the shade of her white parasol.

He was compelled to confess it.

Fantozzi, interrupted in the recountal of recent personal experience with an electric tram-car, raised his eyebrows superciliously.

"Pooh," said Captain Stanley, "everybody gets out of form at times."

Clifford looked gratefully at his generous rival; Amyce also raised her eyes to the well-knit military figure. Generosity is sometimes its own reward— sometimes it even receives perquisites.

Fantozzi continued his dramatic recital of the discourteous tram-car.

"I would come in a tram electrique—Mademoiselle—behold me on the corner street!—the tram approach!—I nod my head!—he do not hear me—"

"Couldn't hear you nod your head?" inquired Stanley sympathetically.

"Wonder his brains didn't rattle," muttered Clifford to himself.

"I nod! I nod!" repeated Fantozzi with mercurial passion; "I permit myself to make observation to stop! Cease! arrest ze tram! He regard me insolent! the tram vanishes itself! I am left on the corner street! The miserable laugh!"

"Are you sure you called to the motor-man to stop?" asked Stanley gravely.

"Parbleu! I did say stop! I said it! I did hear myself say it!"

"Mr. Clifford," said Amyce, "who is shooting?" She raised her lorgnettes: "Oh, Count Routier! Do you know I am not pleased to see little birds shot. Captain Stanley, it is your turn next. Have you no pity for those poor pigeons?"

"Monsieur Clifford had," said Count Fantozzi.

Amyce frowned a little; Fantozzi, prepared to laugh at his own wit, winced at the silence.

"Well," said Stanley, "I must go and perform. Shall I miss every bird—is it your pleasure?" he added, looking at Amyce.

Amyce smiled, her face was an enigma.

"Do as you please, I wish you good fortune in any event," she said.

Fantozzi pretended to shudder for the pigeon victims; Stanley walked thoughtfully across the lawn; Clifford, on fire with mixed emotions of jealousy and love, pretended to be absorbed in the shooting. He glanced indifferently at the gaily-dressed groups on the green, recognised some people and bowed, returned the salutes of other people who recognised him, and finally sat down on a camp-stool near Amyce.

Others were joining the group; a lieutenant of hussars, in sky-blue and silver, a brilliant-eyed diplomatic group from Brazil, one or two tall Englishmen, scrubbed pink, and finally his Excellency the United States Ambassador.

Clifford loathed them all; yet, Amyce was very kind to him. While Captain Stanley stood shooting, she scarcely glanced at the traps, and when that sober-faced young cavalryman sauntered back and confessed he had killed every bird, she scarcely raised her eyebrows. Was it displeasure?

"It is but a sport brutal," whispered Fantozzi close behind her.

"Like your bull-fights," said Clifford, seriously. He and Stanley were quits. It was war with Fantozzi.

The Spanish attaché with the Italian name glared blankly at Clifford who returned his glance wickedly.

"Croquet is better sport," bleated his Excellency, accepting a glass of champagne and a thin slice of bread-and-butter.

Clifford's turn came again at the traps; he missed right and left. He heard Fantozzi laugh. When he came back Amyce had gone away with his Excellency and Captain Stanley. However, Fan-

tozzi was there and Clifford succeeded in picking a
quarrel with him and followed it with a smile and
the slightest touch on the Count's shirt front.

Fantozzi turned a delicate green, then crimson.
Then he went away to the club-house and called
for a cab, and drove to his Embassy at a speed that
interested pedestrians along the Champs Elysée.

Clifford withdrew a little later to the Café Anglais
where he sullenly brooded and dined too freely.
About nine o'clock, he went to see Stanley; at half-
past ten a handsome young Spaniard called to pay
his respects and bring courteous greetings from
Fantozzi.

Clifford left the Spaniard and Stanley deeply interested in each other's society, and took a cab to
the United States Embassy, where, as an artist, he
was to oversee the decorative preparations for next
evening's garden-party. His Excellency had requested it; Amyce appeared pleasantly cordial; so
Clifford went to direct the hanging of lanterns and
gaily-coloured scarfs, and, incidentally to propose
marriage to his Excellency's only daughter.

His Excellency was smoking a cigar on the lawn
as Clifford entered, mentally thanking all the saints
that it was too late to play croquet. Servants
moved through the shrubbery; a few lanterns threw
an orange light among the chestnut branches.

His Excellency was in good humour; he pattered
about, as though driven by improved mechanism;
he chuckled at times that irritating chuckle incident
to victory at croquet.

" We'll have electric lights next week," he said;
" ever play croquet by moonlight? "

" There is no moon to-night," said Clifford, triumphantly.

" I know it," sighed his Excellency.

Preseftly the Ambassador exhibited a desire to
interfere with Clifford's directions to the servants;
he insisted on mounting a ladder and fussing with
a string of crimson lanterns. The first, second, and
third Secretaries of the Embassy were summoned to
steady the ladder; Clifford saw an opportunity and
seized it.

Amyce, who had been standing on the porch, observed Clifford's advance with mixed sentiments.

" Are all the lanterns hung? " she asked.

" No," said Clifford, " his Excellency has proposed
modifications."

" Man   proposes—" began   Amyce, gaily, then
stopped.

The silence was startling.

Presently Amyce picked a rose from the vine at
her elbow.

" Is it mine? " asked Clifford.

" Yours?   I—I don't know."

She held it a moment, then he took it. .

" And the giver? " he whispered.

" I—I don't know," said Amyce.

" Then," said Clifford, " I shall take her—as I
took the rose; " and he moved toward her up the
steps.

At that moment Fate, who had been listening as

usual, somewhere among the shadows, took a hand in the proceedings; there was a crunch of footsteps on the gravel walk, the dim glimmer of a cigar, and Captain Stanley entered the house, bowing pleasantly to Amyce and casting a look at Clifford that meant, " Follow me."   ●

Before Clifford could move, Amyce passed him with a pale smile and crossed the lawn toward the lantern-hangers.

His emotions were indescribable ; he damned Stanley, then, buoyed with the intoxicating thought that Amyce had not refused him, he went into the house and found Stanley waiting in the smoking-room.

" Well," said Clifford ungraciously.

Stanley appeared a trifle surprised but said : " I'm sorry you are in this mess, old fellow. Fantozzi naturally wants a shot at you."

An unpleasant sensation passed through Clifford ; Fantozzi and his shot were repulsive at the moment.

" When ? " asked Clifford.

" To-morrow at sunrise.   I've notified Bull."

Clifford grew angry: " Then he can have his shot," he said savagely, and sat down for a conference, interrupted about eleven o'clock by his Excellency.

The Ambassador was in no mood for bed.   Perhaps something in the lighted lanterns had roused the long smouldering spark of revelry, dormant in every masculine bosom.   Being an Anglo-Saxon he knew of no lighter gaiety than heavy drinking.   He

began to tell stories—quite pointless tales—and he
would not let Clifford go, and he spoke vaguely of
wonderful brands of whisky past and whisky to
come. He sat there, his limpid hazel eyes meeker
than any lambkin's, a carefully dressed lay-figure,
irresponsible to God and man, and for whom nobody was responsible except his Constructor.

About midnight he became entirely automatic ; his
eyes seemed to plead for somebody to wind him up
and set him going again.

" When he gets this way he has a tendency to
wander," whispered Stanley ; " I usually lock him in
his room ; if I didn't he'd be all over town—like an
escaped toy."

Clifford went out on the porch ; Stanley followed.

" At sunrise," said Clifford soberly. " Will you
call for me in a carriage ? "

" At sunrise," replied Stanley offering his hand.

Then Clifford went away, and Stanley, lingering
to watch him to the gate, walked slowly back to the
smoking-room.

To his horror his Excellency had disappeared.
The west porch door swung wide open.

" He'll be all over Paris ! " groaned Stanley smit-
ing his head with both hands.

IV.

Clifford did not go back to the studio; he took a long drive in a cab to steady his nerves. He alternately thought of Amyce, of Fantozzi, of his Excellency's incoherent stories, of Elliott and the studio,—and, perhaps, of Jacquette. Two hours before dawn he found himself standing in front of Sylvain's; and, wondering why he had wandered there, he went in and upstairs. The long glittering room reeked with cigar smoke ; voices rose harshly from the disordered tables; a piano tinkled faintly on the floor above. He looked at his watch; it lacked an hour of the appointed time when he was to meet Stanley with the carriage at the studio. He turned toward the portal impatiently ; somebody entered as he opened the leather doors ; he glanced up and met his Excellency face to face.

His Excellency began a mechanical trot into the room ; Clifford involuntarily detained him and the Ambassador stopped obediently as though somebody had arrested his running-gear. He examined Clifford with mild vitreous eyes as though he had never before seen him. He was perfectly docile, perfectly contented to be started again in any new direction. He needed a few repairs ; Clifford saw that at once. It would never do to send his Excellency home

with such a hat and collar and tie ; the personnel at
the Embassy must never see his Excellency in such
disorder.

"Come," said Clifford gently. There was a cab
at the door ; he stowed his Excellency away in one
corner and followed, ordering the cabby to hasten
to the studio in the rue Notre Dame. There was
not much time to lose when they reached the studio.
Clifford attempted to adorn his Excellency with
clean linen, but found that it might take some hours
as the machinery had run down and the Ambassador
evinced an unmistakable inclination to slumber. He
seated his Excellency in an arm-chair, and hurriedly changed his own evening dress for morning
clothes. Then he went up to Elliott's bedroom, but
that young man's bed was untenanted and undisturbed. The Ambassador slept peacefully in the
studio ; after a moment's thought Clifford scribbled
a note :

" DEAR ELLIOTT :—

When you come in please give this gentleman
clean linen and a new hat and brush his clothes and
send him to the United States Embassy p. d. q.
							" Yours,
									" CLIFFORD."

As he finished he heard carriage-wheels in the
street outside and he thrust the note into his Excellency's hat-band, jammed the hat on the slumbering
diplomat's head, and hurried out to the street where

Stanley and Bull were waiting in the dim grey of the coming dawn.

"Not had coffee!" exclaimed Bull; "nonsense, it's traditional!"

"We'll take it at St. Cloud," said Stanley. "Are you ready, old fellow?"

The carriage door slammed, the wheels rattled faster and faster.

"By the way," said Clifford, "his Excellency paid me a visit this morning. I'll see he gets home in good shape."

"Thank heaven!" cried Stanley; "I've been hunting him all night!"

A moment later he looked earnestly at Clifford: "Is your hand steady?"

"Yes," said Clifford pleasantly.

"You'd better shoot closer than you did at the pigeons," suggested Bull.

"Why? Is Fantozzi a good shot?"

"Rotten," said Stanley.

"He's the more to be feared then," observed Bull cynically.

"Why, you know," confessed Clifford with a frank smile, "I feel certain that I'm not going to be hit. I was nervous last night, but not on that account."

And he smiled confidently, thinking of Amyce.

"But," insisted Bull, "are you going to hit your man?"

"Perhaps. What bosh it all is, anyway," laughed Clifford.

_c   V.

It was not yet sunrise when Elliott, entering the studio with Selby, lighted the gas and started to prepare for bed.   As Elliott turned up the gas Selby encountered the owl-like eyes of his Excellency, blinking, limpid, vacant.

"What's that?" he said nervously.   But when he saw the evening dress, the disordered tie, the hat, he approached the Ambassador curiously.   Presently he reached up, slipped the note from his Excellency's hat-band, opened it, read it in silence, then passed it to Elliott without a word.

"May I ask who you are?" said Elliott.   His Excellency bleated and waited for somebody to set him in motion, with placid confidence.   Elliott frowned.   This then was one of those who had lured Clifford from the fold!—this wicked old creature, apparently paralysed by depravity, planted in an arm-chair!   His ruffled hat accused him!   His crumpled tie, coyly peeping from behind one ear, convicted him!

"Call a cab," said Elliott thickly.

His Excellency betrayed no emotion; his round eyes followed Elliott's movements with trustful tranquillity.   When Selby returned, saying the cab was there, Elliott assisted the Ambassador to his feet; but, what was his surprise and indignation to see that his Excellency was entirely capable of movement. For, once set in motion, the Ambassador began trotting all about the room with perfect solemnity and, apparently with keen satisfaction.

" I beg your pardon," said Elliott coldly, " your cab is waiting." He might as well have talked to the statues in the Louvre. Then he lost his self-control and, taking his Excellency by one sleeve he led him to the arm-chair and seated him.

"Aged man," he said, "are you not mortified? You have dragged my comrade into your depraved society! You've taken him away from the Latin Quarter, you've stuffed his head full of marriage nonsense, of ambition, of desire for wealth and position. How dare you come here and ask for a hat and a collar!"

" Do you intend to ruin Clifford at baccarat?" demanded Selby.

"Or marry him to anybody?" added Elliott hoarsely.

"Who are you?" cried Selby; "are you a corrupt diplomat? Or are you merely a wicked old man on a spree?"

"He can't wear that hat; it won't stay on," observed Elliott. Selby took a woman's bonnet from the manikin, placed it on his Excellency's head and tied the strings under his chin. Elliott threw Clifford's covert-coat over his Excellency's shoulders.

" That bonnet will keep him from catching cold,"

he said," it may teach him a lesson, too, when his wife
sees it."

His Excellency unmoved, serene, surveyed Elliott
from under his bonnet.

"Come," said Selby, and they set the Ambassador in motion again, out the door, along the garden to the street where the cab stood. The cabby
stared a little, but Elliott said grimly: "Take
him to the United States Embassy with Mr. Clifford's compliments. And leave word that he can
keep the bonnet for future use."

*   *   *   *   *   *

About that time, several miles away in the forest
of St. Cloud, Clifford was taking careful aim at Fantozzi's anatomy, and Fantozzi was returning the attention. A moment later two insignificant reports
broke the silence; both men, very pale, stood motionless; two tiny shreds of smoke floated upward
through the tender foliage above.

Captain Stanley turned to Fantozzi's second, they
conferred for a moment, then Stanley turned away
to avoid a smile and went hastily up to Clifford.

"He says he doesn't want another shot; he says
honour is satisfied; look out, I believe he's prepar-
ing to embrace you!"

In vain Clifford attempted to shun the fervid recon-
ciliation, in vain he dodged Fantozzi's tears and
hugs. Fantozzi would not leave him, not he! Clifford dexterously escaped a kiss aimed at his cheek.

There were compliments from seconds, from the

surgeon, from the principals.   Undismayed, Stanley
tackled the procés-verbal.   Bull locked up his instru-
ments, the carriages were summoned by handkerchief signal ; the duel was at an end.   Gaily they
drove back to breakfast—a red-hot Spanish breakfast at Fantozzi's apartments.   They toasfed each
other, they toasted the two nations, Spain and the
United States.

Stanley, obliged to report at his Embassy, excused
himself and promised to return.   The breakfast continued ; Fantozzi played exquisite Spanish airs on
the guitar between courses ; his handsome attaché
accompanied him on the piano.

Bull, tactless to the back-bone, sang " Cuba
Libre," but nobody cared and everybody laughed.
Afternoon came ; they still breakfasted.   Fantozzi
insisted on a bout with the foils ; Clifford accepted ;
they broke a handsome vase and some saucers.

About four o'clock, while Bull was singing
" Cuba Libre " for the eleventh time by special request, Stanley entered, glanced gravely around, and
motioned Clifford to come outside.   Clifford went,
closing the door behind him, troubled by the stony
solemnity of Stanley's visage.

" What's up ? " he inquired.

" This," said Stanley with inscrutable eyes.   " His
Excellency was sent home in a cab this morning,
wearing a woman's bonnet and your covert-coat ! "

" What ! " gasped Clifford.

" Also with your compliments and a request that
his Excellency keep the bonnet for future use."

Cold sweat broke out on Clifford's brow.

"It's Elliott!" he moaned. "It's Elliott's work! Oh, Heaven, he didn't know what he was doing!"

Stanley was silent.

"I'll go to the Embassy," cried Clifford, "I'll go now." ⸿

"Better not," said Stanley kindly.

There was a pause.

"Does—does she know?" faltered Clifford.

"Yes," said Stanley.

"And—and she—*she* believed I did it!"

"No—I told her you were incapable of such a thing. But she is perhaps a little prejudiced—that is—I mean—you understand, I found her much distressed."

Clifford raised his eyes, searching the handsome young face before him. Something in that face made his heart turn to water.

"Stanley!" he blurted out, "it isn't *you*, is it, she has promised to marry—"

"Yes," said Stanley slowly.

Clifford went and leaned over the banisters. After a long time he straightened up, mopped his brow with his handkerchief, smiled, and came up to Stanley holding out his hand.

"Before I take it I want to say that this incident had nothing to do with it," said Stanley; "I proposed and was accepted at the pigeon match."

Clifford was staggered for a moment; then he recovered and held out his hand again.

"She is one in a million," he said cordially,

thinking to himself, "and the rest of the millions are just like her, oh, Lord! just like her!"

Stanley grasped his hand; they stood looking at each other with kindly eyes. Fantozzi's voice came through the closed door:

> "Espagne! Espagne!   •
> Bravo! Toro!"

Somewhere in there Bull still chanted "Cuba Libre!" Presently they bowed to each other, shook hands again, and parted.

" My compliments to His Excellency and to Miss Amyce," said Clifford. Then he went in and took leave of Fantozzi and the others despite their united protests. An hour later he entered the studio, fell upon Elliott and beat him madly. They fought like schoolboys until tired; perspiring and breathless, they retreated to separate sofas and panted.

" Confound you!" gasped Elliott, "what do you mean by it?"

" I mean that I forgive you," said Clifford grimly; " go to the devil!"

They smiled at each other across the studio.

" Was *that* the Ambassador, then?" asked Elliott.

" It was,—Ambassador Extraordinary and Minister Plenipotentiary."

" He isn't red-headed," suggested Elliott, "your Ambassador Extraordinary."

" Nevertheless," said Clifford "he is a most extraordinary Ambassador. Where shall we dine?"

" In the Quarter?"

" In the Quarter."

" With me?"

" With you."

" And Colette and Jacquette?"

" And Colette and Jacquette."

Elliott, choking with emotion, nodded, and picked up a ruffled silk hat from the floor.

" His Excellency's," said Clifford softly, and hung it over an easel.

YO ESPERO

YO ESPERO.

God be merciful to me, a sinner. Thou hast already been merciful to the virtuous by making them so. —*Arabian Prayer.*

I.

" Good morning," said the young fellow, lifting his cap.

" Good morning," said the girl.

It was the third time they had met ; they had never before spoken. The young fellow buttoned his tweed jacket to the throat, glanced over the wooden railing of the foot-bridge, and then looked up at the sky. The sky was pale blue, fleckless and untroubled save for a shred of filmy vapour floating all alone in the zenith ;—that was all, except the gilt incandescent disc of the sun ;—all, except a speck, high in the scintillating vault, that circled slowly, slowly southwards, and vanished in mid-air.

The speck was a buzzard.

The young fellow turned from the glimmering water and looked diffidently at the girl. She bent her grey eyes upon the stream.

" Would you mind telling me whether there are trout in this river? " he asked, moving a step toward her.

She raised her head instantly, smiling.

119

"Gay Brook was a famous trout stream—once," she answered.

"Then I suppose there are a few still left in it," he asked, also smiling.

"But," continued the girl, "that was very, very long ago." She was looking again at the water, pensively.

"How long ago?" he persisted, drawing a little nearer.

"About seventy-five years ago," she replied without raising her head; "Buck Gordon says so. Do you know Buck Gordon? His boys are the telegraph agents at the station above. I don't know the Gordon boys; I have spoken twice with old man Gordon. I do not suppose," she continued reflectively, "that there has been a trout in Gay Brook for fifty years. Do you know why?"

"No," he said, "but I should be glad to know."

He had drawn a little nearer and now leaned on the wooden railing of the bridge, his back to the water, his hands in his pockets. A leather rod-case was slung over one shoulder. The southern sun crisped the edges of his short hair and shorter moustache.

"The reason," said the girl, gazing dreamily into the stream again,—"the reason is because they cut off so much timber in the mountain notch yonder that now the freshets come every spring, and for weeks the water is nothing but yellow mud. Trout can't live in mud,—can they?"

After a silence he said: "And so there are no more

trout." She shook her head. The sun burnished her dark hair and tinged the delicate contour of cheek and throat with a warmer flush. Her white cambric sunbonnet swung from her waist by both strings. Presently she put it on and turned toward him, holding the tips of the strings between the forefinger and thumb of her left hand. Her right hand lay indolently along the grey railing of the bridge. It was dimpled and tanned to a creamy tint.

"I have seen you three times here at the bridge," she observed.

"And I have seen you," he said; "I wish I had spoken before."

She tore a tiny splinter from the sun-bleached railing and dropped it into the water. It danced away through the trembling sunbeams.

"I wondered why you came to fish in Gay Brook," she went on; "I might have told you that there are nothing but minnows here;—I nearly did tell you—"

"I wish I had asked the first time we—I saw you," he said; "it would have saved me no end of disappointment. Why did you not tell me?"

"Because—you didn't ask me. I might have told you anyway if I had not seen that you were from the North."

"You dislike Northern people?"

"I? Oh, no,—I don't know any."

"But you say that if—"

"I mean that I do not understand Northern strangers."

The young fellow looked at her curiously.

"Why, I thought you also were from the North," he said; "you do not speak with a Southern accent—"

"I am from Maryland, but I have lived here in North Carolina nearly all of my life. The reason that I do not speak with a Southern accent is because my uncle is from the North and I have lived alone with him,—ever since I can remember."

"Here?"

"Yes. I am very glad you spoke to me. When do you go away to the North again?"

The young fellow touched his short moustache and gave her a sharp glance. His sunburned cheeks were tinged with a faint colour.

"I am very glad too," he said; "I find it a bit lonely at the hotel."

"The hotel," she repeated; "there are two hundred people there."

"And I am lonely," he said again.

"You can't be,—how can you be?" she persisted, raising her grey eyes to his.

"Because," he replied; "I haven't anything in common with any of them,—except Tom O'Hara."

"I don't understand," she insisted. "It seems to me that if I had the happiness of being with a great many people I should have all in the world that I long for. I have nobody,—except my uncle."

"You have your friends," he said.

"No, nobody except my uncle. I do not count Zeke, and the boys."

"Zeke?"

" Zeke Chace."

" Oh," he said; " I've heard of him. He runs the blockade, doesn't he ? "

" Does he ? " she asked demurely.

He laughed and rested his head on his wrist, looking into her face. Her face was half hidden in the shadow of her sunbonnet, so she met his gaze placidly.

" Doesn't Zeke Chace run the blockade ? " he repeated.

" What blockade ? " she asked. Her grey eyes were very round and innocent.

" Have you never heard of blockade whisky ? " he insisted.

She had to laugh.

" I might have heard something about it," she admitted.

His pleasant serious face questioned hers and her lips parted in the merriest laugh again.

" How silly ! " she cried ; "everybody has heard of blockade whisky."

" Oh," he said, " I have often asked, but the people around here won't talk about it ! "

" Perhaps they take you for a Revenue Officer," she ventured gravely.

" Very probably," he answered.

At this she laughed outright. It occurred to him that she was making fun of him and he glanced at her again sharply.

" How do you know that I am not a Revenue Officer ? " he asked.

Her laughing eyes met his.

"Can you tell a coon from a possum?" she asked in return.

"I? Of course."

"So can I," she said, trying hard to look serious. After a moment they both laughed outright.

"You have teased me unmercifully," he said; "don't you think you ought to tell me where I can catch a trout or two?"

"Then I will," she answered impulsively, moving a step nearer; "but Zeke won't like it. There are trout in the Buzzard Run."

"The Buzzard Run?"

"It's yonder, behind Mist Mountain. Zeke won't like it," she repeated.

"Why? Does Zeke fish too?"

"Zeke? Hm! Not exactly. Never mind,—I shall tell Zeke about you and nobody will bother you. But you must be a little careful; there are snakes on Mist Mountain."

"Not dangerous snakes,—are there?"

"I don't know what kind you are used to," she said; "there are rattlers in the rocks on Mist Mountain."

After a pause he asked her if there were many rattlesnakes there.

"Sometimes one sees two or three, sometimes none at all," she answered. "They give you warning; they run if you let them. It might be better if you kept to the path. There is a path all the way."

"Then I'll stick to it," he said lightly ; "I suppose it's too late to go to-day." He looked at his watch and raised his eyebrows. "Why, it's twelve o'clock!" he exclaimed.

She refused to believe it and bent her dainty head over his shoulder to see.

"Dear me!" she cried, "uncle will question me!"

They stood looking at each other with new-born awkwardness. She took one short step backward.

"Are you going?" he asked, scarcely conscious of what he said.

"Why, yes,—I must."

He leaned over the bridge railing and looked at the crinkling ripples. After a while she also bent over, resting her elbows on the railing. A brilliant green beetle ran across the bleached board, halted, spread its burnished wings, and buzzed away across the stream. A small fluffy honey-wasp alighted between her elbows and crept quickly into a hole in the splintering plank.

"Yes," she repeated, I must go."

He raised his head and looked her frankly in the eyes:

"I should like to see you again," he said.

"Really? Oh, I suppose I shall pass the bridge again before you go."

"How do you know? Suppose I should go to-morrow?"

"You said you were going fishing to-morrow,—didn't you?"

"Why no,—I didn't say so," he said eagerly ; " I would rather talk with you."

"Why don't you go fishing?"

" I would rather talk to you," he repeated.

" What shall we talk about—blockade whisky ? "

They both laughed. He had moved up beside her again.

" I want to see you again," she said, " I think you can see that I do. I could come to the bridge to-morrow. I would rather the people at the hotel did not know. My uncle has forbidden me to speak to anybody except Zeke and the boys. When I was a child I did not feel very lonely ; now I have the greatest longing to know people—girls of my own age. I dare not."

" Have you no girl friend at all? "

" No. I should like to know older women too. At night in bed I often cry and cry—there !—I should not tell you such things—"

" Tell me," he said soberly.

But she only smiled and shook her head saying ; " It is lonely at Yo Espero."

He looked into her grey eyes ; they troubled him.

"I dare not wait any longer," she said,—"good-bye,—will you come to-morrow ? "

" Here ? Yes. Shall I come early ? "

" Oh, yes."

" At seven ? "

" Yes."

He offered her his hand but she did not take it.

" Wait," she said, " I do not know your name,—
no,—don't tell me now,—let me think a little of what
I have done.   If I come to-morrow—then you may
tell me."

He watched her hurry away up the woodland path
that leads to Yo Espero.   When she wa* gone he
stood still, idly tearing dried splinters from the
bridge railing.

II.

The piazzas of the Diamond Spring Hotel were
empty ; the guests came trooping through the great
square hall and into the big dining-room to be fed.

Young Edgeworth arrived late and silently took
his seat, bowing civilly to his neighbours.

There were fifteen people at his table, including
the Reverend Dr. Beezeley, who presided, flanked
by his wife, his progeny, and a bottle of Diamond
Spring water.   Near to the Reverend Orlando
Beezeley sat another minister, a little pink gentleman
with bulging eyes.   His name was Meeke and he
looked it.   But he wasn't.

Now the Reverend Orlando Beezeley and Dr.
Samuel Meeke were both of a stripe, differing on
one or two obscure questions.   One reverend gentleman was a pillar of the " Pure People's League ; "
the other wore the badge of the " Charity Band."
And they squabbled.   .

For their leagues, their bands, and their squab-
bles, Edgeworth cared nothing.   He believed that

all people should be allowed to worship God in their
own fashion,—even by squabbling if they chose. He
was disposed to be courteous to the two ministers
and their wives and young. It was difficult, however, partly because they were inquisitive, partly on
account of the Reverend Orlando's personal habits,
which were maddening. He put his fingers into
everything, including his mouth; they were always
sticky, and this, combined with cuffs that came too
far over his knuckles, oppressed Edgeworth. The
Reverend Orlando's fingers were obtrusive. When
he walked they spread out, perhaps to stem the
downward avalanche of cuff. He also twiddled
them when he had no other use for them, and
Heaven knows he put them to uses for which they
were never intended.

All this interfered with Edgeworth's appetite and
he shunned the Reverend Orlando Beezeley. Once,
at the table, the minister asked him why he didn't
go to the Sunday services which he, Dr. Beezeley,
held in the hotel parlours, and when Edgeworth
said it was because he didn't want to, the Reverend
Orlando sniffed offensively. For a week the atmosphere was surcharged with unpleasantness; but one
day Dr. Beezeley asked Edgeworth what he did
for a living, and Edgeworth pleasantly told him that
it was none of his business. The atmosphere at
once cleared up and the Reverend Orlando became
irksomely affable. This was because he was afraid
of Edgeworth and disliked him.

Therefore, when Edgeworth entered the dining-

room and slipped quietly into his chair, Dr. Beezeley
said : " Hey ! been a-fishin ? "

" No," said Edgeworth.

" Where've you been then ? " urged Mrs. Beezeley,
devoured by curiosity. She had contracted this
disease in the little Boston suburb where she lived,
and she had infected her whole family.

" I have been out," said Edgeworth pleasantly.

Dr. Samuel Meeke, who had pricked up his ears,
relapsed into a dull contemplation of Mrs. Dill
again.

But Mrs. Beezeley was not defeated. She turned
to the pallid lady beside her, Mrs. Dill, and said in
a thin high voice : " Pass the trout to Mr. Edgeworth ; he can't seem to catch any—even off the
old foot-bridge."

Edgeworth was intensely annoyed, for it was
plain that some of the Beezeley brood had been
spying. He looked at Master Ballington Beezeley
who grinned at him impertinently.

His father was busy feeding himself with mashed
potato, but he observed his heir's impudence and
was not displeased.

" I seen you," cried the youthful Beezeley,
writhing with the pressure of untold secrets,—" you
was mashin' a country-girl, Mister Edgeworth,—I
seen you ! "

" Te-he ! " tittered Mrs. Dill.

" ' I *saw* you,' would perhaps be more correct,"
said Edgeworth ; " unless perhaps your parents have
instructed you to the contrary—"

"Ballington!" cried Mrs. Beezeley, turning red, "how dare you use such grammar?"

Edgeworth surveyed the defeat of the Beezeleys without any particular emotion.

Mrs. Dill attempted to save the day but choked on an olive and was assisted from the room by Dr. Samuel Meeke. Then the Beezeleys made Mrs. Meeke wretched with significant looks and smiles and half-suppressed coughs, until she rose to find out why Mrs. Dill and her husband did not return. Poor little woman! her bosom friend, Mrs. Beezeley, had long ago quenched for her what little comfort in life she ever knew.

When the Reverend Orlando Beezeley had fed to repletion, he removed the napkin from his chin, cleared his throat, picked his teeth, and finally took himself off to the piazza.

"I can't stand this table full much longer," muttered Edgeworth to himself, and he called to the head waiter, a majestic personage of colour, and also a Baptist deacon.

"Deacon," said he, "give me a place at another table to-night, can you?"

"Sho'ly, Sho'ly, Mistuh Edgewurf," said the majestic one; "might you prefer to be seated at Mis' Weldon's table, Mistuh Edgewurf?"

Edgeworth looked across at Mrs. Weldon and then at her pretty daughter, Claire.

"Go over and ask Mrs. Weldon whether she objects," he said.

Mrs. Weldon did not object and neither did

Claire, so Edgeworth walked over and said some polite things which he forgot a minute afterward. So did Mrs. Weldon. I am not sure about Claire.

When Edgeworth went out on the veranda to smoke his pipe, a young fellow in tweeds and scarlet golf-jacket, who was sitting astride the railing said: " Hello, Jim, it's all over the hotel that you're sweet on some country girl."

" Tommy," said Edgeworth, in a low pleasant voice, " go to the devil ! "

O'Hara smiled serenely.

" I suppose it's that Beezeley whelp, eh, Jim ? "

" I fancy it is. A fellow can't brush his hair but it's reported in Diamond Springs."

" Oh, there's truth in it then," laughed O'Hara.

" That," said Edgeworth, " is none of your confounded business ; " and they strolled off together, arm in arm, smoking placidly.

" These Beezeleys," said O'Hara, " are blights on the landscape. They ought to be exterminated with Paris-green."

" Or drowned in tubs," said Edgeworth.

" Like unpleasant kittens," added O'Hara.

" Come," said Jim Edgeworth, " what was that yarn you wanted to spin for me this morning ? "

" Yarn ? 'Tis no yarn," said O'Hara ; " it's the truth and it troubles me. Sit down here on the grass till I tell you. Look at the veranda, Jim ; it's like a circus with the band playing."

" The girls' frocks are very pretty ; I like lots of colour," said Edgeworth.

"There's plenty in Claire Weldon's cheeks," observed O'Hara, gloomily.

"It's natural," said Jim.

"It was before you came. Now she puts more on in your honour;—confound it, man, can't you see the lass is forever making eyes at you?—and, Jim, it's death to me!"

Edgeworth stared at him.

"Oh, you're blinder than the white bat of Drumgilt!" said O'Hara; "you've eyes in your head, but they're only there for ornament. Didn't you know I am in love with Claire Weldon now?"

"Why no," said Edgeworth, "are you really, Tommy?"

"Am I really, Tommy? Faith, I thought even the fish in Gay Brook knew it."

"Well," laughed Edgeworth, "go in and win, then!"

"Do you mean it?" said Tommy gravely.

"Mean it? My dear fellow, why shouldn't I?"

O'Hara beamed upon him and grasped his hand.

"There!" he cried, "I knew it! I've told her ye didn't care tuppence for any lass, and if she didn't take me she'd be doin' herself but ill service."

Edgeworth burst into fits of laughter. "Is that the way you woo a girl, Tom O'Hara?"

"There are ways and ways," said O'Hara doggedly.

"How about Sir Brian?" asked Jim, checking his mirth.

Sir Brian was Tommy's father. The several

thousand miles that separated father and son did not lessen Tommy's uneasiness concerning his father's approval.

" I can't help it," said Tom ; " if he disowns me I'll go to work, that I will ! and Claire knows it."

" They say," said Edgeworth, " that the O'Haras always get what they want."

" They do. My grandfather loved a lass who died, so he blew out his brains and caught her in heaven."

" Hm ! " coughed Edgeworth.

" Do you know to the contrary ? " demanded O'Hara.

" No," said Jim, " I'll have to wait a bit to verify this story. Have you any tobacco ? Thanks, my pipe's out. Look at the sky, Tom ; it's pretty, isn't it ? "

They sprawled on their backs and kicked up their heels ; two bronzed young athletes,—as trim a pair as one might see anywhere betwixt the poles of this planet.

" Hark," said Edgeworth, " hear Beezeley and Meeke squabbling over their Maker. Do you suppose He hears them ? He is so very far away. Hark how they wrangle over their future blessedness. I should think they would be ashamed to have God hear them."

" Beezeley says he believes in hell, but doesn't want to go there," said O'Hara, lazily.

" There's no hell," said Edgeworth. He hadn't lived long enough to know ; he was nineteen.

O'Hara raised himself on one elbow and looked at him.

" No hell?" he asked.

" No."

If he had seen the lines in O'Hara's young face,—the faint marks about the eyes and mouth, he might have answered differently.

The afternoon sunlight lay warm across the level meadow. The locust trees were in full bloom, deep laden with heavy, drooping clusters of white blossoms. Every wandering breeze bore the penetrating sweetness of the locusts and the delicate odour of hemlock and pine. Great scarlet trumpet-flowers swayed in the May wind; from the nearer forest came the scent of dogwood and azalea. Over the greensward butterflies fluttered, little white ones, chasing each other among the dandelions, great swallow-tailed butterflies, yellow and black, flopping around the phlox, or pursuing a capricious course along the river bank. There were others too, gay comma-butterflies, delicate violet or blue swallow-tailed butterflies, and now and then a rare shy comrade of theirs, pale sulphur and grey, striped like a zebra, that darted across the flower-beds and flitted away to its dusky haunts among the shrub-oak and holly of the mountain sides. An oriole, gorgeous in orange and black, uttered a sweet call from the lower branches of an oak. A bluebird dropped into the lower grass under the bushes. Then a catbird began to sing and trill and warble until the whole air rippled with melody.

"'Tis a nightingale or I'm in Drumgilt!" said O'Hara, sitting up.

"It's a male catbird," said Edgeworth, rising; "come on, Tom!"

O'Hara picked himself up from the grass, scraped out his pipe, ran a grass-stem through it, aɪd looked at the sun.

"We have loafed the whole afternoon away," he said.

"I was anxious to kill .time," said Edgeworth. He was thinking of the girl at the bridge.

"Kill time! kill time!" said O'Hara impatiently, —"why, man, 'tis time that kills us! I'm going to find Miss Weldon, and I'd be obliged to ye to stay away."

"Bosh!" said Edgeworth, "you're worth twenty like me."

"That I am!" said Tom, "but I'll be saying good night, lad! And for the love of me, stay away from Claire Weldon. You don't want my curse?"

"Oh, no," laughed Edgeworth; "but I'm going to dine at their table. I asked the Deacon to fix it. I can't stand the holy alliance any longer."

"All right," said O'Hara, "when a girl has to see a man eat three times a day, she loses her illusions concerning him."

"What's that?" demanded Edgeworth.

But O'Hara swung off across the clover, whistling "Terry Bowen" and buttoning his scarlet golf-jacket with an irritating air of self-satisfaction.

"The mischief take Tom and his girls!" said

Edgeworth to himself, but he looked after Tom and smiled, for he thought the world revolved about O'Hara. Still he began to be lonely again, now that O'Hara was gone.

"Why the deuce can't he spend a half hour now and then with me?" he muttered to himself; "what can he find to talk about all day to that one girl?"

III.

That night after dinner he found himself joining the procession upon the veranda, walking with a pretty girl whom he did not remember meeting, but, from whose conversation, he knew he must have danced attendance on somewhere or other.

In the half light of the mellow Japanese lanterns, he caught glimpses of familiar faces in the throng; Dr. Beezeley, unctuous and sticky-fingered, the faded Mrs. Dill with Dr. Samuel Meeke, poor little Mrs. Meeke, anxiously smiling when she caught the protruding eyes of her husband, Mrs. Weldon, gracious and serene, walking with some tall, heavy-whiskered Southerner, Tommy O'Hara conducting Miss Claire Weldon, with something of the determination that one notices in troopers who convoy treasure-trains. In and out of the lights they passed him, vague impressions of filmy draperies and lantern-lit faces, with now and then a shadowy gesture or a sparkle of eyes in the twilight. Beyond, the dark foliage of sycamore and maple loomed motionless, with never a wind to stir the tender leaves, but the locust-trees, where the grape-like bunches of white blossoms hung, were all hazy with the quivering wings of dusk-moths. Slender sphinx-moths darted and turned and hovered over the phlox, grey wraiths of dead humming-birds, poised above phantom flowers. Below the fountain spray, drifting fine as a veil of mist across the shadowy blossoms of white iris, a hidden tree-frog quavered a sweet-treble, and on every twig-tip gauzy-winged creatures scraped resonant accompaniment.

"Of what are you thinking, Mr. Edgeworth?" asked the girl beside him.

He started slightly; he had quite forgotten her. He had been thinking of the girl at the bridge and the tryst next morning, but he said: "I was listening to the tree-frog. It means rain to morrow."

"I am very sorry," said the girl, "I was going to Painted Mountain on horseback. Shall we sit here a moment?" She shook out her skirts and seated herself, and he found a place on the veranda railing beside her.

"Painted Mountain?" he asked; "that is beyond Yo Espero, isn't it?"

"Yo Espero is on the southern slope. I heard such an interesting story about Yo Espero to-day; shall I tell you?"

He looked at her sharply, then nodded, saying: "Tell me first what Yo Espero means. It's Spanish, isn't it?"

"I don't know,—I suppose so. I believe it

means '*I hope*.' The village,—there's only one house you know,—was named Yo Espero by the only inhabitant. They say he took the name from the label on the lid of an old cigar-box that he found among the rocks."

"Very unromantic and intensely American," said Edgeworth laughing.

"Ah, but wait,—there's more to come. The man who lives at Yo Espero has a niece, a beauty they say, and would you believe it, the man, her uncle, named her also Yo Espero!"

"Oh!" said Edgeworth musingly.

"Poor girl,—named from a cigar brand! It is wicked—don't you think so, Mr. Edgeworth?"

"Yo Espero," he repeated softly,—"I don't know, —Yo Espero."

"Her uncle calls her Io for short when he does not call her Yo Espero. He must be a brute. They say he knows things about the blockade too."

Edgeworth became interested.

"I have never seen the girl," she continued, "but Mrs. Weldon has, and she says the girl is simply a raving beauty. Dr. Beezeley tried to call on the uncle but was shown the door without ceremony. They say the man is well educated and from the North, but he won't allow anybody to enter his house or speak to his niece."

"Do you know his name?" asked Edgeworth.

"Mrs. Beezeley says it is Clyde. He is some broken-down Northern man of good family who has sunk low enough to mix himself up with the blockade. People say the Revenue Officers are after him and will get him sooner or later. I wonder what the girl will do then?"

"I wonder," repeated Edgeworth under his breath; "hello! here's Tommy O'Hara, the pride of Drumgilt!"

"And the Pride has had a fall," said O'Hara sentimentally;—"did—did you notice if Miss Weldon was passing this way, Jim? Ah, did you see her pass, Miss Marwood? With Colonel Scarborough? Oh, the mischief!"

"Come," laughed Miss Marwood, "we'll go and find them; Mr. Edgeworth doesn't care; he likes solitude—"

Edgeworth attempted to protest, but was bidden to go with them or stay, as he pleased. And he stayed,—to smoke and muse and ponder on the long dim porch while the dew dripped from the perfumed vines, and the great stars spangled the sky, and the million voices of the night sang of summers past and summers to come. And the burden of the song was always the same, Yo Espero, Yo Espero.

At seven o'clock next morning, Edgeworth stood on the little foot-bridge, leaning both elbows upon the wooden railing. Between his elbows was a fresh white cut in the weather-stained plank, from which a shaving of wood had recently been planed, and on this white space was printed in pencil:

"I shall not see you again."

He never doubted that the message was for him He leaned idly upon the rail, reading and re-reading it. A fine warm rain, scarcely more than a mist, was falling through the calm air. The tiny globules powdered his cap and coat, shining like frost-dust.

Presently he fumbled in his pocket, found a jack-knife, opened it, and deliberately shaved the writing from the plank. Then, in his turn he wrote:

"If you will not see me I shall go to-morrow."

"Let the Beezeley whelp read that and make the most of it," he muttered, turning away with an unaccustomed feeling of wistfulness.

What he longed for he did not know; perhaps for a little of O'Hara's society, so he lighted his pipe and started toward the hotel, his hands deep in his pockets, his tanned cheeks glistening with the fine rain.

After a few moments it occurred to him that he had put it rather strongly;—in fact it was an un-warranted and idiotic thing to write. Why in the world should he leave Diamond Springs because a girl whom he had met three times and spoken to once, refused to meet him again? He hesitated, mused a little, and finally resumed his course. Let it stay as it was; it mattered nothing to him any-way. He would leave the hotel,—he would leave the state too, for that matter, for he was sick and weary of the Carolinas, and of the big hotels, filled with invalids who sat in hot baths or drank bottles of nasty "waters." Would O'Hara go with him? He thought of Claire Weldon and frowned.

"She's spoiled O'Hara, that's what she's done!" he pondered bitterly.

When he came in sight of the hotel he saw Dr. Beezelcy pottering about the croquet ground. When the reverend gentleman walked, his flat feet scraped the gravel and lapped over each other in front, like the toes of a Shanghai rooster.

" Hey ! " said Dr. Beezeley, " been a walkin' ? "

Edgeworth nodded.

" Want to play croquet ? " asked Beezeley, looking at him over his glasses ; " it ain't goin' to rain much more."

Edgeworth said he never played croquet.

Beezeley straightened a wicket, hammered a painted stake, and sniffed.

His face, with the bunchy chop-whiskers cut a little close, reminded Edgeworth of the countenance of some big buck rabbit. The reverend gentleman also had other rabbit peculiarities, such as a perpetual appetite, a prehensile lip, and an enormous progeny.

O'Hara hailed him from the tennis courts and he went over, puffing his pipe moodily. But when he found that Tommy intended to invite two girls to make up doubles, Edgeworth flatly refused to play.

" Confound it, Tommy," he said, " you are good enough company for me, and I ought to be for you. What's the use of lugging in strangers every minute? "

" Ladies are never strangers," said Tom airily ; " one of them is Miss Weldon."

" That's all right," said Edgeworth savagely, " but she can't play tennis. Is it a kindergarten you're

setting up, Tom O'Hara? Call your caddy and
come on to the links."

"Listen to the lad!" said O'Hara; "why, man,
I'll go with you where you like and I'll do what you
like,—only," he added, "I have an appointment to
ride at ten—with Miss Weldon."

"Ride then," said Edgeworth with a scowl, and
turned on his heel, leaving O'Hara a sadly puzzled
man.

"What the mischief is the matter with me, any-
how?" muttered Edgeworth, striding wrathfully
away across the meadow; "why can't I let Tommy
alone with his girl. I'm making a nuisance of myself I fancy."

The restlessness which possessed him he did not
even attempt to analyse. That it was caused by
something or somebody outside of himself he was
convinced.

"These people here," he thought, "are empty-
headed and common—when they're not sanctimonious and vulgar. I'll be hanged if I'm going to
spend the time talking platitudes to girls in golf
gowns."

Of course it was their fault that he felt irritable
and bored. He thought of his book, "The Origin
of the Cherokee Indian," but the prospect of shut-
ting himself in his room to drive a pen over reams
of foolscap had small attraction for him. The
rain had ceased, the heavy perfumed air, vague with
vapour, oppressed him, and he looked up at the
mountains, half veiled in mist. But climbing was

out of the question,—he didn't know exactly why,
—but it was clearly out of the question. He would
not go fishing either ; neither would he read. What
was there left to do? Nothing, except to go back
to the foot-bridge.

So when at last, by the highways and byways of
cogitation, he had completed the circle, and had arrived at the point from which he started, he found
that his legs had secured the precedence of his
brain, for already they were landing him at the foot-
bridge.

He was really a little surprised when he found
himself there. He stepped to the railing to find his
inscription. Somebody had shaved it off with a
knife, and, in its place was written :

"Good-bye."

It was then that Edgeworth experienced a most
amazing, not to say painful, sensation. It started in
the region of the heart, and, before he was aware, it
began to affect his throat.

"Good-bye."

He looked stupidly at the word, repeating it aloud
once or twice. Presently he pulled out his knife
and hacked away the writing with a misty idea that
it might bother him less when it was obliterated.
On the contrary it bothered him more than ever.
A desire possessed him to go away, but, when he
pictured himself in a train, rushing northward, the
prospect was not as alluring as he felt it should be.
Perhaps it was because he knew O'Hara would not
go with him.

"The devil take Tom O'Hara!" he blurted out.

The effect of this outburst did not soothe him; it did, however, frighten a small hedge-sparrow nearly to death.

He looked up at the sun-warped sign-post on the end of the bridge. It bore the following valuable information.

HOG MOUNTAIN................................	6 miles.
BUZZARD RUN.................................	10 miles.
RED ROCK....................................	1 mile.
YO ESPERO...................................	3 miles.

"Yo Espero," he repeated aloud.

There was a step on the creaking planks behind him,—a light step,—but he heard it.

They faced each other for a moment in silence. The sun shone out of the mist above and tinged the edges of her hair with a mellow radiance.

"Come," she said, "we can't stay here."

"Where—then?"

Their eyes met. Her lips were slightly parted; perhaps she had walked fast, for her breast rose and fell irregularly. In that silent exchange of glances, each read, for one brief second, a line in the book of fate;—each read,—but whether they understood or not, God knows, for they smiled at each other and turned away, side by side into the forest.

IV.

"Yo Espero! Yo Espero!" Asleep, awake, the words haunted him, night and day they rang in his ears, "Yo Espero, Yo Espero." The brooks sang it; in the hot mid-day the cadence of the meadow creatures took it up; the orioles repeated it across the fields, the thrushes' hymn was for her alone: "Yo Espero, Yo Espero."

Days dawned and vanished, brief as the flash of a fire-fly wing. The locust-trees powdered the greensward with white blossoms, the laurel, dainty and conventional, spread its flowered cambric out to dry, and the dogwood leaves drifted through the forest like snowflakes.

O'Hara, the triumphant affianced of Claire, provoked the wrath of all unaffianced gods and men. He simply mooned. Guests arrived and guests left the Diamond Spring Hotel, but the Beezeleys stayed on for ever. There were captains and colonels and generals from the South; the names of Fairfax and Marmaduke and Carter and Stuart were heard in corridor and card-room. There were Rittenhouses and Appletons, and Van Burens, too, and the flat bleat of Philadelphia echoed the colourless jargon of Boston and the semi-civilized accent of New York.

It was the middle of May. The catbirds had ceased their music and now haunted the garden, mewing from every thicket. A crested blue jay, ominous prophet of distant autumn, screamed viciously at the great belted kingfishers, but wisely avoided these dagger-billed birds, and also the occasional cock-of-the-woods that flew into the oak-grove, and tapped all day on the loose bark.

Edgeworth loved all these creatures. A few weeks previous he hadn't cared tuppence for them. But now it was different; he felt at home with all the world; he smiled knowingly at the thrushes, he nodded gaily to the great blue heron, and laughed when that dignified but snobbish biped cut him dead. Flowers too he was on good terms with; he haunted the woods, now all ablaze with azaleas, he sat among blue and violet larkspurs and felt that he was among friends. The little wood-violets peeped up at him fearlessly; they knew he would never pick them; the big orange lady-slippers arranged themselves neatly, two by two, as he passed, but he laughingly disregarded their offers. True, the girl at his side,—for he never rambled alone,—was worthy of such self-sacrifice on the part of any lady-slipper, orange or maroon.

" Io," he said, as they lay in the forest on the heights above Diamond Springs, " can you realise it all? I scarcely can. Was it yesterday, was it last week,—was it years ago that I said good morning to you there on our bridge?"

" Jim, I don't know."

Her hair had fallen down and she flung it like a glistening veil from her face. She lay full length across the soft pine needles, her scarlet lips parted, tearing bits of flame-colored azalia blossoms from a cluster at her belt.

" See the lizards," said Edgeworth sitting up beside her, "see them race over the dry leaves! There! They've run up a tree! Look, Io."

" I see," she said. But she was looking up at him.

He bent over her and kissed her, both hands clasped in hers.

" You didn't look at all," he said.

" Didn't I?" whispered Yo Espero.

It was true that she had not looked. When her eyes were not fastened upon his face, they were closed.

So he sat smiling down at her with her slim fingers twisted in his; and that shadow of wistfulness that ever hovers close to happiness, fell over his eyes. And he said: " Do you ever regret—anything—Io?"

She smiled faintly.

" No—nothing, dear."

" Nothing?"

" Nothing."

" Then you are happy."

" Yes."

What had she to regret? She loved him. To him she came, sick at heart for the companionship which she had never known. He had delivered her

from her loneliness.   First she listened to him with
the fierce happiness of the lonely ; then she idolized
him ; then she loved him.   Love was all she had to
give ; and she gave it, even before he asked,—gave
it without thought or regret.

"Do you know," he said, "that you have the
prettiest hands in the world?"

"Have I?"

"Don't you know that your whole figure is exquisite?"

She raised one hand indolently and placed the
fingers across his lips.

"What do I care,—if you love me?" she said.

"But I care," he said; "to think that you,—all,
all of you,—with your beautiful eyes and your neck
and your lips and these two little hands, are mine—
all mine!—"

"And that brown hair above me—is mine,—isn't
it?" murmured the girl; "I never asked you before,
but don't—don't I own some of you too?   I have
given you all of myself."

It was little to ask ;—the question was a new one
though, and he suddenly began to wonder how much
of him she did own.   He looked at her half curiously as she lay there, her innocent face upturned,
her young figure flung across the pine-needle mat-
ting of the forest.   Her eyes told him she loved
him ; every line and curve of her sweet body solem-
nized the vow.

"Io," he said, "all of me that is worth owning
you own."

"This hand?" she asked, locking her fingers in his.

"Both," he said.

"Everything? All—all?"

"All, Yo Espero."

"You never said so—before."

"I say it now; all! all! all!"

*   *   *   *   *   *

"We will go to Silver Mine Creek," said Yo Espero, "and we will fish there for a little fish. There are bass in the French Broad, and you shall catch them from the rifts below Deepwater Bridge. We will gallop on horseback to Sunset Sands and we will go to Bubbling Spring. All this will take time, you know, but you are never going away, are you? Hush! I could not live until sunrise. Then, in the fall, we will go across to the little Hurricane where there are deer. You shall shoot a great wild-turkey also! Dear me! What more can a man ask for? And then there are teal and mallard on the French Broad before the ice has bridged the Little Red Horse. You will love the South."

"Yes, dear," he answered, soberly; but his eyes were turned to the North.

"I know lots of springs in the forest," she said, watching his face.

"And blockade stills?" he smiled.

She laughed outright and sat up, gathering her heavy hair into a twist.

"There is one within a few steps of where we sit; you could never find it," she said, tauntingly.

"Oho!" he exclaimed, "whose?"

"Zeke's," said the girl, "I could go to it in two minutes,—hark!—was that a gunshot from the valley?"

"I think it was," he said, "it came from that way," and he pointed to the west.

"From Painted Mountain! Did it sound like a rifle, Jim?"

Her eyes were very bright. Two red spots glowed on either cheek.

"I don't know, dear," he said, "why?"

As he spoke he rose and stepped back two paces. And as he took the second step there came a whirr, a girl's scream, and a rattlesnake struck him twice above the ankle.

For one second the forest swam before his eyes; then a cold sweat started from the roots of his hair and he bent and picked up a stick, shaking in every limb. It was over in a moment; the snake lay dead, shuddering and twisting among the rocks, but it was Yo Espero who had crushed it, and now she turned to him a face as bloodless as his own.

"Wait!" she panted, "there's whisky at Zeke's!" and she sprang across the mountain-side and vanished among the thickets.

He bent over and tore down his stocking; then his head whirled and he sank trembling upon the ground.

As he lay there great throbs of pain swept through him in waves, succeeded by momentary numbness, but through the mist of faintness and the delirium of pain he heard the dead snake thumping among the leaves. Then all was one great thrill of agony, but, as his senses reeled again, a touch fell upon his arm and he heard her voice:

" Drink,—quickly—all—all you can!"

And he did, blindly, guided by her arm. She held the demijohn until his head fell back.

Then she knelt, ripped her own sleeve from wrist to shoulder and stared at her round white arm. Two blue marks, close together, capped the sum-mit of a terrible swelling, and she cried out once for help. With all the strength that remained, she dragged the demijohn to her mouth and stretched out on the ground, the crystal clear liquor running between her teeth. She tried hard to swallow. Once she murmured, " I knew there was not enough for both,—I guess there isn't much left; I guess—it's—too late—"

After a minute or two she wandered in her de-lirium, but still she swallowed desperately until the demijohn rolled away from her nerveless grasp, and she seemed to lose consciousness. With the last spark of understanding left in her numbed brain, she turned over and stretched out, her lips crushed against his face.

Zeke found them. Whether it was the smell of blockade whisky, coupled with the absence of his demijohn, or whether it was Providence, cannot be successfully argued here. But he found them, and he carried them into his ramshackle cabin and laid them side by side across his mattress.

After he had looked at them for half an hour's absolute silence, he spat the remains of a hard-chewed quid into a corner, picked up his gun, and wended his way down the mountain-side to the Diamond Springs Hotel.

Here he was promptly arrested by two pale-faced Revenue Officers, and here, for the first time, he learned that Clyde, the tenant of Yo Espero on Painted Mountain, had been shot dead, two hours before, for resisting arrest at the hands of United States officers.

The hotel was in commotion, but when Zeke drawled out his story, panic reigned supreme, and the Beezeleys started in a body for Zeke's hut. How they got lost on the mountain and were frightened by snakes, and how Dr. Samuel Meeke headed a rescue party in their behalf, has no place in this story,—nor, I imagine, in any story. O'Hara went on Zeke's bond, and Zeke, followed by O'Hara and the proprietor of the Diamond Springs Hotel, started for the blockader's burrow. The proprietor's name was Eph Doom, but, unlike his namesake, nothing about him was sealed, not even his lips, and he chattered continually until Zeke drawled out: "O shet up, yew mewl o' misery!"

Once O'Hara spoke:

"You left them both lying across your bed, Zeke?"

"'Bout a foot apart," drawled Zeke.

But when O'Hara burst into the cabin, he cried:

"Thank God!" For they were in each other's arms.

*   *   *   *   *   *

And that is all there is to say.

Eph Doom recounts a great deal more;ﾍhe tells how those two striplings, dazed by alcohol and numbed with poison, clung together blindly; he tells how he, personally, drove a shoal of Beezeleys and Meekes and Dills from the door of the cabin, and he relates with fire how young Edgeworth sat up, pale, trembling, and demanded that he, Ephraim Doom, should, as a Justice of the Peace, then and there instantly unite in holy wedlock James Edgeworth and Yo Espero Clyde: which he did not do, because O'Hara whispered: "Wait till he's sober."

How Zeke escaped the clutches of the law needs a story by itself.

How Dr. Samuel Meeke and Mrs. Dill—but that is scandal.

How Yo Espero and Edgeworth loved is all that concerns this story.

COLLECTOR OF THE PORT

" ' Why do you limp ? ' asked the maid.
   ' I always stumble when the path is smooth,' said Love."

COLLECTOR OF THE PORT.

I will grow round him in his place,
Grow, live, die looking on his face,
Die, dying clasp'd in his embrace.

TENNYSON.

In winter the Port is closed, the population migrates, the Collector of the Port sails southward. There is nothing left but black rocks sheathed in ice where icy seas clash and splinter and white squalls howl across the headland. When the wind slackens and the inlet freezes, spotted seals swim up and down the ragged edges of the ice, sleek restless heads raised, mild eyes fixed on the turbid shallows.

In January, blizzard-driven, snowy owls whirl into the pines and sit all day in the demi-twilight, the white ptarmigan covers the softer snow with winding tracks, and the white hare, huddled in his whiter " form," plays hide and seek with his own shadow.

In February the Port-of-Waves is still untenanted. A few marauders appear, now and then a steel grey panther from the north frisking over the snow after the white hares, now and then a stub-tailed lynx, mean-faced, famished, snarling up at the white owls who look down and snap their beaks and hiss.

The first bud on the Indian-willow brings the first

157

inhabitant back to the Port-of-Waves, Francis Lee,
superintendent of the mica quarry. The quarrymen follow in batches; the willow-tassels see them
all there ; the wind-flowers witness the defile of the
first shift through the pines.

On the Cast day of May the company's flag was
hoisted on the tool-house, the French-Canadians
came down to repair the rusty narrow-gauge railroad, and Lee, pipe lighted, sea-jacket buttoned to
the throat, tramped up and down the track with the
lumber detail, chalking and condemning sleepers,
blazing spruce and pine, sounding fish-plate and rail,
and shouting at intervals until the washouts were
shored up, windfalls hacked through, and landslide
and boulder no longer blocked the progress of the
company's sole locomotive.

The first of June brought sunshine and black
flies, but not the Collector of the Port. The Cana-
dians went back to Sainte Isole across the line, the
white-throated sparrows' long dreary melody broke
out in the clearing's edge, but the Collector of the
Port did not return.

That evening, Lee, smoking his pipe on the headland, looked out across the sunset-tinted ocean and
saw the white gulls settling on the shoals and the
fish-hawks soaring overhead with the red sunglint
on their wings. The smoke of a moss smudge kept
the flies away, his own tobacco smoke drove away
care. Incidentally both drove Williams away,—a
mere lad in baggy blue-jeans, smooth-faced, clear-
eyed, with sea-tan on wrist and cheek.

" How did you cut your hand ? " asked Lee, turn-ing his head as Williams moved away.

" Mica," replied Williams briefly.   After a moment Williams started on again.

" Come back," said Lee ; "that wasn't what I had to tell you."

He sat down on the headland, opened a jack-knife, and scraped the ashes out of his pipe.   Williams came slowly up and stood a few paces behind his shoulder.

" Sit down," said Lee.

Williams did not stir.   Lee waited a moment, head slightly turned, but not far enough for him to see the figure motionless behind his shoul-der.

" It's none of my business," began Lee, " but per-haps you had better know that you have deceived nobody.   Finn came and spoke to me to-day.   Dyce knows it, Carrots and Lefty Sawyer know it,—I should have known it myself had I looked at you twice."

The June wind blowing across the grass, carried two white butterflies over the cliff.   Lee watched them struggle back to land again.   Williams watched Lee.

" I don't know what to do," said Lee, after a silence ; " it is not forbidden for women to work in the quarry—that I am aware of.   If you need work and prefer that sort, and if you perform your work properly, I shall not interfere with you.   And I'll see that the men do not."

Williams stood motionless; the smoke from the smudge shifted west, then south.

"But," continued Lee, "I must enter you properly on the pay-roll; I cannot approve of this masquerade. Finn will see you in the morning; it is unnecessery for me to repeat that you will not be disturbed."

There was no answer. After a silence Lee turned, then rose to his feet. Williams was weeping.

Lee had never noticed her face; both sun-tanned hands hid it now; her felt hat was pulled down over the forehead.

"Why did you come to the quarry?" he asked soberly. She did not reply.

"It is men's work," he said; "look at your hands! You cannot do it."

She tightened her hands over her eyes; tears stole between her fingers and dropped, one by one, on the young grass.

"If you need work—if you can find nothing else —I—I think perhaps I may manage something better," he said. "You must not stand there crying—listen! Here come Finn and Dyce, and I don't want them to talk all over the camp." Finn and Dyce came toiling up the headland with news that the west drain was choked. They glanced askance at Williams, who turned her back. The sea-wind dried her eyes; it stung her torn hands too. She unconsciously placed one aching finger in her mouth and looked out to sea.

" The dreen's bust by the second windfall," said Dyce, with a jerk of his stunted thumb toward the forest. " If them sluice-props caves in, the timber's wasted."

Finn proposed new sluice gates ; Lee objected, and swore roundly that if the damage was not repaired by next evening he'd hold Finn responsible. He told them he was there to save the company's money, not to experiment with it ; he spoke sharply to Finn of last year's extravagance, and warned him not to trifle with orders.

" I pay you to follow my directions," he said. " Do so and I'll be responsible to the company; disobey, and I'll hold you to the chalk-mark every time."

Finn sullenly shifted his quid and nodded ; Dyce looked rebellious.

" You might as well know," continued Lee, "that I mean what I say. You'll find it out. Do your work and we'll get on without trouble. You'll find I'm just."

When Dyce and Finn had shuffled away toward the coast, Lee looked at the figure outlined on the cliffs against the sunset sky,—a desolate, lonely little figure in truth.

" Come," said Lee ; "if you must have work I will give you enough to keep you busy; not in the quarry either,—do you want to cripple yourself in that pit? It's no place for children anyway. Can you write properly?"

The girl nodded, back turned toward him.

"Then you can keep the rolls, duplicates, and all. You'll have a room to yourself in my shanty. I'll pay quarry wages."

He did not add that those wages must come out of his own pocket. The company allowed him no secretary, and he was too sensitive to suggest one.

"I don't ask you where you came from or why you are here," he said a little roughly. "If there is gossip I cannot help it." He walked to the smudge and stood in the smoke, for the wind had died out and the black flies were active.

"Perhaps," he hazarded, "you would like to go back to—to where you came from? I'll send you back."

She shook her head.

"There may be gossip in camp."

The slightest movement of her shoulders indicated her indifference. Lee re-lighted his pipe, poked the smudge, and piled damp moss on it.

"All right," he said, "don't be unhappy; I'll do what I can to make you comfortable. You had better come into the smudge, to begin with."

She came, touching her eyes with her hands, awkward, hesitating. He looked gravely at her clumsy boots, at the loose, toil-stained overalls.

"What is your name?" he said, without embarrassment.

"My name is Helen Pine." She looked up at him steadily; after a moment she repeated her name as though expecting him to recognise it. He did not; he had never before heard it, as far as he knew. Neither did he find in her eager, wistful face anything familiar. How should he remember her? Why should he remember? It was nearly six months ago that, snow-bound in the little village on the Mohawk, he and the directors of his company left their private Pullman car to amuse themselves at a country dance. How should he recollect the dark-eyed girl who had danced the "fireman's quadrille" with him, who had romped through a reel or two with him, who had amused him through a snowy evening? How should he recall the careless country incident,—the corn popping, the apple race, the flirtation on the dark, windy stairway? Who could expect him to remember the laughing kiss, the meaningless promise to write, the promises to return some day for another dance, and kiss? A week later he had forgotten the village, forgotten the dance, the pop-corn, the stairway, and the kiss. She never forgot. Had he told her he loved her? He forgot it before she replied. Had he amused himself? Passably. But he was glad that the snow-plows cleared the track next morning, for there was trouble in Albany and lobbying to do, and a rival company was moving wheels within wheels to lubricate the machinery of honest legislation.

So it meant nothing to him, this episode of a snow blockade; it meant all the world to her. For months she awaited the letter that never came. An Albany journal mentioned his name and profession. She wrote to the company and learned where the quarry lay. She was young and foolish and nearly brokenhearted, so she ran away. Her first sentimental idea was to work herself to death, disguised, under his very eyes. When she lay dying she would reveal herself to him, and he should know too late the value of such a love. To this end she purchased some shears to cut her hair with; but the mental picture she conjured was not improved by such a sacrifice. She re-coiled her hair tightly and bought a slouched hat, too big.

When, arrived at the quarry, she saw him again, she nearly fainted from fright. He met her twice, face to face, and she was astounded that he did not recognise her. Reflection, however, assured her that her disguise must be perfect, and she awaited the dramatic moment when she should reveal herself—not dying from quarry-toil—for she did not wish to die now that she had seen him. No—she would live—live to prove to him how a woman can love—live to confound him with her constancy. She had read many romances. Now, when he had bade her follow him to the headland, she knew she had been discovered; she was weak with terror and shame and hope. She thought he knew her; when he spoke so coolly she stood dumb with amazement; when he spoke of Finn and Sawyer and Dyce she understood he had not penetrated her disguise, except from hearsay, and a terror of loneliness and desolation rushed over her.

Then the impulse came to hide her identity from him,—why, she did not know. Again that vanished when he called her to come into the smoke. As she looked up at him her heart almost stopped; yet he did not recognise her. Then the courage of despair seized her and she told her name. When at length she comprehended that he had entirely forgotten her—forgotten her very name—fright sealed her lips. All the hopelessness and horror of her position dawned upon her,—all she had believed, expected, prayed for, came down with a crash.

As they stood together in the smoke of the smudge, she mechanically laid her hand on his sleeve, for her knees scarcely supported her.

" What is it ; does the smoke make you dizzy ? " he asked.

She nodded ; he aided her to the cliff's edge and seated her on a boulder. Under the cliff the sunset light reddened the sea. A quarryman, standing on a rock, looked up at Lee and pointed seaward.

"Hello ! " answered Lee, " what is it ? The Collector of the Port ? "

Other quarrymen, grouped on the coast, took up the cry ; the lumbermen, returning from the forest along the inlet, paused, axe on shoulder, to stare at the sea. Presently, out in the calm ocean, a black triangle cut the surface, dipped, glided landward, dipped, glided, disappeared. Again the dark point came into view, now close under the cliff where thirty feet of limpid water bathed its base.

" The Collector of the Port ! " shouted Finn from the rocks.

Lee bent over the cliff's brink. Far down into the

clear water he followed the outline of the cliff. Under it a shadowy shape floated, a monstrous shark, rubbing the rock softly as if in greeting for old acquaintance' sake.

The Collector of the Port had returned from the south.

II.

The Collector of the Port and the company were rivals; both killed their men, one at sea, the other in the quarry. The company objected to pelagic slaughter and sent some men with harpoons, bombs, and shark-hooks to the Port; but the Collector sheered off to sea and waited for them to go away.

The company could not keep the quarrymen from bathing; Lee could not keep the Collector from Port-of-Waves. Every year two or three quarrymen fell to his share; the company killed the even half-dozen. Years before, the quarrymen had named the shark; the name fascinated everybody with its sinister conventionality. In truth he was Collector of the Port,—an official who took toll of all who ventured from this Port where nothing entered from the sea save the sea itself, wave on wave, wave after wave.

In the superintendent's office there were two rolls of victims,—victims of the quarry and victims of the Collector of the Port. Pensions were not allowed to families of the latter class, so, as Dyce said to Dyce's dying brother: "Thank God you was blowed up, an' say no more about it, Hank."

There was, curiously enough, little animosity against the Collector of the Port among the quarry-men. When June brought the great shark back to the Port they welcomed him with sticks of dynamite, but nevertheless a sense of proprietorship, of exclusive right to the biggest shark on the coast, aroused in the quarrymen a sentiment akin to pride. Between the shark and the men existed an uncanny comradeship, curiously in evidence when the company's imported shark-destroyers appeared at the Port.

" G'wan now," observed Farrely, "an' divil a shark ye'll get in the wather, me bucks! Is it sharks ye'll harpoon? Sure th' company's full o' thim."

The shark-catchers, harpoons, bombs, and hooks, retired after a month's useless worrying, and the men jeered them as they embarked on the gravel train.

" Drhop a dynamite shtick on the nob av his nibs!" shouted Farrely after them—meaning the president of the company. The next day, little Cæsar l'Hommedieu, indulging in his semi-annual bath, was appreciated and accepted by the Collector of the Port, and his name was added to the un-pensioned roll in the office of the company's super-intendent, Francis Lee.

Helen Pine, sitting alone in her room, copied the roll, erased little Cæsar's name from the pay-roll, computed the total back pay due him, and made out an order on the company for $20.39. Then she rose, stepped quietly into Lee's office which adjoined her own room, and silently handed him the order.

Lee was busy and motioned her to be seated. Dyce and Finn, hats in hand, looked obliquely at her as she leaned on the window-ledge, face turned toward the sea. She heard Lee say, " Go on, Finn ; " and Finn began again in his smooth plausible voice :

" I opened the safe on a flat-car, an' God knows who uncoupled the flat. Then Dyce signalled go ahead, but Henderson he sez Dyce signalled to back her up, an' the first I see was that flat hangin' over the dump-dock. Then she tipped up like a seesaw an' slid the safe into the water—fifty-eight feet sheer at low tide."

Lee said quietly : " Rig a derrick on the dump-dock, and tell Kinny to get his diving kit ready by three o'clock."

Finn and Dyce exchanged glances.

" Kinny he went to Bangor last night to see about them new drills," said Finn defiantly.

" Who sent him ? " asked Lee angrily. " Oh, you did, eh ? "

" I thought you wanted them drills," repeated Finn.

Lee's eyes turned from Finn to Dyce. There was, in the sullen faces before him, something that he had never before seen, something worse than sinister. The next moment he said pleasantly : " Well then, tell Lefty Sawyer to take his diving kit and be ready by three. If you need a new ladder at the dump-dock send one there by noon. That is all, men."

When Finn and Dyce had gone, Lee sprang to his feet and began to pace the office. Once he stopped to light his pipe ; once he jerked open the top drawer of his table and glanced at a pair of heavy Colt's revolvers lying there, cocked and loaded. He sat down at his desk after a while and spoke, perhaps half unconsciously, to Helen, as though he had been speaking to her since Finn and Dyce left :

" They're a hard crowd—a tough lot—and I knew it would come to a crisis sooner or later. Last year they drove the other superintendent to resign, and I was warned to look out for myself. Now they see that they can't use me, and they mean to get rid of me."

She turned from the window as he finished ; he looked at her without seeing the oval face, the dark questioning eyes, the young rounded figure involuntarily bending toward him.

" They tipped that safe off the dock on purpose," he said ; " they sent Kinny to Bangor on a fool's errand. Now Sawyer's got to go down and see what can be done. I know what he'll say !— He'll report the safe broken and one or two cash boxes missing, and he'll bring up the rest and wait for a chance to divide with his gang."

He started to his feet and began to pace the floor again, talking all the while :

" It's come to a crisis now, and *I'm* not going

under! I'll face them down; I'll break that gang as they break stone! If I only knew how to use a diving kit—and if I dared—with Dyce at the life-line—"

Half an hour later Lee, seated at his desk, raised his pale face from his hands and, for the first time, became conscious that Helen sat watching him beside the window.

"Can I do anything for you?" he asked pleasantly.

She held the order out to him; he took it, examined it, and, picking up a pen, signed his name.

"Forward it to the company," he said; "Cæsar's family will collect it quicker than the shark collected Cæsar."

He did not mean to shock the girl with cynicism; indeed it was only such artificial indifference that enabled him to endure the misery of the Port-of-Waves,—misery that came under his eyes from sea and land,—interminable hopeless human woe.

What could he do for the lacerated creatures at the quarry? He had only his salary. What could he do for families made destitute? The mica crushed and cut and blinded; the Collector of the Port exacted bloody toll in spite of him. He could not drive the dust-choked, half-maddened quarrymen from their one solace and balm, the cool, healing ocean; he could not drive the Collector from the Port-of-Waves.

"I didn't mean to speak unfeelingly," he said. "I feel such things very deeply."

To his surprise and displeasure she replied : "I did not know you felt anything."

She grew red after she said it ; he stared at her. " Do you regard me as brutal ? " he asked sarcastically.

" No," she said, steadying her voice : "you are not brutal; one must be human to be brutal."   .

He looked at her half angrily, half inclined to laugh.

"You mean I am devoid of human feeling?"

"I am not here to criticise my employer," she answered faintly.

" Oh—but you have."

She was silent.

"You said you were not aware that I felt anything."

She did not reply.

He thought to himself : " I took her from the quarry, and this is what I get." She divined his thought. She could have answered : "And you sent me to the quarry—for the memory of a kiss." But she did not speak.

Watching her curiously, he noticed the gray woollen gown, the spotless collar and cuffs, the light on her hair, like light on watered silk. Her young face was turned toward the window. For the first time it occurred to him that she might be lonely. He wondered where she came from, why she had sought Port-of-Waves among all places on earth, what tragedy could have driven her from kin and kind to the haunts of men. She seemed so utterly alone, so hopelessly dependent, so young that his conscience smote him, and he resolved to be a little companionable toward her, as far as his position of superintendent permitted. True, he could not do much; and whatever he might do would perhaps be misinterpreted by her, certainly by the quarry-men.

"A safe fell off the dock, to-day," he said pleas-antly, forgetting she had been present at the an-nouncement of the disaster by Finn and Dyce. "Would you like to see the diver go down?"

She turned toward him and smiled.

"It might interest you," he went on, surprised at the beauty of her eyes; "we're going to try to hoist the safe out of fifty odd feet of water—unless it is smashed on the rocks. Come down when I go at three o'clock."

As he spoke his face grew grave, and he glanced at the open drawer by his elbow, where two blue revolver barrels lay shining in the morning light.

At noon she went into her little room, locked the door, and sat down on the bed. She cried steadily till two o'clock; from two until three she spent the time in obliterating all traces of tears; at three he knocked at her door, and she opened the door, fresh, dainty, smiling, and joined him, tying the strings of a pink sun-bonnet under her oval chin.

III.

The afternoon sun beat down on the dump-dock where the derrick swung like a stumpy gallows against the sky.   A dozen hard-faced, silent quarry-men sat around in groups on the string-pieces ; Far-rely raked out the fire in the rusty little engine ; Finn and Dyce whispered together, glowering at Lefty Sawyer, who stood dripping in his diving suit while Lee unscrewed the helmet and disentangled the lines.

Behind Lee, Helen Pine sat on a pile of con-demned sleepers, nervously twisting and untwisting the strings of her sun-bonnet.

When Sawyer was able to hear and be heard, Lee listened, tight-lipped and hard eyed, to a report that brought a malicious sneer to Finn's face and a twin-kle of triumph into Dyce's dissipated eyes.

"The safe is smashed an' the door open.   Them there eight cash-boxes is all that I see."   He pointed to the pile of steel boxes, still glistening with salt water, and already streaked and blotched with orange colored rust.

"There are ten boxes," said Lee coldly ; "go down again."

Unwillingly, sullenly, Lefty Sawyer suffered him-self to be invested with the heavy helmet ; the lines and tubes were adjusted, Dyce superintended the descent and Finn seized the signal cord.   After a minute it twitched; Lee grew white with anger; Dyce turned away to conceal a grin.

When again Sawyer stood on the dock and reported that the two cash-boxes were hopelessly engulfed in the mud, Lee sternly bade him divest himself of the diving suit.

" What you goin' to do?" said Finn, coming up.

" Is it your place to ask questions?" said Lee sharply. " Obey orders or you'll regret it!"

" He's going down himself," whispered Dyce to Sawyer. The diver cast a savage glance at Lee and hesitated.

" Take off that suit," repeated Lee.

Finn, scowling with anger, attempted to speak, but Lee turned on him and bade him be silent.

Slowly Sawyer divested himself of the clumsy diving suit; one after the other he pushed the leaden soled shoes from him.

Lee watched him with mixed emotions. He had gone too far to go back now—he understood that. Flinching at such a moment meant chaos in the quarry, and he knew that the last shred of his authority and control would go if he hesitated. Yet, with all his heart and soul he shrank from going down into the sea. What might not such men do? Dyce held the life-line. A moment or two suffocation—would such men hesitate? Accidents are so easy to prove and signals may be easily misunderstood. He laid a brace of heavy revolvers on the dock.

As Dyce lifted the helmet upon his shoulders, he

caught a last glimpse of sunlight and blue sky and green leaves—a brief vision of dark, brutal faces—of Helen Pine's frightened eyes. Then he felt himself on the dock ladder, then a thousand tons seemed to fall from his feet and the dusky ocean enveloped him.

On the dump-dock silence reigned. After a moment or two Finn whispered to Sawyer ; Dyce joined the group ; Farrely whitened a bit under his brick-red sunburn and pretended to fuss at his engine.

Helen Pine, heart beating furiously, watched them. She did not know what they were going to do—what they were doing now with the air tubes. She did not understand such things, but she saw a line suddenly twitch in Dyce's fingers, and she saw murder in Finn's eyes.

Before she knew what she was doing she found herself clutching both of Lee's revolvers.

Finn saw her and stood petrified ; Dyce gaped at the level muzzles. Nobody moved.

After a little while Dyce's right hand twitched violently. Finn started and swore ; Sawyer said distinctly ; " Cut that line ! "

The next instant she fired at him point-blank, and he dropped to the bleached boards with a howl of dismay. The crack of the revolver echoed and echoed among the rocks. Presently, behind his engine, Farrely began to laugh ; two quarrymen near him got up and shambled hastily away.

" Draw him up ! " gasped the girl with a desperate glance at the water.

Finn, the foreman, cursed and flung down his lines
and walked away, cursing.

" Take the lines, Noonan," she cried breathlessly ;
' Dyce, pull him up ! "

The great blank-eyed helmet appeared ; she
watched it as though hypnotised. When, dragging
his leaden feet, Lee stumbled to the dock and flung
one of the two missing cash-boxes at Dyce's feet,
she grew dizzy and her little hands ached with their
grip on the heavy weapons.

Sawyer, stupid, clutching his shattered fore-arm,
never removed his eyes from her face ; Dyce unscrewed the helmet, shaking with fright.

" There, you lying blackguard ! " panted Lee,
pointing to the recovered cash-box, " take them all
to my office where I'll settle with you once and for
all ! "

Nobody replied. Lee, flushed with excitement
and triumph, stripped off his diving-dress before he
became aware that something beside his own episode
had occurred. Then he saw Lefty Sawyer, bedab-
bled with blood, staring with sick, surprised eyes at
somebody—a woman,—who sat huddled on a heap
of sun-dried sleepers, sun-bonnet fallen back, cocked
revolver in either hand, and, in her dark eyes, tears
that flowed silently over colourless cheeks.

Lee glared at Dyce.

" Ask *her*," muttered Dyce doggedly.

He turned toward Helen, but Farrely, behind his
engine, shouted : " Faith, she stood off th' gang or
the breathin' below wud ha' choked ye ! Thank

the lass, lad, an' mind she's a gun whin ye go wor-
ritin' the fishes for the coompany's cash-box ! "

.   .   .   .   .   .

That night Lee made a speech at the quarry.
The men listened placidly. Dyce, amazed that he
was not discharged, went back to nurse Sawyer, a
thoroughly cowed man. Noonan, Farrely, and
Phelan, retired to their shanty and got fighting
drunk to the health of the " colleen wid the gun ; "
the rest of the men went away with wholesome convictions concerning their superintendent that promised better things.

" Didn't shanghai Dyce,—no he didn't," was the
whispered comment.

Lee's policy had done its work.

As for the murderous mover of the plot, the plausible foreman, Finn, he had shown the white feather
under fire and he knew the men might kill him on
sight. It's an Irish characteristic under such circumstances.

Lee walked back from the quarry, realising his
triumph, recognising that he owed it neither to his
foolhardy impulse, nor yet to his mercy to Dyce
and Sawyer. He went to the house and knocked
at Helen's door. She was not there. He sat alone
in his office, absently playing with pen and ruler
until the June moon rose over the ocean and yellow
sparkles flashed among the waves. An hour later
he went to the dock and found her sitting there
alone in the moonlight.

She did not repulse him. Her hour had come

23

and she knew it, for she had read such things in romances. It came. But she was too much in love, too sincere to use a setting so dramatic. She told him she loved him ; she told him why she had come to the Port-of-Waves, why she had remembered the kiss and the promise. She rested her head on his shoulder and looked out at the moon, smaller and more silvery now. She was contented.

Under the dock the dark waves lapped musically. Under the dock Finn, stripped to the skin, plunged silently downward for the one missing cash-box, trusting to his sense of touch to find the safe.

But what he found was too horrible for words.

" Hark," whispered Helen ; " did you hear something splash ? "

Lee looked out into the moonlight ; a shadow, a black triangular point cut the silvery surface, steered hither and thither,—circled, sheered seaward, and was lost. Then came another splash, far out among the waves.

" The Collector of the Port," said Lee ; " is making merry in the moonlight."

THE WHISPER

I' bruinait. . . . L'temps était gris,
On n'voyait pas l'ciel . . . L'atmosphère
Semblant suer au-d'ssus d' la ville,
Tombait en bué su' la terre.

"FANTAISIE TRISTE."

As I entered the alley the bells of the dim city tolled for the passing night. Far in the black maze of filthy lanes and mist-choked streets a policeman whistled; I heard the distant din of an Elevated train, rushing through the fog, nearer, nearer, duller now, now smothered in the vapour which rolled from river to river, thick, heavy, stifling.

In the gloom of the alley a shadowy form loomed up and passed, leaving no sound of footsteps in my ears, but all around me the vapour became faintly tainted with opium and a flare of yellow light streamed out across the fog from an opening door. There was a momentary murmur of voices, the soft shuffle of felt-shod feet, the rustle of silken sleeves. A painted paper lantern swung from the doorway, dipped, and disappeared. I heard the deadened slam of the door and the black night veiled my eyes again.

An empty truck, with broken shafts buried in the mud of the gutter, blocked the sidewalk, and I crossed the greasy pavement to avoid it.

Around the pale flame of a gas lamp the fog spun an iridescent oval; the wet sidewalk glimmered un-

derneath. Far down the reeking throat of the alley
an arc-light shone like a grey star.

I raised my eyes to the dark house before me
where from a rusting balcony a sign hung low above
the doorway.

"This was her house," I said aloud to myself;
but I passed on to the next house. Here I paused
a moment, looking back at the bamboo sign dripping with fog, then turned and descended some
wooden steps to an iron door. Before I could find
the handle, wrought in bronze like a dragon's claw,
the door flew open and I heard McManus' angry
bellow; "Git t' hell outer here, yer dope suckin'
yap!" and a Chinaman was hustled into the area
beside me.

"Chin chin thlough hattee!" snarled the Chinaman, "walkee where dlam please!"

"I'll walkee you on yer neck!" growled McManus,
and kicked the Chinaman half way up the steps.

"Dlam! Dlam! Dlam!" screamed the Chinaman, dancing with rage, but Charley, the bouncer,
burst out of the door, and the Chinaman fled chat-
tering like an infuriated ape.

I stepped into the low-ceilinged room and took a
chair at a cherry-wood table beside the wall. Two
young men sitting there said, "Hello, Jim!"

"Good evenin'," said McManus, leaning over the
bar, "did you see me givin' de bounce to Wah-Wo?"

"Yes," I said, "when did he come back?"

"He jest come in. I told him to git an' he give
me de ha-ha, so Charley trun him down. What

t'hell, sez I, an' he gives me back talk! Say, I won't do a t'ing to him!'"

One of the young men at the table beside me looked up from the Welsh-rabbit he was eating and called for ale. McManus brought it himself, a brimming pewter mug, and wiped his hands on his blue apron. Then he bawled for Charley to take my order.

"Sure," said Charley coming in from the street where he had been patiently waiting for a scrap, and he leaned with both fists on the table and winked pleasantly at the company. Lynde, of the "Herald," advised me to try a rabbit, and Penlow, of the "Tribune," spoke well of the chops, so I left it to Charley and he retired to the grill, whistling, "Oh I don't know!"

"It's a wonder to me," I said, hanging my wet mackintosh on a peg and kicking off my overshoes, "it's a wonder to me that Wah-Wo was discharged."

"There was no evidence to hold him," observed Lynde after a moment's silence.

Penlow lighted his pipe and rattled his mug on the table.

"No evidence," I repeated; "do you fellows doubt that Wah-Wo did it?"

"I suppose he did," said Penlow, "it was my scoop too."

"We may scoop yet," said Lynde, "the man's bound to be caught. What did they do with that young tough from Hell's Kitchen?"

" Sheehan?   Oh, his alibi is good," said Penlow.
" Mac, fill her up will you?"

McManus replenished the pewter and stood for a
moment beside us as if undecided.

"Gents," began McManus, " youse is dead off—
excuse me."   He shifted his toothpick and rubbed
his thumb on the polished bar.

" Wah-Wo ain't in it," he said contemptuously:
"I give him de t'row-down,—fur why?—fur because
I don't give de glad hand to no dope suckin' come-on
—an' he's dopy.   But he didn't do no dirt to the gal
whut youse gents was stuck on—he ain't that kind '
He give me the laugh an' I t'rowed him down,
see?   An' I won't do a t'ing but push his face in.
See?"

" But," said Penlow, "her dog flew at him when
he went to the house.   Kerrigan, you know—' Happy
Days Mike'—said that Wah-Wo tried to cut a girl
in Doyers Street."

" Nit! I don't think," said McManus scornfully:
" Kerrigan's a stuff—"

" Well, Mac," said Lynde, "what's your theory?
You know as much about it as anybody.   The girl
came in here every night, didn't she?   People say
that she lived alone, but of course she had company
when she wanted it.   What's your idea, Mac?"

McManus looked out of the window and drummed
on the bar with the blade of his oyster knife.
Charley, clad in a blue checked jumper, arrived with
some chops and ale.   I unfolded my napkin and began my supper.

For a while I ate in silence, thinking of Wah-Wo and the dead girl.

Caithness of the Consolidated Press came in looking cold and ill, and we hastily made room for him at our table.

" You're sick," said Lynde sharply, " you ought to be in bed."

" I'm all right," said Caithness, glancing at us with his large dark eyes : " Mac, get me something hot."

I swallowed my ale and turned again to the chops, scarcely listening to the hum of voices beside me, for I was thinking again of the dead girl.

I had no doubt that Wah-Wo had killed her. Again and again I had seen his eyes fastened upon her as she sat chatting with us, here at this very table. The motive was clear to me. I had spoken of this to the others but they laughed at me. The District Attorney took no stock in it, either ; the result was the discharge of Wah-Wo.

How could anybody but a Chinaman, crazed with jealousy and opium, harm the child ? For she was a mere child, this pallid victim whose soul had mounted to the Judgment seat from the filth of Chinatown.

Pale, slim, childish, depraved, she had never haunted Chinese resorts nor, to my knowledge, had she ever touched needle to flame. She had shunned the women of the quarter. I seldom saw her speak to any man except the reporters and newspaper

artists who came to McManus's for a midnight chop
or rarebit.

Her acquaintance with us had been open and
guileless. She chatted with us about our business,
discussed the latest police shake-up or the newest
Tammany scandal, gave us her views on politics and
the City Hall, and glided away into the street
again followed by her dog. Her dog! A great
hulking brute, black as night, with sombre eyes and
low hanging jowl,—a creature silent, unmoved except when she bent her pale face to his ear and whispered. Then and then only he would rise, shuffling
from the sawdust floor under the bar, and stalk after
her into the night.

He never paid the slightest attention to us.
Calls, caresses, threats, left him unmoved.

" What is it you whisper into his ear, Lil ? " we
often asked, but she would only smile and answer :
" His name."

And so, as none of us knew his name, we called
him simply, " her dog."

It had been two months now since Lil was found
on her bed with a bullet in her heart and the dog
lying stolidly across her bare little feet. And after
we had clubbed together and buried her, we were
kinder to her dog.

Every night he came gravely into McManus' to
lie down under the bar just as he had done when
Lil sat there chatting with us.

At first McManus was afraid that the dog would
" hoodoo the place," but he left the silent brute un-

disturbed, and, after a while, began to grow fond of it.

"That dog ain't no mutt," McManus would say as he stood behind the bar opening oysters; "no an' he ain't no rube! Say! he's in it all the time when Charley trims the steaks."

As I sat thinking of all these things and sipping my ale meditatively, I heard the iron door creak on its hinges and the knocker fall once. Then something heavy and hairy rubbed its body against the door outside. McManus stood up saying: "Here he comes, gents!"

Her dog entered.

Lynde held out his hand as the brute passed, and Penlow flung a bone on the floor. The dog noticed neither the caress nor the bone, but lay down under the bar and stretched his great limbs across the floor, sighing heavily.

"There is one thing certain," said Lynde, looking at the dog: "the man who killed the girl was in the habit of visiting her,—and that dog knew him."

"I also believe the murderer was known to the dog," said Penlow."

"The murderer," said Caithness, "was her lover."

"It is strange," said I, "that none of us suspects anybody except Wah-Wo."

"Why strange?" asked Caithness, then he added impatiently, "yes, it is strange! Do you think she would have looked at a Chinaman?"

"The Chinaman looked at her; I saw him," I replied,

"After all, she was a common girl of the street," said Penlow unaffectedly, "and I guess pride cut no figure with her."

"That is where you lie," said Caithness in a low voice.

There was a dead silence. Then Penlow said: "Did I understand you, Caithness?"

I rose and laid my hand on Penlow's arm, which was twitching though his face was calm.

"Are you crazy?" I said to Caithness.

"I think I am," said Caithness slowly, "I beg your pardon, Penlow."

Lynde turned his puzzled eyes from Penlow to Caithness and lifted his mug mechanically. Penlow straightened in his chair but said nothing, and I leaned back motioning McManus to remove the covers.

After a few moments the constraint became irksome. "Red," the tortoise-shell cat, mascotte of McManus and exterminator of mice by special appointment, had cornered a vicious rat in the backyard, and now came marching in to display the game for our benefit.

"Git!" said McManus with pardonable pride, "the gents here don't give a damn fur to see rats."

Charley hustled the cat out again and McManus assured us for the hundredth time that "Red" was the only cross-eyed cat in New York.

None of us had ever before seen a cross-eyed cat, so we did not deny it, although I remonstrated

with McManus concerning his pride in " Red's"
ocular misfortune.

" What's that ?" demanded McManus.

" I don't see why," said I, "a cat should be the
more valuable because it happens to be afflicted
with strabismus."

" Sure !" said McManus doggedly.

" No, I don't," I repeated.

" It's a mascot," said McManus.

" How do you know?"

" Did youse gents ever see another cross-eyed
cat ?" demanded McManus hotly.

We all said no.

" Then what t'hell do youse gents know about
mascots ?" he exclaimed triumphantly.

The constraint still weighed upon us, however, for
Caithness had neither spoken nor smiled, and Penlow, it was easy to see, had not forgotten.

Lynde picked up a paper and ran it through, unaffectedly searching for his own matter ; after a
while Penlow did the same.

I looked at Caithness, and he felt my eyes, for
presently he moved a little and passed his hand
over his sunken cheeks.

"What's up?" I asked, dropping my voice and
bending toward him.

" Nothing—why ?"

" You look like the last rose of summer,—you've
got a beastly cough."

He smiled faintly. " It's consumption," he said,
" I found out to-day."

I stared at him stupidly.

"I don't mind," he said; "I'm dead sick of the whole business."

"How do you know it's consumption?" I asked at length.

"I went to three doctors to make sure; I tell you I don't care."

Little Penlow was listening now; before I could speak again he leaned over and took Caithness's hand affectionately.

"Brace up, old boy," he said, "go to California and get well."

"Of course," I cried, "you're a fool to stay in this cursed climate, Caithness!"

I spoke harshly for I was more affected than I cared to show.

"Chuck up your job! Let the Consolidated Press go to the devil!" urged Lynde.

"I have resigned," said Caithness quietly. A fit of coughing shook him, and he raised his napkin to his lips. He continued, "I thought I'd come around to-night and say good-bye."

The dog shifted his position under the bar and sighed again. One of the gas jets behind the bar blazed up suddenly; McManus turned it lower, cursing the gas company.

"Do you fellows know that I have scooped?" said Caithness abruptly.

"Not—not the fellow who shot Lil," faltered Penlow, who had thrown his whole soul into solving the mystery.

"Yes—the murderer of Lily White," said Caithness. In the silence I could hear McManus grinding his toothpick in his yellow teeth.

"I'm out of the Consolidated now," continued Caithness calmly,—"the scoop is yours if you want it, Penlow."

"But—but you "—began Penlow.

"I?" said Caithness fiercely, "what do I care for newspapers? What do I care who knows it now,— what paper prints it first?"

Lynde leaned over the table, his head in his hand; Penlow's pipe went out; he did not relight it.

"Did you never know," said Caithness with a touch of scorn in his voice, "that I also loved the girl? Do you think I am ashamed to confess it? Do you know what I have been through since she died? Hell? Oh, yes, that's what they say in books. It doesn't matter;—Penlow, when you are ready—"

Penlow started, then groped in his pocket for pencil and pad.

"I am ready, Jack," he said.

"This is the story," said Caithness, almost eagerly. "On the 13th of last November, Lily White, a girl living next door, was shot through the heart by a man who was jealous of her. He knew that she came into McManus's and gossiped with the newspaper men, and he knew that Wah-Wo had offered her all his money, which was a great deal. When she was chatting with us here, this man was not jealous,—have you got that, Penlow?"

"Yes," said Penlow, scratching away on his pad.

"He was not jealous when Lily chatted with us, but when he saw Wah-Wo talking to her one night under the electric light by the Joss-house, he watched the girl night and day. She said that she loved him—she laughed at him when he offered her marriage,—so he watched her. Have you got that, Penlow?"

"Yes."

"Then a day came when Lily was to go to the country to see her sister,—that is what she said,—to see her sister, and this man went with her to the train and saw her off on her journey. But something told him to watch the next in-coming train, and he did. And Lily was on it.

"He followed her. She came straight to Doyers Street, heavily veiled, and entered a house that you all know,—the house with the paper lanterns and red signs. Wah-Wo lives there. A week later she returned to the man who had followed her. He was waiting for her,—have you written that?"

"Yes, Jack."

"He was waiting in her room,—alone with that dog there. He accused her, and she denied it. She called Heaven to witness her innocence. He offered her marriage again; she laughed at him. Then he shot her through the heart."

Penlow ceased writing and looked up expectantly.

"The murderer's name? Have patience," said Caithness grimly smiling. "The man called to the dog,—her dog there, and, because he was the only living soul who knew the brute's name, the dog answered and followed him out into the street.

"All day long he wandered about the city, and at night he went back to look upon the dead. He did not care who saw him,—he courted discovery, but no one paid him any attention, and, as it now appears, nobody even saw him. About midnight he went away, leaving the dog crouched at the dead girl's feet, and since then he has moved like a living death among the people of the city, unsuspected, unnoticed by any,—except me." He paused and looked at us. Tears had quenched the pale flame in his eyes, and the hair clung to his damp forehead.

"That man killed the woman I loved," he said, "and now I am going to give him up!" Then he rose trembling. The sleeping dog sighed heavily; his hind legs quivered.

Caithness bent and touched the massive head, muttering, "Come!"

At his touch the dog raised its head and looked at him with grave eyes.

Then, moving toward the door, he whispered again, *calling the dog by name;* and the great brute rose stiffly, yawned, and slowly followed him out into the night.

The iron door slammed behind them; the damp odour of fog came from the black street. Lynde

13

buried his head in his hands; McManus leaned heavily on the bar, pale as a corpse. Presently I heard the sound of rustling paper.

It was Penlow, tearing up his pad.

THE LITTLE MISERY

f

THE LITTLE MISERY.

If you be dead also and are come hither to join us, I pity your lot, for you will be stunned with the noise of the dwarfs and the storks.

VATHEK.

I.

THERE was a river-driver beyond the Northwest Carry who respected neither moose nor man. Because he was the best river-driver on the 'West Branch they let him alone until he struck an Indian with a pick-pole.

The Indian's head was damaged and while he waited for it to heal, he selected his revenge. His revenge was simple and effective. He hunted up the moose-warden and told many lies. Deftly concealed among these lies, however, was a truth that infuriated the warden.

The river-driver, whose name was Skeene, sat on his haunches and sneered when the moose-warden glided into camp. But when he dug out a head and antlers behind a shanty, Skeene picked up his rifle, looked obliquely at the moose-warden, tied his blanket and fry-pan, hoisted his canoe onto his head, and walked away to the southward, still sneering. I don't know what they said about it in Foxcroft, but Hale, who owned the timber, and who thought

197

he owned Skeene, hunted him up and sent him to
work on the new cut-off, hoping the affair might
blow over in time for Skeene to drive logs again.
But Skeene turned lazy and lined the dead water
with traps and set-lines, and when Hale remonstrated, Skeene laughed. Then Hale threatened
him and hinted about moose-wardens, and $500
fines, but Skeene thrashed Hale before the whole
camp, packed his kit and canoe, and paddled
serenely away down the West Branch.

That really began the trouble, for Hale never
forgave him. When Skeene started to guide for
Henderson on the upper Portage, Hale heard of it
and ran him out. That, of course, marked him
among the guides in the lake-country, and Skeene
perhaps felt the ostracism, for he quietly went to
work for Colby on the new sluice that ran from the
carry-pond to the lake. Possibly, if they had let
him alone, he might have turned out as tame as a
moose-bird,—he was only twenty-three,—but Hale
remembered, and the Indian remembered, and one
day a man came in to the Carry Camp with a 44
bullet in his wrist and an unserved warrant in his
pocket. The man was a moose-warden, and the
warrant was for Skeene.

When the news spread that Skeene had shot a
warden, the guides from Portage to Lily-Bay con-
demned him. Down at Greenville a sheriff and
posse boarded the " Katahdin," and spent several
weeks cruising about at public expense. The lake
steamboat was comfortable, the food good, and the

sheriff and posse were in no hurry to quit. Possibly they expected Skeene to come down to the
shore and sit on the rocks; perhaps they fancied he
might paddle across their bows in his sleep. Naturally he did neither. When at length somebody
suggested that the sheriff and posse take to their
canoes, that official steamed back to the foot of the
lake in a huff, and presently the rumours of Skeene's
misdoings became scarcely more definite than camp-
fire gossip.

Perhaps even then, if they had given him a
chance, he might have surrendered and taken his
punishment, but they didn't give him the chance.
A warden saw him building a lean-to, on the island
that divides the West Branch. The warden waited
until dark, crawled in outside the fire, and caught
Skeene asleep. That is all the warden recollects,
merely that he caught Skeene asleep. What Skeene
did to the warden when he awoke, the official cannot remember distinctly.

Three weeks after that, Skeene walked into Kineo
store, handling his rifle in a most alarming fashion.
He suggested that they place certain provisions and
ammunition in his canoe, which lay on the beach
below. The three clerks complied with an enthusiasm borne of fright. Twenty minutes later Skeene,
in his canoe, was seen making for Moose River.
Two guides, just from Lily Bay, refused to fire at
him, arguing it was not right to drown a man for
stealing pork and powder. The hotel had not yet
opened, and the people at the annex objected to a

man-hunting trip, so they only notified the sheriff again and secretly wished Skeene in hell.

Of course, at the hotels they denied the very existence of Skeene; but the Bangor "News" printed the story, and people fought shy of Moose River and the lake beyond which is called Red Lake. In vain the guides declared the region safe. It was safe as far as they were concerned. It is not the nature of a guide—that is, a white guide—to inform on or interfere with any man. Skeene let them alone. The Indians, too, paddled about Red Lake when they wanted to. The Indian log-driver, however, stayed away after Skeene had shot a hole in his canoe. The canoe being bark, it was through Providence and a patch of gum that the log-driving half-breed ever paddled out of the mouth of Moose River.

Now if they had not started to hunt Skeene from the Lakes, he would never have troubled anybody, except possibly Hale and the half-breed. He went to Canada for a year, worked at anything that came along, and sent money to Kineo store to pay for his pork and powder. That, of course, won him the guides again. So when home-sickness drove him back to Red Lake, he expected to be let alone. Hale, sluicing at the Northwest Carry, heard he had returned, and started for Red Lake with the log-driving half-breed and six men. Two days later they returned; Hale had a bullet in his leg above the knee and the half-breed carried a similar gift in his forearm.

This incident, while relieving the conversational monotony at camp and landing, bothered the sheriff cruelly. He went to Foxcroft where they said unpleasant things to him; he went back to the Landing and they made fun of him.

There was a captain on the lake named Snow,—a white-bearded, mild-eyed giant. When the local paper wanted an item it filled in with, "Extraordinary weather on the Lake in July! Steamboat 'Red-Deer' in port with six feet two inches of Snow in her pilot house!"

The sheriff went to see Snow, and, after a long confab, summoned his posse, boarded the Red-Deer, and left Greenville, as the local paper expressed it, "under sealed orders, bound for Moose River." Naturally, half a dozen canoes were aboard, some lying bottom upward on the superstructure, some lashed to the rail. The posse carried Winchesters, although no game was in season.

Off the Grey Gull, an island, the little steamboat slowed down and stopped, the canoes were hoisted over the rail and dropped; the posse embarked. The sheriff said good-bye in a voice made loud by nervousness, and the Red-Deer swung about and steamed back to the foot of the lake with six feet two inches of Snow in her pilot-house.

At the mouth of Moose River two more canoes were waiting; Hale sat in one, paddle glistening in the pale spring sunshine; in the other sat the Indian log-driver, nursing the hammer of a rifle.

Below the long ridge the water is nearly dead,

although a canoe might drift to the point in twenty-four hours. It was paddling for a mile to the first wing-dam, and there, the sheriff, who led, flung his stern-paddle into the bottom of the canoe, flourished the setting-pole, and stood up. At the same moment a jet of flame leaped from the edge of the wing-dam and a bullet passed through the sheriff's hat. The amazed official promptly fell overboard, sank, rose, grasped the edge of the canoe, and swamped it, turning the bow-paddler into the river. The swift current landed them on a shoal before the sheriff could shriek more than twice, and they crawled up on a rock, sleek and wet as half drowned flies in a sap-pan.

The other canoes had halted; some of the posse waved their rifles, but nobody fired at the wing-dam except Hale. He banged away as fast as he could pump the breach-lever, and Billy Sebato, the Indian, took to the bushes and lay patiently waiting for a mark, purring with eagerness.

"Jim Skeene, you darned thief!" shouted Hale, "come out from them stones! Jest you come out on to that there wing-dam once!"

Above the rush and gurgle of the river they heard Skeene's voice: "You let me be or I'll shoot to kill!"

"Thief! Thief!" yelled Hale, dancing in his seat with anger, until the canoe heeled and almost swamped.

"I ain't no more thief than you be, Josh Hale!" bawled Skeene, "I paid for them rations and

ca'tridges and you know damn well I did!" Before
he could add anything, the Indian, Sebato, fired
twice.

"If that nigger Sebato don't quit shootin' I'll let
loose on all o' ye!" called Skeene, shaking his rifle
above the wing-dam edge.   "Git back to your
dreen, Josh Hale, I tell you."

Hale had reloaded his magazine, and now, swinging his setting-pole with one hand, started to push
his canoe among the rocks where he could hold it
and fire under cover.   Skeene evidently saw him for
he slid suddenly to the corner of the wing-dam and
fired three shots through the canoe, cutting a swale
lengthwise at the water's edge.

"Oh, you sneaky bob-cat!" yelled Hale, white
with rage.   In another moment he was working cup
and sponge to bail his canoe, which swung away on
the current and drifted broadside across the sand-
bar below, where it settled in two feet of limpid
water.

"Now 'll you let me be?" called Skeene.   "I
hain't done nothin' to you.   If that there moose-
warden wants me let him come and get me.   Ain't
you ashamed to go huntin' a man like a Lucivee?
I tell ye I'll shoot to kill, b' God I will, at the next
man that fires!"

"You dasn't," shouted the sheriff from behind his
rock; "you ain't half.a man, Jim Skeene!"

"I be," said Skeene calmly, "but I don't want no
fuss.   You keep off'n this river, and you keep off'n
this here wing-dam.   And you stop sneakin' along

the woods there, Billy Sebato! Git back there! Git back, or I'll shoot to kill!"

"You'll hang if you do!" bawled the sheriff.

"Then tell that nigger Indian to git back! Tell him quick! I see him—I—"

Sebato's rifle cracked, and the shot was repeated by Hale, wading out on the shoal. Then a forked flame flashed from the wing-dam, there came a crash and crackle of dry twigs, and the Indian pitched heavily over the bank into the swirling river.

The echoes of the shots died out among the trees; for a minute the gurgle of the river ripple alone troubled the stillness. A kingfisher wheeled up stream, the sun flashing on his blue wings; a fish soused in a calm pool below the dam. Presently the changed voice of the sheriff broke the silence:

"Jim Skeene, God help you, you'll swing for this."

Skeene's pale face appeared above the dam, but nobody shot at him.

"You drove me to it," said Skeene. He spoke huskily. "I told him to git back,—I warned him to quit sneakin' up on me."

"Come down off'n that wing-dam," commanded Hale.

"Not for you, Josh Hale," replied Skeene, "nor not for any man o' ye! An' I won't be took neither. I'm goin' away to live quiet if they let me."

He crouched and watched them as they pushed their canoes out into the main channel. The sheriff and Hale advanced to the pool where Sebato lay.

A slender fillet of blood, a mere thread hung in the water just below the surface, and stretched out, following the current, floating like a red string.

" Bring them settin'-poles," said the sheriff soberly, " paddles won't stand the heft, an' he's, hefty." Hale suddenly turned, snarling at the wing-dam ; " Jim Skeene, you sneakin' muskrat !—" he said ; but Skeene was gone when Hale's bullet stung the rock above.

II.

They gave Skeene little peace for two months. Week after week a string of canoes passed the swift water under the first and second wing-dams, poled to the point-trail, and, disembarking a file of rifle-men, poled on again to the discharge at Red Lake. Week after week the distant flash of a paddle startled the deer at sunrise among the lily-pads. At evening, too, silent canoes stealing through the sedge-grass, roused the great blue herons from their heavenward contemplation and sent the sheldrake scuttling and splashing across shoal water with a noise like a churning twinscrew.

But they did not catch Skeene.

Once they saw him for a moment standing in the stern of his canoe. The canoe lay at the mouth of the Little Misery, that dead stretch of water and dead-fall, winding through the bog to the southward. They gave chase, trailing Skeene's canoe by the wake bubbles until they ran plump into quick water.

But the Little Misery is a strange stream draining
a strange land, and there, in that maze of cuts and
channels, of "logans" and quick water, of swamp,
shoal, sedge, and spectral ranks of dead trees, tow-
ering above swale and deadwood, they stood no
more chance of flushing Skeene than a caribou has
of raising three fawns in a season.

What he did with his canoe nobody might know.
Certainly he left the main channel.   Did he himself
hide in the bog or dead-falls?   Where do young sand-
pipers vanish on a shingle beach?   Oh there were
sounds in the swamp as the sheriff's posse steered
through the even with silent paddle,—sounds that
stir only in lonely places, faint splashes, a sound of
a swirl in still water, the breeze in the swale-grass.

And so they hunted Skeene at twilight, at dusk
of morning, at high noon, from the Northeast Carry
to the Northwest Carry, from the West-Branch to
Seboomook, from Portage to Lily Bay, and through
a hundred miles of lake and stream, up and down,
up and down.   But Moose River bore no tales on
its placid breast, and the wing-dams towered silent
as twin Sphinxes, and the sounds that startled the
silence where the Little Misery coils through the
strange country, are mysteries even to those who
interpret them.

It was in May that the ice went out, in company
with Skeene; it was in July that they felt the bite
of his bullets below the wing-dam; it was in August that they gave up the chase.

That evening, Skeene stood on a wind-fall in the

depths of the Little Misery and watched three canoes file out of the discharge and glide into the swift water of Moose River. The next morning he started a lean-to on the ridge back of the Little Misery, and the sharp crack and thwack of his axe rang out over Red Lake. At sunrise a moose-cow heard it and ploughed hastily shoreward through the lily-pads with an ouf! woof! ouf! as she struck the pebbles on the beach. One by one the great blue herons flapped up from the dead pines, circled, sailed, and turned over to pitch head downwards into the sedge with dull cries.

At noon the echoes of axe-strokes died away and the hut was thatched with balsam, blue side skyward. By three o'clock a spike buck, a yearling, lay across a log on the ridge, and at four o'clock Skeene had satisfied his hunger.

He sat on the shore under the ridge, pensively picking his white teeth with the enjoyment of the abandoned. Across the lake the mountains turned to sapphire and ashes; a pale sky deepened into flame colour; the sun hung a globe of crimson in gilded mist.

One by one the last sunbeams reddened the trunks of the trees to the eastward, the foliage burned, the shore line glimmered. Like changing hues on a bubble, the colours deepened, and played over the placid lake. A single snowy bank of cloud, piled up in the east, glowed where the sun stained its edges. The midges danced above the sedge; the lake-wash rocked the swales, to and fro, to and fro.

A trout broke in shallow water, flapped up and splashed again, and the red sky crimsoned the widening rings, spreading slowly shoreward.

In the days that followed, Skeene learned to talk to himself. When he did this he forgot that he had killed Sébato; after a while he forgot it altogether.

When the August afternoons were ablaze with brazen sunlight and the lake glistened like a sheet of steel, Skeene sprawled on a log in the shade and watched the great blue herons. When they "drove stakes" he mocked them with the same note until they answered "Ke-whack! Ke-whack! Ke-whack!" The red squirrel's thin treble he imitated; he called the chipmunks with a tsip! tsip! and laughed until his white teeth glistened when a carrion-jay alighted on his knee for a shin-joint half hacked. The great belted-kingfishers knew him, the sheldrake, stringing along the creek at evening, turned their bright eyes to his, the osprey who lived above the ledge, wheeled above him for hours, knowing that he also was a savage thing and hunted when hungry.

He was hungry several times between sunrise and sunset. The swift water of the Little Misery gave him a trout to every set-line; the deeper pools by the sedge gave him pleasure.

On the Little Misery deer swarm at evening, and he had meat for the price of a cartridge.

The white nights of August brought that vague unrest that all forest creatures feel. The deer girdled the roots of the ash-trees and the spike bucks grew bolder; the great blue herons danced their contre-dance, evening after evening, at first solemnly, advancing, retreating in stately quadrilles, lifting their slim shins high in the sedge; but, as the month ended, the contre-dance lost dignity and gained in abandon, until the lone loon out on the lake shook the silence with his demon's laughter. As the moon waned, the forest world stirred; its attitude was expectant; it waited. The cow-moose began to cast evil oblique glances on her calves, now turned darker; and the little bull moose-calf, frisked until his tiny bell swung like the wattle on a turkey.

An impatience, almost a sadness fell upon Skeene. And with sadness came fear. He covered his lean-to and built a smoke-hole through which blue haze rose in the calm morning air. But, like wild things in winter, he was wary, and the steam-hole of a beaver's house might be more easily located than the chimney of Skeene's hut.

When September came a hush fell over the forest; and and water were silent; the trout no longer broke water or leaped full length in the after-glow; the deer picked a silent path along the shore; the herons stood all day, heads stretched heavenward; the loon's maniac laughter was stilled. Silent and more silent the woods grew as the new moon, a faint tracery above the hills, rose in the evening sky. At its first quarter the silence deepened, at its half, the stillness was intense. Then one black night the Full Moon of September flashed in the sky, and before the last shore ripple had caught its glitter, a gigantic

14

black shadow waded out into the lake and a roar shook the hills.

The first bull-moose had bellowed, and the rutting season had begun.

Instantly the forest, the lake, the shore, the stream were alive; the meat-birds cried from every cedar; the deer barked from the sedge; a lynx howled and miauled in the second growth. Everywhere plumage and fur were growing glossy and gay. Even Skeene sewed porcupine quills into his boot-moccasins, and sang fragments of a song he had heard in Quebec.

III.

Now there is a season for all things; in the fall the black moose grows blacker and sleeker; in the fall the red buck rubs the tattered velvet from every prong; in the spring the mewing cat-bird whistles dreamily as a spotted thrush; in the spring the snow-bird changes its feathers, chameleon like, as the snow drifts or melts; and the dry chirring of the red squirrel grows sweeter.

" Each after its kind," says the quaint Book, and so the spruce-grouse drums in the long summer days, and the crested wood-duck ruffles its rainbow plumes, and the painted trout hang over the gravel beds in September, and the antlered moose barks at the September moon.

As for Skeene, he sewed porcupine quills in a semicircle over the instep of his moccasins, laced a string of scarlet trout-flies across his slouch hat, and listened to the bull-moose, bellowing out on the moonlit ridge.

At times he sang his Quebec song, at times he sighed. Twice he spared a yearling buck,—he could not tell why. He caught a big red sable, bigger than the coon-cat at the Carry House. It scratched and bit him, but he was very good to it. A lazy beaver, driven from the colony by his industrious relatives, bored a hole in the bank under Skeene's shanty. Beaver-tail and hindquarters are good, cold boiled, but Skeene let him live in peace and even piled enough poplar saplings at his door to last any lazy beaver a year. And all this time he was sorry he killed Sebato at the wing-dam ; he wished he had shot him a year before in the bog-country,— it was a good chance and nobody would have been the wiser.

When the September moon waxed full and the water lapped softly along the lake ledge, Skeene's heart grew full, and the blood in his neck and cheeks ebbed and surged like moon-tides. So, on the second night, he took his rifle and dragged the canoe to the beach. But his heart failed him and he feared the Carry House, and he went back to his camp and rolled and grunted through a sleepless night. On the third evening he started on foot, but he hesitated when the lamp in the Carry House broke out, a red beam in the night. He stood, wretched, wistful, un-decided, fingering his rifle butt, and his heart beat to suffocation. Something near him stirred and moaned among the rocks,—a miserable gluttonous fisher-cat, its head bristling with porcupine quills. And Skeene, sick with self-compassion, trailed the wounded creature to the water's edge and killed it,— pitying it as he pitied himself. Then, worn out with the fever in his veins, he slept openly where he lay, wondering if he should wake on Red Lake shore or on the shores of a redder lake.

On the fourth night of the full of the moon, he went swiftly across the ridge, unarmed, and the miles of woodland and shore sped away like mist, so eagerly he ran. On that night he heard the moose-cows calling the barking bull, and the whoof ! of the dun doe in the sedge. Far on the shore the red beam of the Carry lamp signalled him and his blood flamed the answer in his face. And, as he strode up to the house, he saw a woman on the shore looking out into the night across the spectral lake. It was Lois, servant at South Carry. He had danced with her two years ago at Foxcroft Landing, he had sent her six otter pelts a month before he shot Sebato.

She was the girl he had come for.

Is it possible she expected him ? The restlessness of September had drawn her to the lake and something had led him to her.

The moon, a silver lamp, traced a shining trail across the shadowy waters ; his canoe grated softly on the shoal, a string of bubbles followed the paddle sweep, the foam whispered secrets to the clustered sedge-grass.

*　　*　　*　　*　　*　　*

And so, together, they glided away on a trail of silver water to the strange country, drained by strange streams, stirred by strange winds. The red spark of the Carry lamp died out in the night, the little grey stars twinkled over the dead waters, pale sparks from phantom nuptial torches flaring in the north.

At dawn the sky crimsoned the Little Misery. They slept. At sunrise a moose roared a salute to the coming day.

They awoke and kissed each other.

IV.

When the public-spirited citizens of Foxcroft offered $500 reward for the capture of Skeene, Placide L'Hommedieu scratched his greasy chin, licked his lips, and went out to buy cartridges. Placide had trapped in the Province and thought he could trap as well in Maine.

" Monsieur L'Hommedieu what will you do with $500 ? " asked the Mayor of Foxcroft.

"Le Hommydoo won't need it," observed a grizzled portage guide who had once shot a match with Skeene. And he was right for they found L'Hommedieu a week later peacefully floating down Moose River in his canoe, with a bullet in his brain.

When Skeene paddled away with Lois, there was trouble in Foxcroft. Hale left sluice, drain, and chain, and wired the Sheriff at the Landing to meet him at Moosehead Inn.   The Mayor went also, and next morning the reward was doubled for " James Skeene, Murderer, dead or alive."

Hale had never forgiven the blow at the cut-off, but a busy man would scarcely have left his sluice to hunt another man to death for that alone.   No, Hale had other reasons, and they concerned neither Billy Sebato nor Placide L'Hommedieu.   They concerned Lois, servant at South Carry ; for when she left with Jim Skeene she took Hale's betrothal ring with her.

After Skeene had set Placide L'Hommedieu afloat, with mud on his face and a bullet in his skull, he shoved the canoe into swift water at Moose River, broke both paddles, splintered the setting-pole, and solemnly watched the canoe out of sight.

Lois, waiting for him when he poled into the Little Misery, looked at his knife in the scolloped leather sheath, then at his rifle, and finally into his sombre eyes.

" I heard,—only one shot.   Was it a deer ? "

He nodded muttering that he had missed ; but that night she caressed him, taking his curly head into her arms, and wept over him till daybreak crimsoned the world.

After that they were almost gay.   He notched logs and built a hut and rammed moss into the cracks.   Lois brought clay from the sweet water, and cut balsam until her little hands were stained to the palm.   Twice he passed the three carrys to the C. P. R. and hung to a freight as far as Sainte Croix.   They knew nothing and cared less in the

Dominion, and he bought salt and pork and flour and cartridges with the proceeds of Hale's ring. The third trip he walked on the C. P. fearing the train, and he got his price for ten pelts, including musk-rat.

They knew that happiness that is bred in haunting fear, that fierce, that intense love whose roots are imbedded in terror. Lois had been to school and these were the things she knew;—that two and two make four, that Moose calves are born in May, that bark peels best in June, that Moose-calves are weaned in September. She knew also how to use Skeene's knife, and when he found beaver above swift water and told her so in the evening, she cut saplings and whittled trip-sticks and notched chokers while he hewed out the bed-pieces for the traps, and sharpened enough young ash to build the fences for winter traps. Mink traps, too, were no mystery to Lois, and they talked long and wisely concerning standards and cubbies and spindles while the embers died under the simmering tins and the deer whistled on the windy ridge.

Snow came, a phantom flurry through the pale sunshine, and Skeene lugged more deer hides into his hut. A hot week followed, sending the trout to the bottom-sands and the deer to the shallows; then came the ice; at first a brittle, glittering skin, encasing stem and reed, and wrinkling hidden stagnant pools. The wind in the grasses grew harsher, the reeds rattled at evening; vast flocks of little birds circled high in the sky for the winds of the

South called them, and the geese were drifting overhead.

One day the snow came again, and at evening it had not ceased falling. A week later the lake froze and Skeene dragged his canoe into the hut and daubed it with white-lead, while Lois crept close to his side and strung snowshoes. At times she sang. He listened, lying beside the canoe. When she had sung the same song until evening he taught her the song he had learned in Quebec;

> " Mossieu Meenoose
> Mossieu Meenoose
> Mon dieu que tu as
> Un villain chat la."

And she sang it and sewed scarlet braid across her moccasins.

During these weeks Hale was busy in Foxcroft. When the smaller lakes froze he leered sideways at the Sheriff and ordered a dozen pairs of snowshoes. Once or twice he went back to his sluice and cursed, but the River Drivers regarded him with evil eyes, and the sluicers drove their props sullenly until he went away leaving a string of oaths in his wake. There were men of the stamp he wanted on the Province side of the C. P. R. ; there was Achille Verdier, one-eyed and idle ; there was greasy little Armand Fleury, dirtier for his fox-skin cap, dingier for the red braid on the tail. There also resided Wyombo, pigeon-toed, furtive, aboriginal. Much could be done with these gentlemen and $1000.

The value of Hale's ring was $150, therefore the people of Foxcroft gossiped.

Snow fell on the frozen lake; the Little Misery was mantled, the carrys choked. All day long the meat-birds whined in the fir-trees and at night the sleet pelted the frozen snow. The deer yarded on the ridge, the moose on the slope above; the black bear buried his feeble nose in his stomach and dreamed, and the otters frisked over their slide. As for Lois, she was learning things; she learned that the fur on the belly of a young panther is wavy, she learned that men are brutes, and that Skeene was all the world to her; she learned that she also had her value, for she saw him swim the swift water of the Little Misery when she screamed affrighted by an impudent lynx. She learned that he sometimes preferred solitude to company, that he sometimes preferred sleep to caresses. She learned that he went hungry that she might eat, that he shivered while she slept under skin and blanket.

Sometimes they played together, Skeene and this slender girl, like young foxes in the snow. She would often hide, too, in the hollow of a great swamp-oak, and when he came home she would call: " Jim ! Jim ! find me !"

But God lives, and the world spins, and the hare turns white in winter, and the routine of the beginning and the end never varies.

And so it came about that Skeene, laughing up at Lois in the hollow swamp-oak, glanced over his shoulder and saw six black dots clustered upon the frozen lake to the southward. He said nothing but looked into the north. There were more dots there, more also on the ice in the west. For a moment he thought the east was still open; after a while he heard the scrape of a snow-shoe very near. Lois also heard and her face was like death as she reached down and took the rifle from Skeene's hand.

When he had climbed up into the hollow tree beside her and looked out from the hole above the great branch, he saw Hale peering at him from a dead-fall.

"Come down," said Hale.

Skeene clapped his rifle to his cheek and fired.

"Come down," repeated Hale from behind his dead-fall. Lois, trembling at Skeene's feet, shrank at the sombre voice from the woods. Skeene bent and kissed her and caressed her, muttering things she could not understand, but she caught his hand in hers and tore off the fur mitten and pressed it to her hot lips, moaning and sobbing.

"Come down for the last time, Jim Skeene," said Hale slowly. Suddenly a rifle shot rang through the frozen forest. The hand that Lois held tightened against her lips, quivered, relaxed. Something outside fell clinking and clattering to the ground at the foot of the tree. It was Skeene's rifle; and Skeene sank forward, hanging half out of the hole in the tree, head downward, like a dead squirrel.

And beside him, the other wild thing sobbed and whimpered and moaned among the branches while below the swift axes bit into the tree from which the dead game hung, head downward.

" Look in the hut for the woman ! " bawled Hale.

The tree swayed and crackled and fell crashing into the snow.

" Where's that woman? " shouted Hale from the hut ;—" G—d d—n her ! "—

But when at last he found her he changed his mind and let her stay with Skeene there in the snow.

ENTER THE QUEEN

« Votre amour me ferait dieu.
M'aimez-vous, mademoiselle ?
Soupirez un mois, dit-elle.
Un mois ! C'est la mort ! Adieu ! »

ENTER THE QUEEN.

Souvenir cher à mes pensées !
Grâce à la fraîcheur qu 'il leur rend,
Je souris aux heures passées,
Je m'arrange du jour mourant.

BERANGER.

I

THE middle of the studio was occupied by a rug. The middle of the rug was occupied by Clifford. He sat on the floor playing a dirge on a brass cornet. Around him lay bureau drawers, empty trunks and satchels, flanked by cabinets and chests littered with palettes, underclothes, colour-tubes, pipes, and paint-rags.

When Elliott came in, an hour later, he found Clifford still performing on the cornet. He played "Hark! from the Tomb," and "Death and The Maiden"; and while he played he winked ominously at Elliott.

Now, when Clifford played on his cornet, something was amiss. Elliott knew this and watched him sideways, sullenly removing overcoat and gloves. Every dismal bleat of the brass prophesied calamity. The hollow studio echoed with forebodings of disaster.

"Stop that," said Elliott, flinging his hat on a chair; "what's the matter with you?"

"O Commander of the Faithful," said Clifford, "behold the end of the world! J'ai beau cherchai— je n'en trouve point—"

"Money?" asked Elliott, sitting down; "stop blowing into that cornet."

"I know of no other way to raise the wind," said Clifford,—"get your cornet and we'll play duets."

"You mean we are actually without means?"

Clifford threaded his way through an abatis of easels, canvasses, books, and bird-cages to the Japanese tea-table.

"Have some tea?" he inquired.

"No, I won't," snapped Elliott, "and you can tell me where our funds have gone."

Clifford poured himself a cup of tea, raised his eyes piously, sipped it, and looked at Elliott over the edge of the cup.

"Where's our money?" repeated Elliott; "you had charge of the common account for the last three months—"

Clifford sighed, unrolled a sheet of paper, shoved it toward his confrère, and offered himself more tea. Elliott examined the figures anxiously.

"You hopeless ass!" he blurted out. "Why didn't you draw the purse strings?"

"I can deny you nothing, my son," protested Clifford, casting furtive glances toward his cornet again.

"But we're ruined!" bawled Elliott in sudden fright.

"Utterly," admitted Clifford pleasantly.

Through the broad glass roof the pale winter sunlight fell over piles of rugs and weapons on the floor; in the garden the sparrows chirped unceasingly around the frozen fountain. Elliott sat motionless, hypnotised by the column of figures before him. Clifford regarded his canary birds with vague reproach.

At last Elliott broke the silence:

"We had enough,—more than enough to live on decently; we threw our money away! Ass that I am, I didn't realise I was such an ass."

"I didn't either," said Clifford.

"Oh, you didn't?" sneered Elliott; "who was it that spent five hundred francs on those idiot birds?"

They frowned at the two dozen canaries. The birds hopped aimlessly from pole to perch and from perch to pole.

"I didn't buy a coupé for a lady," retorted Clifford.

"No, but you gave garden parties with fireworks and Chinese lanterns, and the company broke windows and set the curtains ablaze, and the police fined us for shooting rockets without a permit—"

"Accidents," observed Clifford; "our social position in the Latin Quarter required us to entertain."

"Our social position on this planet will also require us to eat,—occasionally."

"There's the furniture."

"I won't! I won't! You hear me, Clifford! I'll not sell a chair. Isn't there any money in any of those bureau drawers?"

"No,—look for yourself," replied Clifford cheerfully.

"Now I'll not mortgage our furniture," said Elliott; "so you needn't finger my carved chairs. We must pull through,—I don't know how,—but we must pull through. I shall cut down my tobacco, I shall drink cheap wine, I shall see Colette at once—"

"Do you think she can stand the blow?" inquired Clifford.

"Your wit is unseasonable," said Elliott haughtily; "how much can you get for your canaries?"

Clifford flatly refused to sell the birds and played a dirge on his cornet. Then the horror of poverty laid hold of Elliott and drove him out into the Luxembourg where he sat in the fading sunshine until the drums boomed from the southern terrace and the challenge of the sentinels, droning, monotonous, sounded and resounded across the windy park.

There was a hint of snow in the air as he passed out into the Place de Medici. He clinked the few gold pieces in his pocket as he walked. This appalled him, and he stepped more quickly.

On the Boulevard, a slim white-browed girl, exquisitely gowned, called to him from a coupé. When he motioned the coachman to stop and stepped to the curb, she buried her nose in a bunch of violets and laughed.

"Colette," said Elliott gloomily, "Mr. Clifford

and I are compelled to retire for the space of three months. Therefore, most charming and most wise Colette,—therefore—"

He raised one hand and opened his fingers as though releasing a butterfly.

II.

All that week Clifford roamed about the studio blowing melancholy blasts from his cornet. Elliott sold a picture to Solomon Moritz for twenty francs, regretted it, tried to get it back, beat Mr. Moritz with a mahl-stick and resisted an officer. To his horror the French Government insisted on entertaining him for a week at Mazas, whither Clifford visited his comrade daily until Saturday and freedom arrived.

"This is a hell of a country," observed Elliott as he shook the dust of Mazas from his heels in company with Clifford. "It's no place for the breadwinner; the Jews have the country by the throat."

"They said," observed Clifford, "that you had Moritz by the throat."

"I did; the ruffian refused me thirty francs for my 'Judgment of Solomon.'"

"Dear me!" exclaimed Clifford with an impudent gesture, "wasn't it worth it?"

"You will refrain," said Elliott furiously, "from poking me in the ribs,—now and hereafter."

Half an hour later they entered the studio and sat down opposite each other in silence. The canaries filled the room with their imbecile twittering, and hopped and hopped until Elliott jumped up and seized his hat.

"Is this studio a bird-cage?" he demanded bitterly.

Clifford said something about jail-birds and picked up his cornet. For an hour he played "'Tite Femme" and "Place aux Gosses." But when he attacked "The Emperor's Funeral March," Elliott seized him.

"Let go," said Clifford sullenly.

"No. See here, Clifford, let's be friends and let's try to be practical. We've got to make our living for the next three months. Let's stop squabbling and hold a conference. Will you?"

"Yes," replied Clifford amiably.

"Then where do we dine?"

"We haven't lunched yet."

"This is awful," muttered Elliott, staring at the canaries; "do you suppose we could eat those birds?"

In the silence that ensued a piano began in the studio above, and a voice sang:

> "Et qu'elle est folle dans sa joie,
> Lorsq'elle chante le matin,—
> Lorsqu'en tirant son bas de soie,
> Elle fait; sur son flanc qui ploie,
> Craquer son corset de satin!"

The piano ceased; there came a laugh, a double

roll on a Tambour-Basque, and the clicking of castanets.

" Who's that ? " said Elliott morosely.   Then with
a sneer he paraphrased the last line of the song.

Clifford pricked up his ears but shook his head.

" Hear her laugh ! I suppose she's dined," continued Elliott with a vicious eye on the birds.
" Well, are we going to eat those cursed canaries ? "

" I never heard you swear like that," protested
Clifford.   " Has poverty weakened your intellect ? "

" Yes," said Elliott savagely.

" If we eat 'em our meal will cost five hundred
francs."

" Then you've got to sell them.   They are no
good,—yellow   birds   are   always   feeble-minded.
Canaries are ridiculous."

The castanets began again, and the voice took up
the Spanish measure :

> " My Picador !   My Picador !
> Thy Spanish customs I adore,
>   Thou garlic loving,
>   Cattle shoving,
> Spick-and-spangled Picador !
>
> .   .   .   .   .
>
> I hear the mottled heifer roar,
>   My Picador !
> The people pounding on the floor,
>   My Picador !
> The ring is clear !
> The cow is here !
> They've had to haul her by the ear;
> The Banderillos linger near !
> Oh, Picador !   My Picador ! "

"She's very gay," observed Clifford, after another silence broken only by the distant click! click! click! of the castanets." Hm! I—er—I suppose we ought to call—"

"Call," repeated Elliott; "when I'm hollow!"

"If we call," said Clifford briskly, "we may be invited to dinner." He smiled, whistled a bar or two, and poked the fire."

"Don't," said the other, "you waste fuel."

The wind showered the sleet across the great windows; in the twilight a chill crept in over the rugs; a distant shutter banged, rattled, and banged again.

Elliott jumped up and paced the floor.

"We've got to do something," he said, "and do it now. Where's your watch?"

"You ought to know," said Clifford reproachfully. "Yours is there too."

After a moment he continued; "I've got those cuff-buttons you gave me—" He went into his bedroom and returned with the cuff-buttons. Elliott took them, jerked on his overcoat, nodded, and opened the door.

"I'll be back in half an hour,—wait for me," he said, and slammed the door behind him.

III.

"Now, what the mischief am I to do for half an hour," mused Clifford, staring out of the blank window, both hands in his pockets, an empty pipe be-

tween his teeth. There was a vacancy in his stomach
that bothered him, and the more he thought about
it, the more it hurt. The canary birds were revel-
ling in bird-seed ; he eyed them enviously for a while,
then walked up and down whistling. Every time
he passed the big gilded cage he could hear the birds
cracking and splitting the seeds, and the noise of
the feast irritated him.

His neighbour on the floor above was singing away
with heart and soul about bull-rings and toreadors,
banging joyously upon the Basque drum or snap-
ping and clicking the castanets.

"Dear! Dear!" he thought, "my neighbour is
really very gay. She must have moved in to-day.
I—I wonder what she's like!"

He listened, sitting close to his dying fire. After
a moment he heard her cross the room and open the
piano again.

"Dear! Dear!" he said to himself, "what a
musical young lady! Probably an embryo actress
from the Conservatoire ;—or—or—"

The piano began ; it was scales this time. For an
hour he sat huddled before the cold ashes, listening
to the five-fingered acrobatic exercises, alternately
yawning with hunger and cursing Elliott. When
six o'clock struck from the concierge's lodge he stood
up, gazing dismally out into the night.

Suddenly he heard the scrape of feet outside, and
he hurried to his door and opened it.

Through the lighted hallway a figure shuffled,
carrying a large tray covered with a white napkin.

It was a waiter from the Café Rose-Croix and Clifford knew him.

" Bon soir, Monsieur Clifford," he said doubtfully.

" Good evening, Placide, Placide,—er—is that little banquet for me? Oh, it's all right ! I suppose Monsieur Elliott paid for it—"

" But, Monsieur," said the waiter, " this dinner is for a lady."

" What's that ? " said Clifford sharply. Then he buttonholed Placide and hauled him inside the studio.

" Who is the lady? The one upstairs ? "

" Yes—Mademoiselle Plessis—she awaits her dinner—let me go, Monsieur Clifford," pleaded Placide.

" Oh, I'm not going to play tricks on you," said Clifford, " here! hold on !—if you move I'll tip the tray. Now all I want you to do is—is—er—dear me !"

The odour of a nicely browned fowl disturbed his thoughts ; his mind wandered with his eyes. Placide gaped at him. He knew Clifford and he dreaded him. " Here you !" said that young gentleman, removing his eyes from the fowl with an effort, " do you think that because I do you the honour of conversing with you that I wish to rob you? Do I look like a man to interfere with a lady's dinner? Placide, you know me ? "

" I do, Monsieur," replied the waiter despondently.

" Then listen ! I am going to make you my confidant ! Think of that, Placide !"

The waiter looked at him obliquely and did not appear to appreciate the honour in store.

" Placide ! "

" Monsieur ! "

" I am in love ! "

" Doubtless—if it is Monsieur's pleasure—"

" Silence ! Idiot ! I am about to bestow gifts ; I am about to—"

" The chicken, Monsieur, is becoming cold—"

" I am," repeated Clifford majestically, " about to offer two dozen—twenty-four—canary birds to my adored. You may ask ; what is that to you—"

" I do," began Placide.

" Silence ! Pig ! These twenty-four canaries are to be carried to her by—think of it, Placide !—by you ! "

Placide rolled his eyes, big with anguish. The chicken exhaled a delicious aroma.

Clifford drew in a long breath of the fragrance. Then he lifted the enormous gilt cage, and placed it in Placide's hands. " Go up-stairs and take these cursed birds with the compliments of Foxhall Clifford, artist, American, 70 rue Bara, first floor, door on the right."

" But—but my tray—"

" Imbecile ! Do you think I'm going to eat your tray ? Come back for it and—tell me what the lady says."

Placide shuffled sullenly to the door ; Clifford opened it.

" My tray—" began the unwilling waiter.

" Placide," said Clifford, " I have not dined—er —re—cently and my temper is uncertain. You are discreet. I wish to dine. Do you understand?"

Placide smirked.

" Then use your wits—and when I have ten francs-ᐸ well—hasten, my good Placide."

When the waiter had gone, Clifford tiptoed over to the tray and sniffed at the napkin.

" Dear! Dear!" he said, " what a wonderful congregation of perfumes. Now if she doesn't shut the door on Placide's nose—I—I hope—I delicately hope that I may receive my reward."

He paced to and fro, whistling, but never taking his eyes from the tray. After a few minutes he heard Placide's slippered tread on the stairs, and hastened to admit him.

" The young lady says," began Placide, lifting the tray, "—the young lady says that Monsieur is too amiable—"

Clifford's heart sank.

" And," pursued Placide with dreary deliberation, edging toward the staircase, " the young lady says that she hopes to see you "—

" When?" blurted out Clifford.

" Some day," grinned Placide, and escaped up the stairway, sneering, triumphant.

The blow staggered Clifford for a moment—but only for a moment. Before Placide had descended again, Clifford was changing his clothes; before Placide had passed the lodge-gate, Clifford had fastened a white neck-tie under a spotless collar. Then he tied a bit of crimson silk tightly around his forehead, inserted two feathers from a duster in the fillet where they waved like the plumes of a Sioux War-chief; and ten minutes later, radiant, patent-leathered, but starved, he rang gaily at the door of the studio overhead.

When Claire Plessis opened the door, Clifford bowed profoundly and skipped in, introducing himself with joyous abandon.

"It is the custom," he said, bowing again and again with something of an Oriental salaam, "it is the custom in America—in far distant, sunny America,—to call at once upon distinguished strangers who come to lodge in the building. Therefore, Mademoiselle,"—and although he spoke French flawlessly he brutalised it now to suit his purpose, —"therefore, Mademoiselle,"—He salaamed again, rapidly and said:

"How! How! How!"

"Monsieur," faltered the girl, not knowing whether to laugh or call for assistance,—"Monsieur, I am honoured—pray be—be seated."

"Mademoiselle—it is too much honour!"

"Monsieur—"

They bowed again, and Clifford sank into a chair, his duster plumes nodding on his head.

The girl regarded him with undisguised amazement. She saw his eyes rolling toward the white-covered table and thought, "Oh dear, what shall I do with this foreign savage who sends me canary birds by the gross and who skips like a dancing dervish?"

" Monsieur," she stammered.

" How! How! How!" grunted Clifford absently, sniffing the tablecloth.

" Nothing—nothing, Monsieur," she said hastily; " I wish to thank you for the birds—"

" We eat them in America," he said, and chattered his teeth.

" Like—like chickens?"

" What are chickens?"

She laughed and looked at the uncarved fowl on the table.

" Is that a chicken?" asked Clifford in his most awful French. " Is it good to eat?"

" If you would do me the honour to accept my hospitality, Monsieur, you could prove it for yourself," she said laughing, and a little more at ease. " I have not yet dined,—I am quite alone—"

Clifford accepted, rising with oriental languor, and bowed magnificently. He led her to her place, seated her, drew up a chair opposite, and smiled upon her. His feathers bobbed with every movement.

" Now of course, I must carve," she said, striving hard to repress an hysterical laugh; for Clifford, desiring to play his part of a foreign savage to perfection, was doing impossible things with his knife and fork.

" If she finds me out," he was thinking, " it will not be very gay for me." So he showed his teeth and muttered and salaamed occasionally, while the girl bowed to him over her slender glass of claret

and helped him to more and more and more until
the suffocating desire to laugh brought tears to her
eyes.

" In America it is etiquette to eat until there is
nothing left—at least I have read that is books,"
she ventured.

" It is," said Clifford, uncorking another bottle.

"You seem to like chicken," she said.

" Ah," he replied, "wait until you try my canary
birds ! "

" But," she cried, " I am not going to eat them ! "

Their eyes met across the table.   He felt that he
was going to laugh ; he looked into her big grey
eyes.   Her dark-fringed lashes were trembling too ;
on each cheek a dimple deepened ; between her
scarlet lips the white teeth parted ; then she sank
back, her hands flung helplessly into her lap, and,
looking into each other's eyes, they burst into ringing peals of laughter.

Three times she dried the tears in her eyes, and,
leaning forward, attempted to speak, but when her
eyes met his again, she threw back her pretty head
and laughed until the colour deepened to her throat.
And so they sat there, trying to speak, but shrieking
with laughter, until the glasses and bottles clinked
and vibrated and the window panes sang again.

At last she murmured, " For shame, Monsieur !
I—I ought to be very angry,—but I laugh—oh
dear! oh! dear !   I laugh and I should be furious !
Fie !   You play the foreigner—the—the untutored
one who never saw chicken—oh dear! oh dear !—"

She rose, drying her eyes again on a dainty pocket handkerchief.

"Shame on you! How dared you come to my room and—oh dear—and tell me you eat canary birds—and walk like a dancing dervish, and do such things with your knife, and—what is your name?—mine is Claire."

*   *   *   *   *   *

When, three hours later, he rose to go, he had told her all,—the whole wretched truth, and she had watched him with curious grey eyes, now brimming with laughter, now exquisite in their sympathy. She forgave him—not easily—but when he removed the feathers from his headdress and said he was sorry, she held out her hand to him with brilliant eyes and grave lips.

"So—you are forgiven,—not because you deserve it. Here in the Quarter we are like the leaves in the Luxembourg; we bud with the promise of summer,—we unfold, we nestle and whisper together,—we grow gorgeous and brilliant,—then we fall. Let us live in friendship while we may,—we of the Latin Quarter. I forgive you, mon ami."

IV.

When Clifford reached his own door on the floor below, he heard voices in the studio. A hard world had driven some caution into his head and he listened for a moment to assure himself that the voices were not the voices of creditors.

"It's Elliott and Colette," he murmured, knock-
ing discreetly. Elliott opened the door; on the
piano-stool sat Colette demurely twisting the fur
of her boa. Clifford bent over the extended hand,
then looked at Elliott. The latter felt in his pocket,
produced the cuff buttons, and tossed them on the
table.

"You can keep your jewellery," he said, "I've got
a better scheme ; Colette proposed it—"

"You wouldn't listen to the other plan," she said
shyly, " I don't want that coupé—"

"You mustn't say such things," interposed Clifford gravely ; then, turning to Elliott, "what are we
going to do?"

"Let me tell," cried Colette, fanning her flushed
face with the end of the boa ; "sit down and be
very still,—you also, Monsieur Clifford,—there !
Now listen ! I, Colette, have a very beautiful
plan."

"How to become a millionaire in a week,—by
Mademoiselle Colette," began Clifford, and was
beaten with the fur boa.

"Very well " she cried ; " then I shall not trouble
myself,—oh! you had better say you are sorry!
Now listen ! It is my plan,—mine, Co-lette ! "

She settled herself on the piano-stool, whirled
around until her pointed shoes rested on the rug,
smiled, buried her nose in the point of her boa, and
said ; " To begin, you are poor !—don't interrupt !
It is well to begin at the beginning. Then, you are
poor. You have nothing to live on—you improvi-

dent ones,—for three more months. Comment faire!
Paint and sell pictures? No. Why? Because you
have not yet learned enough at the École des Beaux
Arts! But yet you must live. How? Ah, Dick,
if you would only let me return you that old coupé
—there! I didn't mean it! Now let us begin
again!—You are poor—"

"We're back where we started," began Clifford
but was snubbed.

"So,—you are poor. You must earn *something*.
How? Why, with your cornets!"

"Eh?" stammered Clifford.

"Exactly!" cried Colette; "you shall play
every evening in Bobinot's orchestra and gain many
many francs, industrious ones! Voilà!"

Clifford stared at her. She nodded her head at
him and smiled.

"It's an idea," said Elliott; "Boissy told Colette
that Bobinot's two cornet players had gone, and old
Bobinot is looking for two new ones. It's a chance,—
we need only play in the evenings—it will keep soul
and body together—won't it? Why don't you say
something?"

"It's an idea,—isn't it?" repeated Colette solemnly.

"What!" faltered Clifford, "play a cornet in that
cheap Montparnasse Theatre,—Bobinot's! Suppose
they hear of it in New York?"

"Suppose we have to go to the American Consul
and ask him to ship us home," retorted Elliott.

Bobinot's, the students' theatre on Montparnasse,

was not the Théâtre Français perhaps, but the acting was good,—indeed it was better than that seen in most New York theatres. Clifford had spent joyous evenings at this " Quarter " theatre ; it was often better than the " Cluny "—even " Antonio, père et fils," admitted that.

" Still," he said, "the Quarter will never stop laughing—er—Colette in her coupé and you in the orchestra—"

" I shall not drive in my coupé until Dick wishes it ! " cried Colette, crimson and white by turns. " For your bad taste I—I pardon you."

Too utterly snubbed to have a mind of his own, Clifford meekly made his peace with Colette and opened the door for her and Elliott.

" Are you sure we can get the place ? " he asked. " Perhaps Bobinot won't want us."

" Bobinot must ! " said Colette ; " I shall call upon Claire Plessis who is to sing the première rôles there. She is sweet ; she is also from Tours. That is my country. And I love her very much."

" Where does she live ? " inquired Clifford with a guilty start.

" Upstairs. I shall call upon her to-morrow. Dick, are you coming ? Then good-night, wicked one ! Come, Dick, dear ! To your evil conscience I leave you, Monsieur Clifford "— and she laughed and gave him her gloved hand.

Clifford closed the door gently behind them. For a moment he stood staring at the panels, then raised his eyes to the ceiling.

16

"I wonder," he thought, "I—I wonder whether Claire will tell Colette?"

He shivered. The Quarter is pitiless in ridicule.

Elliott came back late that night, but he was cheerful and he whistled as he shook the snow from hat and coat and stamped around the studio.

"We'll see Bobinot to-morrow," he said; "I tell you it's not a bad idea—all Colette's, too!"

"I thought you and Colette had agreed to disagree," observed Clifford.

The other reddened a little. "We have," he said —"for three months."

Before he was ready for bed he missed the canary birds and questioned Clifford, but the latter told him to mind his business. This Elliott cheerfully complied with and went to bed.

"By the way, did you dine to-night?" he called out before he closed his door.

"Yes," snapped Clifford.

V.

Thanks to Colette and Claire, through the medium of Boissy, the little snare-drummer, who lived on the top floor, Monsieur Bobinot consented to give Elliott and Clifford a trial.

Boissy presented them to Monsieur Bobinot as two eminent American virtuosi, but Bobinot sneered openly.

"Don't try to stuff me," he said; "they're two

students on their uppers. What do I care as long
as they can play ? "

" They—they are very eminent "— pleaded Boissy
—" their—hm !—technique is so original, Monsieur
Bobinot— "

Bobinot turned a pair of hard bright eyes on Clifford.

" En effet, Monsieur Bobinot, we are students,"
said Clifford with magnificent condescension ; " but
we can blow harmony out of a broken bottle ;—
Elliott, kindly play ' The Battle of Buena Vista ' for
Monsieur Bobinot."

Elliott drew his cornet from beneath his overcoat
and gravely performed the stirring war march with
hideous variations, while Clifford imitated a drum
with his knuckles on the window pane.

" Cannon," said Clifford, banging on a sheet of
tin which lay on the floor.

" Let my properties alone ! " shouted Bobinot.

" Drums,—the Mexicans retreating," continued
Clifford serenely, returning to the window.

" Humph ! " snorted Bobinot.

" Cries of the wounded ! " observed Clifford, and
emitted a series of piercing screams while Elliott
continued his variations.

" Ow ! Ow ! Ow ! " wailed Clifford, winking at
Boissy who had sunk helpless on a chair, weak with
laughter.

" Stop ! " thundered Bobinot.

Elliott finished his variations and looked expectantly at the manager of the " Théâtre Bobinot."

"It's d—n fine," said Monsieur Bobinot, "but I could manage to exist and earn an honest living without your artistic collaboration. I say I could dispense with your musical services, but I cannot, Messieurs, afford to lose from my personnel, two such splendid examples of human impudence. Consider yourselves engaged. Boissy, I'll pay you for this!"

"Then," said Clifford artlessly, "let's cement the contract with a bottle!"

"Bottle of what?" demanded Elliott; "we haven't any money! You mortify me!"

Clifford smiled blandly. "Come, Monsieur Bobinot, no hard feelings you know! What shall it be?"

"Whatever you like, Messieurs," said Bobinot grimly; "I'll take it out of your salary."

But Monsieur Bobinot was better than his word. He saw at a glance that the young fellows were in earnest, and he not only acted the host very decently, but, as Boissy dragged the two young men away, he handed them each a week's salary in advance.

"It's for your infernal cheek!" he said; "come to rehearsal at ten!"

The first week passed without a hitch. Elliott played the orchestrated scores for Clifford, and the latter, being quick and instinctively musical, learned his part by heart, to the utter demoralisation of the tenants on the upper floors. Mademoiselle Plessis stood it as long as she possibly could and then sent for Clifford.

"Monsieur Clifford," she said seriously, "this must stop."

"If it stops *I* stop," said Clifford; "I can't live on air."

"No," she said, "you are neither a chameleon nor an angel."

"Not an angel yet, but on the floor below," he said humbly.

Mademoiselle Plessis tapped her foot against the fender and brushed the leaves of her rôle with the tip of one white finger.

"Mon ami," she said, "I cannot learn my rôle if you toot all day on that cornet."

"What am I to do?" inquired Clifford miserably.

"You must have certain hours to practise. Monsieur Boissy plays on his drum from two until four; Monsieur Castro chooses that time for trombone exercise; why can *you* not play your cornet during those hours?"

"I will," said Clifford craftily, "but what shall I do from four until six?" He looked at her with eyes that appealed and languished.

"Do?"

"Ah, yes! It will be lonely up there on the floor above—won't it?"

Mademoiselle Plessis raised her clear eyes to the ceiling.

"Is it so very lonely down there? It is not,—up here."

"Very. I think of you all day."

"Of me? How foolish!"

"Yes; I wish I were able to aid you to learn your parts."

"But you can't—"

"I could if you'd let me read your cues—"

—"I don't need that—"

—"Don't refuse—"

—"I must—"

—"Don't—"

—"But I do! And you are very silly.—"

*   *   *   *   *   *

So it was arranged that Clifford should bleat on his cornet from two until four, during which time Claire would go out for a walk; and from four to six, when Claire was at home, he might aid her by his presence and advice and judiciously regulated sympathy.

"The idea!" she said, with a pretty gesture of disdain; "you will only bother me. You had much better write me a little play."

"A 'lever de rideau!'" exclaimed Clifford; "by Jove, I'll do it!"

"Can you write French well enough, mon pauvre ami?"

"No, but you can supply all the localisms and wit. Will you?"

"We might try," she said with a doubtful smile. She was very much interested, however, and when, a few days later, he brought her a rough sketch of the "Queen of Siam," she read it with serious interest.

"It is a pretty idea," she said, flushing with pleasure. Then, resting her chin on her hand, she invited him to sit beside her.

"You know," she said thoughtfully, "if we are really going to collaborate, we must be very grave and serious for *you* are not working for pleasure and *I* am earning my bread—"

—"And honey,—oh! you'll have woodcock on toast and champagne too if this play goes!"

"Then let us make it go," she exclaimed enthusiastically.

"Let's!" he cried with equal fervour.

There was a pause.

"The play won't go if you don't take your pen in hand," she said.

—"But I will—"

"Then hadn't you better release my hand?"

And so the afternoons wore away while with heads together over the manuscript they chattered about exits and entries, scenarios, cues and "pan coupé's" and Clifford rose to the occasion, displaying a wit which matched her dainty cleverness and struck the quick warm spark of sympathy between them.

"Delicious!" she would laugh at some hastily pencilled bit of dialogue, and then, bending over the table: "Don't you think that we might shorten the King's lines just here? See, I only strike out these three words—ah! see how much better it reads!"

"Much better!—very much better!"

"Very much; it flows smoothly now—oh! oh! how funny to make the Queen threaten them! How did you ever think of that?"

" Why, it follows naturally—you see she is all in armour, and the spurs trip up the archbishop—"

And so the afternoons wore away.

This was all very pleasant, but it had its drawbacks and one winter evening toward six o'clock Clifford jumped up and stared at the clock horrified :

" Good heavens!" he muttered, " they are giving ' Pomme d'Api,' to-night and I haven't practised the music ! What the deuce shall I do !"

" And you can't read music at sight ? Oh, what a shame! It is all my fault, mon ami," she cried in contrition.

" No it isn't—only the afternoon flew, and I never thought. Bobinot will sack me for this !"

" You must get a substitute," she said," it's often done."

" Where can I find one ? "

" Ask Boissy, he knows lots of people who do that sort of thing,—there's his drum now! go down and see him—hurry—go quickly, mon ami,—Oh ! you mustn't !—you mustn't ! There ! my gown is all in wrinkles. I do not wish you ever to return,—no, never,—go quickly now or Boissy will be gone !— hasten !—ah well—then I will try to forgive you, mon ami."

As he galloped down the stairs and out into the street he felt as though he were treading on clouds —rosy clouds.

" Nevertheless," he said to himself, " I must never kiss her again."

VI.

The substitute cornet player was a success but was also very expensive. Clifford paid him thankfully, but it made a large hole in his meagre weekly salary, and he decided to do without substitutes in future. He explained to Elliott how it was, and the latter young gentleman, who viewed Clifford's infatuation for Claire with alarm, shook his head and sighed.

"You can't afford it, my son. Suppose you hadn't been able to get a cornet player? Bobinot would have bounced you."

"Now I am not so sure of that," said Clifford, who had been consulting Claire. "I understand that the leader of the orchestra—what's his name—"

—"Bock—"

—"Bock,—I understand that he's generally drunk and can't tell whether one or two cornets are play.. ing."

"But he would see your empty placé."

"I could get any ordinary man to sit there,— Selby would do it for the lark. If he pretended to play, Bock wouldn't know the difference. I had to pay that substitute of mine twenty francs. Kid Selby would do it to oblige me."

"And he could stuff the cornet with cotton," suggested Elliott.

"Exactly—Bock would never know. So any time we want a vacation we'll call on Selby, stuff his cornet with cotton, and let him blow his cheeks out while the other man does the playing? Where are you going?"

"I'm going to get Kid Selby—it's my turn for a vacation to-night," replied Elliott laughing, and walked out, slamming the great doors.

Clifford opened his desk, took out a pile of man-uscript, and, thrusting them into his pocket, hurried up-stairs to begin his daily collaboration with his fair neighbour. Time flew for them, but the "Queen of Siam" was slowly taking the shape of a curtain-raiser whose fate would soon be determined. The lyrics were fortunately few, and of course Claire rhymed them, for poetry in French was beyond Clifford's ken. And she rhymed them charmingly, setting them to the music of quaint old songs that all France knows. Clifford hung breathlessly over the piano, gaping with admiration.

Monsieur Bobinot had read the piece and had found it suitable,—so suitable in fact, that for a long time he refused to believe that Clifford could be the author.

"Voyons, confess he hashed it up from some old vaudeville!" he repeated to Mademoiselle Plessis, until at last he was constrained to accept it as original. Of course he cast Claire for the "Queen"; she refused to stir a step unless he did; and the other parts were given to Mesdames Paule Nevers, Bonelly, Mario-Widmer, and to Messieurs Max,

Bourdielle, Deberg, Bayard, Brunet, and Simon. Naturally Max was cast for the Archbishop of Ept, and Bayard for the King, while Bourdeille's character, "Syleuse," was written entirely with the view that he should create the rôle.

Bobinot grumbled. It seemed to him that he had nothing to say about anything in his own theatre, but Mademoiselle Plessis had her way and the property man and costumer were already at work on the designs that Elliott furnished gratis. Deberg orchestrated the score.

"It would cost me," shouted Bobinot in a fury, as he blue-pencilled Elliott's voluminous directions on each drawing,—" it would cost me more than my theatre is worth to make these costumes according to Monsieur Elliott's advice. He can save himself literary work, and me several sous worth of blue pencil by sticking to his designing and leaving the execution to a man who wears a head in the proper place!"

The Théâtre Bobinot was flourishing. The " Serment d'Amour," " Princess des Canaries," " Mignapour," "Le Jour et la Nuit," followed successively " Le Panache," and " Pomme d'Api" of Offenbach ; and already in the programme of " Les Domestiques," the comedy by Grangé and Deslandes, appeared the announcement of the preparations for " The Queen of Siam." " A comedy in three acts by M. Foxhall Clifford and Mlle. Claire Plessis ;" for, at Bobinot's demand, the "lever de rideau," had been expanded into a three act musical comedy.

Bobinot said very little in praise of it either to Clifford or to Claire, but he bragged about it to everybody else in the Latin Quarter as well as in the Montparnasse Quarter. He refused to pay any cash for it, but signed a contract for a generous royalty, and Clifford and Claire were more than satisfied. The former promised princely sums to Elliott for his costume designs as soon as the money began to pour in. Elliott was grateful and redoubled his pages of instructions for Bobinot, whose curses rang loud and deep as he slashed through them with his blue pencil.

Clifford took a good many days off from the orchestra, and, finding that a cotton-stuffed cornet in the hands of the untutored and unmusical Selby was perfectly satisfactory, took more days off. Selby for his part, liked the fun and became the envy of the Quarter. At times, however, Clifford had slight clashes with Elliott when they both wanted the same night off.

"Come, come," Clifford would urge, "Claire isn't on to-night you know, and I've promised to dine with her at Thirion's."

"And I've promised Colette to meet her at the Vachette."

"But you can meet her there to-morrow and I can't meet Claire because she takes Nevers' place in ' Pomme d' Api.' "

Then Elliott would mutter; "the deuce take you and Claire!" But he always gave in and tootled away in the orchestra, while Selby, the delighted substitute beside him, puffed and perspired over a noiseless cotton-stuffed cornet. Bock, the besotted, never doubted that both cornets were playing.

" Thank goodness this won't last," thought Elliott ; "our three months' poverty is up on Monday and then !—then this cursed orchestra can go to the devil ! "

Rat-tat-tat— ! rattled Bock's baton as he glanced at Elliott.

"Oh you old ass ! " grumbled Elliott, toot ! toot ! —" go to Guinea ! "—toot—toot—tootle—too-o-ot."

VII.

The humiliating part of it was that neither Clifford nor Elliott could attend the rehearsals of "the Queen of Siam " except in the orchestra. Bobinot was omnipresent, and they were obliged to occupy their places.

Now the orchestra was sunk in a pit so far below the footlights that although the musicians were visible to the audience, nothing on the stage could be seen by the musicians themselves.

When Clifford was not obliged to blow his cornet, he could hear Claire's sweet voice :

" Oh, papa dear I much prefer
My helmet and my steel-ringed shirt,
My jewelled hilt, my gilded spur,
Targe, Casque, Tassett and Bassinet

> So take away my waist and skirt !
> Oh, take away
> Oh, take away
> Oh-h ! take away my maiden's skirt !"

Then he would stretch and crane his neck to see, but Bock always caught him with the angry rat-tat-tat !—" hé ! la bas ! " and he would clutch his cornet and breathe music and anathemas. " It's a pretty state of affairs if I can't see my own play," he grumbled to Elliott, " I'll fix that ass, Bock—just wait ! "

When Claire and Georges Max held the stage, and the repartee made even the prompter chuckle, Clifford's curiosity almost crazed him, and he cursed impartially, Bobinot, Bock, the orchestra and himself.

Claire was delicious, Max irresistible. Clifford squirmed and listened:

Claire; " L'archeveque ! "

Max; Mais non, il faut "—

Claire (excited); " Qu'il vienne ! Qu'il vienne ! J'y suis, J'y reste !—Et quil fait attention à mes éperons ! "

Max; " Mais—mais—c'est moi l'Archiveque—"

Claire (much disturbed); " Té ! je le savais bien, Monseigneur ! "

" That's going to take like wildfire," whispered Elliott lowering his cornet; " I wish I could see the expression on Max's face—"

" And on Claire's ! Hear the prompter laugh ! "

" Look out—here comes the flourish—ready—now ! Enter the Queen, you know ! "

"Tara—ta-ta-tata!" wheezed the cornets for the entry of the Queen, while Boissy's snare drum rattled the salute,

Clifford was sulky and spoke no more that morning, but the next day he went to see Selby.

"I'm d——d if I miss the first night of my own opera," he muttered.

VIII.

Clifford was determined to see the first night's performance but he decided not to tell Elliott, as that youth might also wish to see it. No, he would not mention it to Elliott; he would quietly arrange it for Selby to play the dummy and blow a cotton-stuffed cornet beside Elliott. True, the flourish of trumpets that was to announce the entrance of the Queen would be, strictly speaking, a flourish of one cornet, but Bock could never know and the audience wouldn't either for that matter. So he spoke to Selby and gave him his stuffed cornet.

"There's no cornet in the overture, you know— it's that stringed affair of Lalo's. You are to watch Elliott and pretend to toot when he does. The first flourish is when the Queen comes in," he explained to Selby.

Then he went to bed, chuckling, for he had covertly secured the last seat but one in a prominent box, and he chuckled again as he thought of Elliott's fury on beholding him among the spectators.

All the next day he chuckled too, watching Elliott

furtively. The latter seemed very unsuspicious ; he did not even mention a wish to view the performance. And at last the impatiently expected night arrived.

The Théâtre Bobinot was ablaze ; banners waved from the mansard ; posters flamed under the gas jets outside,—big yellow posters announcing "THE QUEEN OF SIAM !"

Inside the theatre the orchestra was assembling.

IX.

Selby pretended to fuss over the leaves of the score ; he fiddled with his cornet a moment, then he sat down and looked up at the house.

The audience was not what is termed "brilliant," but the house was jammed with the good people of the Montparnasse Quarter, sandwiched in between hordes of Latin Quarter students, actresses, grisettes and vivacious young persons who preside over the counters of the Bon Marché and Grands Magazines of the Louvre. A first night always filled the little theatre, box, pit, and gallery, and the announcement of the "Queen of Siam," with Mlle. Claire Plessis, Mlle. Nevers and Max and Bourdeille, had stirred the Quarter profoundly.

Selby polished the mouthpiece of his cornet and called to Boissy, who left his snare drum and came over.

"Where is Elliott ?" he asked.

"Hasn't come yet. "Oh, you're here to give Clifford a chance ? It's a good house, isn't it ?"

"Great," said Selby pensively, " I bet Clifford makes a lot out of this. Here comes old Bock now."

The leader of the orchestra, vinous as usual, emerged from below, wiping his moustache, and walked straight to his seat.

" I wish Elliott would hurry," said Selby nervously.

" There's no overture,—Bock cut it out because the play's long enough."

" I know—I know, but there he is taking a last look at the gallery and Elliott isn't here. The thing begins with a flourish of trumpets to the Queen."

As he spoke, a figure came out of the little door under the stage, holding a cornet.

" Thank goodness," said Selby, "here he is now,— no,! by jingo, it's a new cornettist! "

The stranger sat down in Elliott's seat, picked pensively at some cotton in his cornet, and smiled at Selby.

" Where's Elliott? " said Selby hoarsely.

" In that box,—see him? He wants to witness the first act. He says "— But Selby sprang to his feet, pallid with fright.

"Can you play a cornet? " he almost shrieked.

" No,—can't you? " stammered the new arrival.

Before the wretched Selby could reply, Bock rapped for attention; there came three heavy knocks on the stage floor behind the curtain, and, as the violins began the " Air of the Petticoat," the curtain twitched, trembled, and began to ascend, exposing a brilliant stage and dozens of glittering limbs.

Clifford in his box, gazed at the chorus in rapture.

17

Then, as the chorus began to sing, he felt a violent tug at his coat, and, looking round, beheld Elliott.

"You!" faltered Clifford, "what are you doing here?"

Elliott's face was shrunken with fright.

"Heavens!" he gasped, "they'll miss the flourish! Those fellows can't play! I—I didn't know you had engaged Selby so I hired a man in the street"—Clifford was rooted to the spot; his eyes fixed on the miserable substitutes below. Then his hair slowly rose as Max cried joyously:

"The Queen! The Queen! Hark—hark to the trumpets' shrill welcome!"

A dismal silence ensued. All eyes were turned on the orchestra where Selby sat frozen stiff with horror, while his companion, scarlet in the face, cheeks puffed out and eyes starting from their sockets, blew madly into his cotton-stuffed cornet from which no sound proceeded.

"Hark! The trumpets ring again!" cried Max, looking anxiously at Bock, who, speechless and furious, waved his wand toward Selby.

"Idiots! Play!" he roared at last.

"We can't!" gasped Selby. The audience screamed.

Claire coolly walked to the footlights, but the sight of Selby's face sent her into wild uncontrollable laughter.

Claire's laughter saved the piece. The house stood by her from that moment, and the "Queen of Siam" went merrily on to the sound of a cornetless orchestra. For Clifford and Elliott and Selby had fled ;—fled away into the snowy night. far, far from the haunts of men.

    *   *   *   *   *   *

This is a story of the Quarter, truer than it ought to be. You have, doubtless, heard it before. It is not original with me. I myself have heard it told in London.

Ah! when shall we be wise, Madame?—When shall we learn wisdom—we of the Quartier Mont-parnasse?

I could tell you how Clifford returned and was forgiven by, Claire and Bobinot,—but I won't. I could tell you how Clifford presented his royalty rights to Claire on the occasion of her marriage to Monsieur Bobin—but there!—I nearly told you a stage secret! So I shall answer no more questions —unless you care to know about Colette and Elliott and Selby.

Do you?

ANOTHER GOOD MAN.

*"Ah ! d'une ardeur sincere
Le temps ne peut distraire,
Et nos plus doux plaisirs
Sont dans nos souvenirs.
On pense, on pense encore
A celle qu'on adore,
Et l'on revient toujours
A ses premiers amours."*

ANOTHER GOOD MAN.

Une conscience sans Dieu est un tribunal sans juge.

LAMARTINE.

I.

WHEN Fradley came to Paris he renounced literature as a means of livelihood, for, although his success as a writer in " Brooklyn Babyhood," had been pecuniarily satisfying, it occurred to him that painting might be less fatiguing than poetry, and he decided to adopt it as his profession.

His illustrations to his own rhymes had been, up to the present time, of archaic simplicity, and were limited to pen and ink productions representing infants afflicted with exaggerated eyes and eyelashes.

Young mothers hovered over the pages of " Brooklyn Babyhood " spelling out his rhymes to crowing infancy. In these jingles, children were told that they were " arch " and " cute," they were assured of their importance, their every action was applauded, solid pages of baby-talk were administered, and baby-ridden Brooklyn writhed with delight.

There were some people, however, who revolted, —some who even declared that Fradley was a public nuisance and that his rhymes inculcated self-

consciousness ; but these people were probably un-
natural parents.

When he wrote his immortal poem, " How many
toes has the Baby ? " the Brooklyn " Banner " pub-
lished the poem in full with a portrait of and a peon
to " Brooklyn's Brilliant Son."

This was all very well but it couldn't last. A
rival poet from Flatbush got hold of the Brooklyn
" Star " and began a series of poems, the baby talk
of which made Fradley's most earnest efforts fall
flat. In vain he demanded to know the exact num-
ber of fingers and toes which the baby possessed ;
in vain he cooed and gurgled and bleated ! The
Flatbush poet was a woman, and she knew her
business. When Fradley cooed, she cooed ; when
Fradley gurgled and bleated, she gurgled and
bleated, backed up by the entire staff of the Brooklyn " Star." In vain Fradley called for a counting
of toes ; she extended her researches into distant
sections of baby's anatomy, and Fradley was
doomed. The last blow fell when the Flatbush
poet produced

" BABY'S ICKLE TOOFY,"

which, translated freely, means " baby's little tooth."
That settled it. Fickle Brooklyn fell down and
worshipped the Flatbush lady, and Fradley sullenly
packed his bag and sailed for France.

When Fradley took up his abode in the Latin
Quarter, he expected that his arrival would create

something of a stir. It did not. He waited a month for appreciation and finally asked Garland what he thought of his illustrations.

" I haven't seen any," replied Garland.

" I didn't know you illustrated," added Carrington, but noticing the mortification on Fradley's face, said good-naturedly, " You know we don't see much over here except the Paris papers ; what do you illustrate for? "

Fradley was speechless.

" What paper are they in ? " asked Garland, yawning innocently.

" In ' Brooklyn Babyhood,' " snarled Fradley and left the café.

Carrington, a modest young Englishman with a high colour and blond moustache, looked troubled. Garland was irritated.

" You know," he said to Carrington, " if he shows that sort of temper the older men will be down on him."

" It's very annoying," said Carrington.

" Very. We new men have got to keep pretty quiet just now or the old men will make it hot for us. This man Fradley is enough to turn the whole studio against us. Did you make the fire this morning ? "

" Oh, yes, of course. Clifford was very decent to me."

" He's all right, but there are some of the older men in Julian's who are spoiling to discipline us. Did you notice it to-day ? "

"I fancy I did," replied Carrington, swallowing his beer.

"This man Fradley," continued· Garland, "is enough to queer the whole batch of this year's men. Confound him, he's effeminate."

"Oh, I don't know," said Carrington pleasantly.

"Well, I do.   His room is opposite mine, you know, and he's trotting in and bothering me all the time about the decorations of his boudoir.   Whew! Why, Carrington, he has tied ribbons all over his furniture, and he has tidies and things about so that you are afraid to sit down.   I don't want to mis-judge the man, for we new men must hang together, but I draw the line at embroidered night shirts stuck all over with lace and ribbon."

"So do I," said Carrington, "does he do that sort of thing?"

"I suppose so.   He brought one in to show me."

"Maybe it wasn't his," suggested Carrington.

"Possibly not.   It would have been more appro-priate for the Queen of Sheba."

II.

Don't," said Clifford, "pat me on the back and tell me to keep my shirt on!"

"Nonsense!" said Elliott, "you are making a mountain out of a mole-hill!"

"And your language," said Selby, "is not ex-actly—"

"Oh, isn't it! Now you listen to me; the Café des Écoles is no boudoir, and if a man can't express his views here then I'm a fossil."

Rowden looked vaguely uneasy and Braith studied Clifford over his pipe.

"The Quarter," continued Clifford, "is going to the devil; do you deny it?"

"Yes," said Elliott cheerfully.

"That makes no difference—keep cool, Elliott, I know you only said it for argument, but it isn't so—"

"Messieurs, you must make less noise," said the proprietor, hurrying over from the desk."

"Stop pounding on the table and yelling," said Clifford to Carroll.

"If you don't," observed Elliott, "the sergot will come back and take our names again—"

"For the last time too, and Elliott's already got three, so he'll go to the cooler and devil a sou will I go bail," growled Clifford; "now listen to me, you fellows, if you want to know why the Quarter is going to the bow-wows. Just look at the crop of this year's men! Are we going to put up with McCloud. He threw the proprietor of the Café des Arts out of doors and ran the Café himself at ruinous rates until the proprietor came back with the police. I paid his fine."

"Well," said Elliott, "McCloud is certainly cocky for a nouveau!"

"Cocky? Well rather. Because he's a sort of infant Hercules and has played on the Australian team is no reason why he should split all the tables with his fist and do cheap feats of strength, and grab a cab by the hind wheels and hold it with the cabby yelling like a demon and everybody laughing at me."

"You!"

"I was in the cab; it was on the Boulevard Montparnasse—"

"And you were going—" began Elliott.

"Never mind where I was going," said Clifford with dignity, "the fact remains that I was inside. It was lucky for McCloud that I was, for when a policeman nipped his budding humour my bail came in very handy."

"And is that," inquired Braith suavely, "the ground for your assertion that the Quarter is doomed?"

"Isn't it enough?" demanded Clifford;—"a nouveau taking liberties,—making me ridiculous before the whole Montparnasse Quarter,—who know me—every one of them,—and to crown all, being with a lady—"

"Oh!" said Elliott tenderly. Osborne smirked and whistled the devil's quadrille, Elliott and Thaxton played phantom trombones with enervating effect and Carroll beat madly upon a bottle.

Clifford became redder and redder. His unrequited affection for that wonderful little creature, the new Bullier star, was a topic for mirth and gentle jest throughout the Latin Quarter. They had recently parted, friends,—it being understood that she liked him, but hardly cared to pin her affections to a man who sat helpless in a cab while somebody held the hind wheels and the boulevard laughed. It was putting it plainly perhaps, but it did no harm, and Clifford was very careful to keep it to himself.

" You fellows," observed Clifford scornfully, " had better stop those monkey shines. Put down that bottle, Carroll, or I'll take it away. You'll be trying to stuff it in your mouth next. Bite on the cork, it's better for teething."

This cruel thrust at the very recent advent of Carroll to full-fledged honours in the studio had its effect.

" I know," continued Clifford, " that you all think I'm blighted, but you're all mistaken. I'm sure you will see that I am right about these new men when I tell you what happened at the studio this morning. I sat down in a front place and waited for the roll call, and, before my name was called, a thing—a nouveau took the place himself."

" What ! " cried the others incredulously.

" It's true," continued Clifford, " this baby—this nouveau violated all precedent, and, because his name came before mine on the list, he actually had the impudence to throw me down ! "

The others looked thoughtful.

" That is going too far," observed Elliott gravely, " we must discipline these young gentlemen."

" There are two or three," said Thaxton, " who seem worse than the rest, for instance, young Garland—"

" Seems to me that was the creature's name who took my place," interrupted Clifford.

" It couldn't be—he's a decent fellow and makes the fire when he's told to," said Selby.

" Perhaps he didn't know you were an old man," suggested Elliott.

" Probably not," said Carroll, who was still smarting from the teething taunt, " Clifford hasn't been twice in the studio since the nouveaux came."

Elliott took out a note-book and wrote down Garland's name.

" I'll keep an eye on him," he said, " but there is another little wretch who ought to have an example made of him at once."

" Who ? " asked Clifford.

" I believe his name is Fradley," replied Elliott lighting a cigar.

" Then we'll fix Fradley," muttered Clifford. " Who cares for a game of billiards ? "

III.

The roll call was over at Julian's and every place had been marked in white chalk on the floor. The model in the first studio had profited by the confusion attendant on the distribution of bread, colours and canvasses, and, shuffling into his trousers and slippers, strolled into the second studio of Boulanger and Lefevre to investigate the cause of the uproar which had arisen and which continued with increasing violence.

The studio was packed with yelling students, some mounted on tabourets, some on the old dust-chest by the door, others on the stove and model stand. From Doucet's two studios a delegation had arrived, all of the Sculptors and most of Bouguereau's men were there, and the noise was terrific. A big blond fellow wearing the uniform of a cuirassier seemed to be directing things, and his bellows shook the windows and rattled the bones on " Pierre," the battered studio skeleton.

The clerk came in and remonstrated, but Clifford put him out and locked the glass door, leaving him gesticulating and taking names as fast as he could write. Then Jules peeped in, smiled sadly and beckoned to Boissy, the cuirassier massier. Boissy opened the door and explained that they were only "organising." That was sufficient, and Jules and the clerk withdrew.

When the classic halls of Julian's echoed with demoniac screams, cat-calls, and howls—when voices were uplifted in every language except German, and the thickets of easels were mowed down in rows by some playful boot-heel, it was generally an indication that the students were " organising." They had a passion for organising, and they seldom failed to indulge it. Just now they were organising under the leadership of that strange creature, Sara, also known as " La Rousse," who was generally the root of all mischief in the Quarter. She stood on the model stand beside Boissy, her fiery red hair coiled along her neck, her wonderful white skin glistening, her mysterious face bathed in the sunshine which streamed down from the glass roof above.

With an inscrutable smile she studied the massed faces below her. Occasionally her eyes rested on some new man, who never failed to feel uncomfortable and look at the floor until the grayish-green eyes swept in another direction. Sara was haughty at best. In her sunniest smiles lurked the lightning of scorn, and in all her brief "affairs," the caprice of passion never disturbed her astounding egotism, never lowered the imperious head, never drove the shadow of irony from her scarlet lips.

Boissy shouted for silence, and banged on the floor with his spurred heels, but nobody paid attention until the girl took a step forward and held up both pink palms as if to shield her ears from the pandemonium. That was sufficient.

Then with a nod to Boissy, who straightened his epaulettes and looked fierce, she began very quietly.

"Messieurs il s'agit—" when an unlucky nouveau fell off a stool and crashed to the floor carrying several easels with him. He was mobbed at once amid cries of "Silence, cochon! Down with the Nouveau! Vive Sara!"

"C'est épatant," observed Sara with superb scorn, "fiche moi cet nouveau au clou!"

No sooner said than the unlucky youth was seized and hustled toward the dust-chest amid cries of "au clou! au clou!"

Elliott opened the lid of the dust-chest and looked at Boissy.

" What's his name," growled Boissy.

" Freddie Fradley," replied Elliott, " shall he go in ? "

Fradley screamed and struggled, but at a sign from Sara they shoved him in, and, inserting some mahl-sticks under the lid to give him air, requested " Fatty " Carriere to sit on the top, which he did with alacrity. Sara tossed her glittering hair and continued, undeterred by the faint screams from the chest :

" Messieurs, you all know that on the night of the Mi-Carême, it is the custom of our studio to go en masse, to the Bullier. Messieurs, the massiers of all the studios have decided to honour me with an escort, but—" laughing proudly, " that is the difficulty ! All of you wish to go with me, which you know very well is impossible. Are there not other girls in the Quarter ? "

" No ! " shouted the students in a spasm of gallantry.

She opened her arms with a peculiarly graceful motion. " You know that I adore you all,—all the Julian men, and I do not wish to show favouritism—"

" Vive Sara ! Vive la Rousse ! " came thundering from the students and was echoed by stifled yells from the dust-chest.

" Fatty " Carriere banged on the lid and uttered awful threats against Fradley's health unless he ceased. Sara smiled. " No, no favouritism," she said—" mais—mais comment faire ? "

" Take us all as escorts ! " cried Clifford, and the

18

Frenchmen understood and took up the cry—" en choisisez pas ! *nous voulons aller tous !* "

The girl's eyes sparkled, and she shook her head at Clifford. " Monsieur the incorrigible ! "

Clifford waved his hat and cried,—" C'est entendu alors ! Vive Sara ! "

" Mais non, mon petit Clifford," smiled the girl, " c'est impossible—"

" Not at all," exclaimed Boissy with a reckless laugh, " Clifford and I—we will arrange that ! "

" Of course," replied Clifford, " we'll fix the police."

Then bedlam broke loose, and impromptu quadrilles began, and " Fatty " Carriere, unwilling to lose his share of the dance, hastily locked the chest, punched some air holes in the lid, oblivious of the danger which Fradley would run if anybody sat down on them, and went lumbering and gyrating about until his elephantine gambols shook the building.

Shortly afterward, the fatherly Monsieur Julian appeared, softly suggesting that work should begin, and ten minutes later the seats were full, the models posed in the various rooms, and the scrape of charcoal and palette knife alone broke the quiet of the studio.

Clifford, who had missed the morning roll-call, roamed about looking for a place. There appeared to be none. The lines of easels radiating in circles from the model-stand were all occupied. He glared at the nouveaux.

"This is disgusting," he observed to Elliott! "fancy a four-year man hunting a place and those fool nouveaux squatting on the tabourets!"

"Come in time,—it's the only way now," replied Elliott.

"Here is a place, Mr. Clifford," said Garland who was sitting in the front row. Clifford threaded his way among the easels to his side.

"It's very good of you," he said; "whose name is that on the floor?"

"Fradley's," said Garland. Clifford rubbed it out and substituted his own signature.

"This begins Fradley's discipline," he muttered, and called to Ciceri to bring him his portfolio. Then he looked at Garland and was prepossessed in his favor.

"You're a nouveau, are you not?" he asked amiably; "what is your name?"

"Garland."

"Mine is Clifford."

"Oh, we all know that," laughed Garland.

"Oh, you do!" said Clifford, "and how the devil do you know it?"

Garland did not think it prudent to mention the cab incident, and Clifford picked up his charcoal and squinted at the model.

"I hear," said Garland, "that you older men are going to discipline us."

"We are," said Clifford calmly.

"Why?"

"Well, you see, we usually receive a certain

amount of respect and deference from new men, and before you fellows came nobody ever heard of a nouveau turning an old man out of his seat."

Carrington looked up from his easel. "I am a nouveau," he said, "and I think, Mr. Clifford, you will find that the nouveaux respect the traditions of the studio."

"I think so, too," insisted Garland.

Clifford looked at him coldly. "Didn't you turn me out last week?" he demanded.

"I," cried Garland, "never!"

"Fradley did," said Cary, "and I noticed it at the time and wondered why you didn't spank him, Clifford."

"Well, by Jove!" exclaimed Clifford, "I thought it was you, Garland."

"I know you did," replied Garland indignantly, "and a pretty life I've led with Rowden and Elliott and all the concour men making it hot for me. I respect the traditions and always will."

"Then I beg your pardon," said Clifford cordially, "come and see me at my studio."

All the nouveaux knew what that meant. It indicated that Garland would soon be released from menial work, and would find himself in the charmed circle of the powers that be.

"By the way," said Clifford, "there is that fellow Fradley in the dust chest. Hadn't I better let him out?"

"Has he enough air?" asked Selby.

"Plenty. I bored some more holes just now and

asked him how he felt.   He said I was no gentleman."

"He says," said Rowden, "that it's a disgrace to
his family and a blot on his honour.   He's an excit-
able customer and screams like a cat when addressed
through the air-holes in the lid."

"Oh, let him out," said Clifford.

"No, he must be taught decency.   He's been
here three months, and that's long enough for the
studio to size him up."

"Why did you put him in?" asked Garland.

"Because," replied Elliott, "he made a racket
trying to go out when Sara was speaking."

"He couldn't help it, he fell off the stool ; let him
out," said Clifford.

"No, he must understand that this studio won't tol-
erate a sneak.   Did you know that he went to old Julian with tales of our doings and said that for his part
he never met such a rude and vulgar set of men before?   He said he had not come to Paris to listen
to models make speeches, but had expected to find
a refined and elevating art atmosphere.   He insisted
that he could not draw if the studio was noisy, and
he asked old Julian to stop the racket.   Fancy the
expression on Julian's face!"

Clifford's face was a study.   "What impudence,"
he said, "what did Julian do?"

"He?   Oh, he told him that he was not obliged
to stay ; that there were other schools in Paris."

Clifford turned to his drawing and shrugged his
shoulders.   "Let him sit in the box then," he mut-

tered, steadying his plumb line with the end of his
pencil ; "dust-chest discipline won't hurt him !"

Clifford was a clever draughtsman. The nouveaux
watched him in respectful admiration as he con-
structed his study, indicated a shadow here and
there, and then, dusting the paper, rapidly sketched
in the essential outlines and began to model the
head with a vigour and dash which did not at
all detract from its value as a serious academic
study.

Mid-day struck, and there was a scramble for hats
and a rush for the stairs. Bouguereau's men came
trampling out of their atelier with the studio band
at their head and the studio mascot, a pale-eyed
goat named " Tapage," bringing up the rear. Following Bouguereau's atelier came Doucet's two
rooms and behind them Chapu's sculptors. The
stairs were jammed, and as Clifford was in a hurry
to get his luncheon, he persuaded " Tapage " to
butt the passage clear, which the goat was only too
glad to do, for he smelled the appetising odour of
brown paper and cabbage leaves in the court
below.

When Clifford had reached the restaurant on the
corner of the boulevard he remembered that Fradley was still in the dust-bin. "The deuce !" he
muttered, " I've got to go back and let the beggar
out !"

Sara, who had been posing in the second studio
for the concour men had also forgotten Fradley, and
it was only when she had finished dressing and stood

alone in the studio twisting up her burnished
tresses, that a rustling in the dust-chest behind her
recalled Fradley's existence to her mind.

"B'en vrai!" she exclaimed, "I forgot you, my
friend!" and she stooped and drawing the bolt,
lifted the heavy lid. Fradley was squatting in a
corner of the chest.

"Ah! mais ça—c'est trop fort!" she cried in
self-reproach ; "I am so sorry."

Fradley snarled.

The girl looked at him curiously for a moment
and then began to laugh. "To think that we all
should have forgotten you, my poor friend! I shall
scold Boissy and Clifford—oh—they shall catch it!
Do you know you are very dusty?"

Fradley arose and surveyed his cuffs. Then he
turned to the mirror and grew giddy with rage.
His long, artistically arranged hair was full of straws,
and his thin egotistical features bore little resem-
blance to Byron's at twenty, which he was confi-
dent they did when not smeared with soot.

"The rude, ungentlemanly creatures! The horrid
brutes?" he cried. "I will complain to Julian, I
will have them dismissed—"

"Comment?" said the girl.

Then Fradley plunged into the French language.

" Vooly voo donny moi—er—a—rest, or vooly voo
pas! Je swee tray fachy,—er—er—tray, tray
fachy!"

"You are angry? Mais mon petit, tu as raison!"

Fradley eyed her with animosity. "C'est votre

faut!" he said; "Je dirais Musseer Julian toot sweet!"

"Comment?" inquired Sara.

"Wee! Wee!" he said with a venomous glance at her, "vooz avvy mis moi dans cette boite!" She did not understand his accusation, but she laughed wickedly and marched straight up to him. Before he knew what she was about she had deliberately thrown her arms about his neck and kissed him.

"There," she said calmly, "we must not be enemies, mon petit; now I forgive you for making a racket when I was trying to speak, and you may tell the whole atelier that Sara has kissed you." Then with an imperious nod she marched out of the studio leaving Fradley petrified.

A few moments later Clifford came in and found him still motionless, gaping vacantly.

"Oh, you're out, eh?" said Clifford. Fradley paid no attention to this salute, but stared at the door through which Sara had disappeared.

Clifford eyed him for a moment and then sat down on the chest.

"Fradley," he said, "you listen to me and I'll give you a pointer or two concerning this studio. Be manly and you'll get along. Don't kick against tradition. Better men than either of us have conformed to the customs here and filled the stove and searched for the 'grand reflecteur' on dark days."

He looked hard at Fradley. "You had better conform to custom or go somewhere else. We seldom haze here,—we never haze a manly man, and if you know anything about the École des Beaux Arts you will appreciate what I say."

Fradley was looking at him, but something in his eyes told Clifford he was not listening.

Then Clifford rose, disgusted, and swung out through the hall and down the stairs, leaving Fradley in an imbecile trance.

IV.

Fradley had delicate tastes. His rooms were hung with pale green draperies, tidies lay on every divan, and his initials were embroidered on his pillow shams. He worked very little at the studio.

"It is not necessary," he told Garland; "mere painting doesn't make an artist,—it's experience; an artist must be broad!" So Fradley began the process of broadening by going to theatres, concerts, exhibitions and museums. He also presented letters of introduction to families who maintained nourishing tables. There was one thing about him that Garland could not understand. Fradley was thin, very thin, but he ate ravenously, and Garland, eyeing him from his meagre face to his spindle shanks, wondered why he did not grow stouter.

"It's most extraordinary," he said to Carrington, "the fellow eats like a pig and grows thin on it. It's very disagreeable to me. I wish he'd stop coming in here every evening."

"You're too severe on him," said Carrington.

"I am? Well just wait until he begins visiting

you with a roll of manuscript poems to read. By Jove, he nearly drives me idiotic!"

"Oh, he's a very decent fellow," said Carrington; "he's a man of splendid morals—"

"—According to himself," said Garland. "Since he arrived in the Quarter he has not missed an evening in telling us how he scorns the immoral students of this immoral Quarter, and how innocent and pure he is himself. I take no stock in that sort of thing. You and I are morally decent, but we don't sound trumpets on that account.

Carrington was silent for a moment, then he said diffidently; "I'm rather sorry for him; he isn't popular, you know. I think we ought to be friendly to him."

"It's his own fault that he is unpopular."

"Perhaps so; anyway I might as well tell you that he asked us to come to see him to-night. I accepted."

"Good heavens," groaned Garland, "he's sure to read us a poem."

"What of it?"

"Oh, I can stand it if you can. I'm tired and cross, but if you have accepted that settles it."

"It's nine o'clock," said Carrington, glancing at his watch, "we might as well go now and get away early. I'm dead tired myself. Come on, old chap, and face the music. We nouveaux should stick together!"

"You're d——n democratic for an aristocrat," laughed Garland, following him across the hallway to

Fradley's door. They found Fradley sitting before the piano. He could not play the piano, but he had an enervating habit of striking single notes with one finger which filled Garland with murderous inclinations.

"Ah!" said Fradley in affected surprise, "Garland?—and Lord Ronald Carrington—"

"How are you, Fradley," said Carrington hastily, "trot out your verses, for Garland and I are going to sport our oak directly—we're dead beat from the studio concour."

Carrington had worked modestly in the Quarter for months, living under his name of Carrington with no prefix, for he hated notoriety and fuss, and was perfectly aware that a fuss would be made over him if people discovered him to be identical with the young Lord Carrington who led his company so gallantly in Burmah, He had resigned from the service to study art, and he worked hard and faithfully to make up for lack of ability. It took Fradley to discover his title and identity and, much to Carrington's chagrin, he spread the glad news and fell down and worshipped.

"Come," said Garland, "let's hear your verses. Got anything to smoke?"

"You may smoke," murmured Fradley, in a trance before Carrington, "for Lord Carrington smokes—"

"For goodness, sake call me Carrington," said Ronald, "and give us some tobacco will you?"

Fradley produced his tobacco and then began to

glide about the room tidying things, arranging knick-knacks, dusting albums, until Garland shuddered.

"Come, Fradley," he said, as amiably as he could, "trot out your grog and poetry and let's get to bed. You know we only have to-morrow on the concour and we must get up early."

Fradley tripped over to the piano, found his manuscript, tripped back again to the fireplace, sat down, throwing one lank leg over the other, and coughed gently.

"It's only a trifle—a little thing I finished to-night. Let me read it to you."

Garland, aghast at the bulky manuscript, lighted a cigar and gave himself up to gloom. Carrington settled back in his chair and determined to enjoy it.

"It is entitled, 'The Kiss of Sin,'" observed Fradley.

"Oh, fin-de-siècle? inquired Carrington.

"I thought you were opposed to immorality," said Garland.

"This is moral!" gasped Fradley, "do you think I would—"

"No—no! go on, old fellow," said Carrington.

"For Heaven's sake," muttered Garland.

Then with a smile the poet began :

"Her burnished hair is red as flame,
  Her red lips burn like fire,
And she has pressed the kiss of shame,
  Upon my lips. Am I to blame?
Away, bold siren! Learn to tame
  Thy culpable desire!"

" Now is that immoral ? " asked Fradley.

Ronald was dozing, eyes wide open.

" No," said Garland, " that's harmless ; go on," and he curled himself up in the armchair and thought of Sara La Rousse. The poem was in cantos and they were numerous. Some cantos were tearful, some tempestuous. Many paid beautiful tribute to temperance, such as the verse beginning :

> "Away! away! with the rose-wreathed cup !"

A little further along, Fradley's morals tottered, for the lines,

> " Oh, never shall lips of mine be pressed
> To thy wicked mouth or thy sinful breast !"

were almost immediately followed by :

> " Beautiful creature, fly with me !
> I'll build thee a house 'neath the hawthorn tree."

" I thought you said you gave her the shake ! " interrupted Garland querulously. Carrington woke up at the same moment and looked terribly ashamed of himself.

" Very charming," he murmured, " it's about Sara, isn't it ? "

Fradley blushed. " Oh, no—er—it's only a poetic fancy."

" Any red-headed girl—eh ? " said Garland rising; " well, I am awfully obliged to you,—we'll have the rest of it soon I hope—come along, Ronald."

Fradley accompanied them to the door.

"Are you going to that—that orgie at the Bal Bullier on Mi-Carême?" he asked.

"I am," said Garland.

"Are you?" he asked of Carrington.

"Oh, yes, I suppose so ; everybody else is going."

"And do you think it right?"

"No—it's not decent ; you would not enjoy it," said Garland with a malicious smile. "Don't go."

"I don't know—I don't know," murmured Fradley ; "an artist must be broad—"

"Especially when he's abroad—"

"Oh, come on!" grumbled Carrington,—"good night, Fradley, awfully obliged you know."

The poet entered his boudoir and lighting a wax candle looked at himself in the mirror. He smoothed his love-locks, touched his lips with glycerine, and crawling into an embroidered night-shirt sank languidly upon the bed, pulling the silken coverlet over his ears. Then he began to think of Sara.

V.

From the Seine to the Bullier, the Boulevard St. Michel lay glistening under the frosty stars. On the fountain in the Place St. Michel, the iron griffins which spat water all summer into the basin below, sat grim and helpless, jaws and claws bound in chains of ice. Above them victorious St. Michel lifted the flat of his sword to spank a prostrate Satan whose nether limbs were now mercifully padded with snow.

The Boulevard, packed from gutter to gutter, echoed with the fanfare of Carnival. Cabs crowded along five deep; tram-cars and omnibuses wheezed and tooted and ploughed their way through the constantly increasing throngs.

With mask and horn and mirliton the crowd swept through the boulevard, while from the terraces and windows of every café, students sprawled, and shouted and chanted strange anthems to celebrate the Mi-Carême.

The Café Vachette was festooned with gas jets, the Café de la Source glowed under clusters of electric globes, the Cafés d'Harcourt and Rouge were ablaze with lanterns and electricity, and the ice-covered fountain in the Place de Medici flashed back from its crystalline basin a million sparkling rays of blue and gold. On top of the hill the Bullier rose terraced with coloured lamps, bathed in a flood of electric light, which traced a trembling network of shadows over the asphalt among the trees of the Avenue de L'Observatoire. And among the shadows which the branches flung across the parkway, partly concealed by the terrace of the café which forms the angle of the avenue, a figure, enveloped in a sealskin overcoat, shivered and peered across the square to where the frivolous and godless were pouring along the sidewalk to the Bullier. On they swept, with horn and song and the rattle of canes on bench and shutter; and past them dashed cab after cab, halting for an instant at the entrance, while visions of light draperies and lighter feet sped across

the foyer to the cloak-room. Now a band of archi-
tects arrived, chanting the slogan of Lalou, now
a masked company of artists in blouse and béret,
locking arms with a dozen of the gentler sex. At
times the throng closed about some favourite who
immediately mounted a boulevard bench to ha-
rangue them on the evil of being serious.

The figure in the sealskin overcoat appeared to be
interested, and ventured a little way along the square,
but was almost immediately frightened back by the
voice of a compatriot, inebriated but melodious;

> " He didn't come back no more.
>   N—o ! "
>   He didn't come more.

> " N—n she sat by the fire—hic ! "

It was Arizona.

> " N—n she sat by the fire—"

here memory proved treacherous, and, after several
attempts to recall the fate of the abandoned one,
Arizona jerked a large felt hat over one eye,
squared his shoulders, advanced his lower jaw and
began to yell. " Come an' pick up the dead—aw !
Come an' rescue the dyin' ! It's my night to
howl, an' a souvenir goes with each an' every
corpse ! "

Across the square somebody in the crowd shouted :
" Arizona, shut up ! "

" W'as that ? " demanded Arizona indignantly ;
and, encircling a tree with one arm, he started the

other in a rapid rotary motion increasing in velocity until it looked like an extinct Catherine-wheel.

"What's the matter, Arizona?" asked Garland who came running across the street; "you know you mustn't yell like that in English."

"A souvenir goes with each corpse," said Arizona sullenly, "I'm a pitiless wolf—"

"You're a pitiful ass," said Clifford, coming up, "whom are you scrapping with now?"

"If I find him I'll jump on to his neck," said Arizona sulkily.

"He means Fradley," said Elliott to Clifford, "he's jealous because Sara forbade him to assault Fradley."

The figure in the sealskin coat shuddered behind his tree.

"Arizona, my son," said Clifford, "you're a nouveau yet, and you'd better not make yourself too conspicuous. You're drunk too, and if I catch you trying to get into the Bullier I'll settle with you in a way you'll remember. Give me that six-shooter —quick. Now don't try any of your cheap cow-boy humor in the Latin Quarter. Go home."

"Look yere, Clifford," said Arizona, "I'm a noovo but I ain't no slouch, an' you fellows never have to tell me to be less fresh. Now I—hic!—I objec' to Fradley chasin' Sara—"

"You have no claims on Sara," said Elliott laughing.

"All right, then I hain't, but I objec' to that fool-hen Fradley scratchin' alkali in my sage-bush.

19

Mebbe Sara ain't my business ; but I'm doin' dooty about thet there public claim, an' I'm death on jumpers like him ! "

At that moment the uproar on the boulevard was redoubled. A battalion of singing students, each clad in evening dress over which was draped a white blouse, was advancing from the Boulevard Montparnasse.

" Come on, Garland,—Arizona, go home ! " said Clifford, and he hurried across the square to join the procession, followed by Elliott and Garland.

In the middle of the procession, enthroned upon the roof of a cab sat Sara. She was engaged in exploding squibs while Boissy held the terrified horse down to a sideway prance. Behind the cab marched Julian's young hopefuls, singing " *Le Bal à l'Hôtel de Ville.*" Sara fired a whole bunch of squibs as the cab came to a halt before the statue of Marshal Ney, then, as it moved on into the flare of light, a mighty shout arose ; " Vive Sara ! " to which that young person politely replied, " Vive l'atelier Julien ! "

A moment later Sara and her cohorts were engulfed in the throng passing through the foyer of the Bal Bullier.

Half an hour later, Arizona appeared at the box office and charged in with a whoop which raised the hair under the silver helmet of the cavalryman on guard. It was, however, nearly twelve o'clock when Fradley, his eyes bulging with fright, sidled into the lobby, bought his ticket and sought the den of the

female harpies who take checks for wraps. He
slipped the sealskin overcoat from his meagre frame,
and a harpy grabbed it. He hurriedly thrust the
zinc check into his pocket, smoothed his love-locks
and tripped timidly to the head of the stairs which
leads down to the floor of the ballroom. Here a
coarse red-necked man relieved him of his ticket,
and he stood face to face with the gilded demon—
Vice! For a moment he thought of flight ; then
something on the floor below made him blush violently.

"Get out of the way! You're blocking the
stairs!" shouted the red-necked man, but Fradley
did not hear him in the din. Then a brutal cavalryman seized Fradley and hustled him down the stairs.

"Stop!" screamed the poet, but somebody in the
crowd below caught him by the leg. It was a fear-
ful struggle. The red-necked man vociferated, the
soldier pushed and the masked figure below hauled
away at his feet. Fradley felt he was losing consciousness ; the scene swam before him. For one
awful moment he saw, in the gaudy surging masses
below, the glittering pit of hell—his ears were
stunned by the crash of demoniac music,—then something gave way, the soldier snickered, and Fradley
found himself jerked headlong into the gulf, only to
be caught in the arms of a stalwart personage wearing a false nose and a tin crown over one ear.

"Welcome to Pandemonium!" yelled the
crowned personage, as he banged Fradley over the
head with a bladder; "and may I ask, Monsieur, if

you generally come into a Royal Presence on your head?"

Before Fradley could reply, a Nautch Girl caught him around the neck and swung him into the crush of dancers. He struggled violently.

"What: you won't dance?" she cried, with a stamp of her bangled sandals.

"No, I won't!" cried Fradley, perspiring with terror.

"You shall!" she insisted.

Then a clown with his face all white, came squealing and tumbling along, neatly floored him in an unexpected flip-flap, picked him up, and laying his chalky face on his shoulder, shrieked and sobbed, "oh, mon frère! mon frère!" This was the last straw. With a wrench and a twist he freed himself and fled to the gallery, where he found a vacant table and sat down to collect his thoughts. Little by little his fright gave way to anger. A waiter dusted the chalk from his coat and told him that there was a mirror behind the musicians' box. Here he smoothed his hair and rebuttoned his collar, keeping a suspicious eye on two young ladies of the ballet who were practising strange steps before an adjoining mirror.

"Monsieur," said one of them, "have the goodness to tell me whether I do the "grand écart," as well as "La Goulu."

"What is the "grand écart," asked Fradley stiffly.

He was instructed, and he withdrew in haste to his table in the gallery.

A quadrille was in progress below. He stood on his chair to see and then sat down again, not to see. This manœuvre he repeated at intervals and ended by remaining on his chair, "For," he argued, "it's life,—and an artist must be broad."

Before the quadrille ended, he was playfully toppled from his chair by a Spanish dancer, who took his place and offered to reward him with a kiss which he refused. After a while the dancer skipped off with an Arab, and a feeling akin to loneliness took possession of Fradley.

The dull red and blue woodwork of the Bullier was hung with the banners of all nations. In the musicians' gallery, Conor and his orchestra banged away at the "March into Hell," and the tables trembled with the crash of the brass. The floor was crowded to suffocation. Imbecile shrieking clowns in ruffles and powder, went madly bounding about, Turks footed it with Russian peasant girls, gendarmes wearing false noses and enormous moustaches locked arms with "ces messieurs" of the Vilette who wore the charming costume of that quarter including "favoris" and "rouflaquettes." Students in evening-dress galloped about playing circus, and a pretty Cupid, mounted on one young gentleman's shoulders, challenged a shepherdess, mounted on another, to a race, so away they went, crying "Allons! houp! houp!" From a near corner a monotonous chanting arose, where some thirty students were squatting in a ring beating upon drums with their hands. It was the rhythmic air of an Egyptian

dance which was being executed in the middle by a
willowy white-veiled girl who swung two gilded
scimitars.   Like sheet lightning the broad blades of
the swords flashed above the silver-flecked veil, as
her slender, supple figure swayed to the music.

"Brava! Bis! Bis!" they cried, and the girl, with
eyes like stars above her veil, whirled the scimitars
into circles of flame.   Suddenly she stood rigid, there
came a clash of steel, the swords lay crossed before
her, and, as the minor air swelled out, she whipped
off her veil and sent it floating and billowing above
her head while her little feet began to move to and
fro among the swords, blade upward on the floor.
The applause was deafening as she tossed back her
head and said with the merriest laugh, " Je veux
bien boire un bock!"

Clifford jumped up from the floor and picking up
the swords presented them on one knee.

" Tiens! c'est toi, mon ami?"

" Yes.   Forgive me the cab, Cécile," he murmured,
drawing her half resisting arm through his.

" I can't forgive you.   It was too ridiculous to sit
there,—and somebody holding the hind wheels."

" Oh, Cécile—"

" No—no!"

" Ma petite Cécile—"

" By Jove, she's going to forgive him," said Elliott
to Rowden who was dancing attendance on the pretty
Cupid.

" Mr. Rowden, I insist," pouted the Cupid, shaking
her curls.

"But I don't enjoy playing circus," pleaded Rowden, as Boissy pranced proudly by, his epaulettes over his ears, bearing Sara as Diana, who prodded him on with a silver-gilt arrow.

Then Cupid became petulant and signified her intention of seeking another steed, and presently Elliott became the pleased spectator of his friend careering about in company with similarly burdened youths.

"I'm not in it," sighed Elliott, until he spied Margot, who stamped her foot and called for a steed. Shortly afterwards he joined the rest in feats of the haut-école.

To say that Fradley was enjoying himself is not strictly true. Once every ten minutes he subdued some bound of a tortured conscience with the thought; "artists must be broad;" but except for these encounters with his doubts he found it all secretly thrilling and pleasant. He was lonely, in a way, yet he hardly knew what he would want of company. As for speaking to any of those bright-eyed young persons who now and then slapped his face with a rose or rattled a tambourine over his hat,—that was out of the question. No, indeed! He would look on, "because an artist must be broad," but he had no desire to contaminate himself with a word or a smile from such as they. No, indeed! No! No! There seemed to be some need of repeating this frequently to himself, but curiously enough it did not assuage his loneliness. Once a black-eyed Mephistopheles poked her pointed red feather into his eyes and then begged pardon with an irresistible smile which, fortunately for history, came several centuries too late for St. Anthony.

What Fradley might have done had not the girl been carried off by Garland, nobody can tell. He felt a thump in his throat and a murderous feeling toward Garland, and yet he was sure that he had been about to wither temptation with a frown. Carrington spoke in his ear.

"Look at Sara! Magnificent!" Fradley turned.

Seated upon a table in the gallery with the air of an Empress, Sara received the homage of the Quarter. Behind her Cécile and Clifford waved gaudy fans and imbibed champagne in tall goblets. The curly-headed Cupid and the black-eyed Mephistopheles were endangering their silken hose by sliding down the balustrade, aided and applauded by a Japanese maid and three fairies.

Fradley had eyes for Sara only. "Vulgar," he said.

"Yes," said Carrington doubtfully. A great wave of loneliness swept over Fradley.

"Shameless!" he gasped.

Then Sara's strange grey eyes met his across the whirl of the carnival; he saw her throw up her haughty head and send to him a wonderful smile,—a smile that scorched and yet healed, and in an agony of doubt he opened his lips to cry again to Carrington—to the world, "shameless!" but his lips were dry, and his voice died in his throat with a click.

The music clashed; Cécile dropped her glass and

clasped Clifford's hand ; Sara sprang into Boissy's arms,—there was a rush, a tempest of cheers, and Fradley, jostled and hustled clung to a pillar,— clung a moment only, then was swept away, into the throng.

" Dance ! " cried a breathless voice behind him, and, " dance ! " cried another voice beside him. He tried to stem the tide,—he shut his eyes, but soft arms were around his neck and a puff of perfume smote him like a blow in the face, and " dance ! dance ! " cried a voice in his ear. He knew the voice, his eyes flew open and he cried out, but "dance ! dance ! dance ! " she panted, and her burnished hair flew in his face. He saw the crescent on her brow, he saw the strange grey eyes below it. Each separate hair in the fiery mane flashed like a perfumed flame, and he reeled and steadied himself with a soft hand that sought his own, while the orchestra thundered and the rosy ring of faces floated away, away, into an endless rosy chain.

When it was that he drank something, he could not remember. He was very thirsty, and iced champagne was but a temporary relief.

" Good ! " cried Boissy with a stare, " so you're going in for it ! "

Fradley looked at him, but Sara dropped her hand on his arm saying, " Toi, tu sais bien danser," and turning scornfully to Boissy, " go away. You dance like a gendarme ! "

The music began again, and with the music bedlam broke loose. There was no pretence of sets. After a couple had danced themselves into exhaustion, they climbed over the balcony and watched the others. Cécile tossed her veil into the human whirlpool below, laughing delightedly as the silver stars were rent from it and sent scaling into the air. Rowden howled through the din for Clifford to pledge him, and smashed glass after glass in a vain effort to make him hear, while the black-eyed Mephistopheles, perched on Garland's shoulders, poured out goblet after goblet of gold-dust and flung it over the throng until heads and shoulders glittered with the golden scales. Elliott had climbed into the orchestra with a bottle of champagne, and while the grateful musicians were quenching their thirst, he pounded on the spare cymbals until the handles came off and Monsieur Conor ejected him.

Then in the height of the delirium, Arizona shook the walls with his war-cry. "Aw! I'm bad! b-b-a-a-d! Me teeth is choke-bored an' a hair-trigger works both feet!" Fradley heard that cry and trembled. It came nearer and nearer.

"Pick up the dead! Pick up the dyin', an' git the souvenir!"

Sara cried: "Arizona, va t 'en!" but it was too late. With a howl from Arizona and a scream from Fradley, they clinched and fell, Arizona on top. He remembered that he punched Arizona and in turn received a tap on the ear which made him forget that he was alive. Garland picked him up, and when consciousness returned he saw Sara, furious, withering Arizona with her scorn.

"Go!" she cried, pointing to the door.

Arizona, humbled and dishevelled, went.

It needed much cooling liquid to put Fradley back where he had been prior to Arizona's assault, and that condition was far from normal. He proffered menaces, he attempted to divest himself of his coat, but Sara, very pale, and paler still after each goblet in which she pledged the exalted Fradley, took possession of him with all the blindness of sudden caprice.

Fradley felt that his hour,—the hour of the truly great, had struck. Dimly he recalled that other Fradley, the normal one, timid as a rabbit, dreading battle, loathing brute force. Vaguely he remembered that other and normal Fradley, moral, temperate in all but feeding. And he scorned him! Buried forever let him be, that *other* recreant Fradley! And all the while he went on talking with the others, capering when they capered, drinking when they drank, returning gibe for gibe, defending his own, claiming and pushing his claim with threats— warlike threats, and all the time, dimly, dully commiserating, scorning that other,—that normal Fradley.

Later he revived enough to have a pang of fright as the cold air of the boulevard blew in his face, but the cab was warm and cosey and he sank back to the cushions with a sigh of content. As in a dream he heard the rattle of wheels and the cries of the driver. Other cabs passed—endless lines of them. It seemed centuries before his cab stopped and when it did he objected to leaving it, but Sara had her way, alas now as hazy as his own, and the porter who opened the door for them at the Café Sylvain, winked solemnly at the ancient cabby, who only shook his white head and drove slowly away.

ENVOI.

The rock-ribbed Planet drifts across the Sun,
   Swarming with creatures creeping on the crust,
   Freighted with fears, and tears, and human dust,
Speaking the blank star-beacons, one by one.

Tossed on the ocean of Ten Million Nights,
   The Moon a battered battle-lantern swings;
   A Meteor a battle-pennant flings,
Lost in the ocean of Ten Million Lights.

Down to the Sea in Ships! Who knows?—Who
    knows
   What Unseen Thing shall climb the mist-hung
    shrouds
   And set the spread of splendid crowding clouds,
And light the signals set in starry rows?

Deep in the Black Crypt of the Universe
   A feeble thing stood sobbing on a star;
   "I live! I live! 'Tis mine to make or mar!"
And Silence was the Answer and the Curse.

Bee-haunted blossoms bud and bloom at Noon;
   Bird-haunted meadows belt the Seven Zones;

And under all lie bedded human bones,
And over all still swings the tarnished moon.

On Men and Haunts of Men—if all Light dies,—
   And, where a million stars hang tenantless
   Whence the last ray is fled,—yet—none the less
A Million Lamps are trimmed for other Skies.

Believe it, O my soul! Arise and go
   Forth among Men and seek the Haunts of Men ;—
   Nor shalt thou, O my soul, return again
To tell thou knowest naught ; We know ! We know !

                                        R. W. C.

April, 1896.

www.ingramcontent.com/pod-product-compliance
Lightning Source LLC
Chambersburg PA
CBHW060550030726

47498CB00005B/1333